Of *Blood* and *Magic*

Cursed by Blood Saga
Book Eight

Marianne Morea

Coventry Press Ltd.

Somers, New York
http://www.coventrypressltd.com

This is a work of fiction. Names, characters, places, and incidents are products of the author's imagination or are used fictitiously and are not to be construed as real. Any resemblance to actual events, locations, organizations, or persons, living or dead, is entirely coincidental.

ISBN-13: 978-1-7325262-3-5
First Edition: Coventry Press Ltd. 2019

Cover Artist: Cover Couture

Printed in the USA

...For the witch in all of us

"The moon has awoken with the sleep of the sun.
The light has been broken, the spell has begun."
~Midgard Morningstar

Chapter One

New York City
One block from Club Avalon
Condemned church-turned-nightclub

"Come out, come out, wherever you are." Blair Cabot splashed blood-laced vodka on the concrete wall in an alley near the club. "You know you want it, you bloodsucking parasites. So, come find it."

She smeared the rest on her inner thighs, listening over her shoulder before climbing the fire escape to wait gargoyle-style in the silent shadows.

Avalon and its surrounds weren't her usual hunting ground. It had been a while since the place had been prowled by the undead. Then again, their dark corner snacking had dropped off all over the city this past year.

HepZ had a lot to do with that happy statistic. The virus made fast work of degrading various supernaturals to their base nature. Vampires especially. The undead bastards were forced to admit they weren't as superior and untouchable as they thought. Tucking tail, they went hat in hand to the Weres for help.

God bless the wolves and their noses. Still, the Alpha of the Brethren had no choice but to help eradicate the paranormal plague before it found its way into the mainstream. That blessed lot saved many lives, even if

some were of the undead persuasion and it meant she had to pick up her blade again.

The pong of New York City and its overflow of homelessness clung to the alley. That and the scent of blood would surely bring a prize or two. The fanged and fucked would never pass up a chance at an easy meal.

As far as she was concerned, the undead were predators. Period. Hiding under a guise of humanity. She knew firsthand what their thirst could do, and she had the memories to remind her every time she closed her eyes. Still, she had a weapon of her own to wield, and it wasn't her blade. It coursed through her very veins.

"Where are you?" Blair peered into the gloom. They were close. She felt it in the night stillness. A rash of recent clumsy attacks had brought her back to the west side. Of course, gangland violence was the convenient scapegoat in all the papers, but she knew better.

"Gangs, my witchy ass," she muttered, shifting in her crouch to let blood flow to her numbed feet. The late October chill was proving too much for her flat, thigh-high boots, let alone the miniskirt that went along with them. Her choice of outfit served a purpose, so she sucked it up.

Muscles coiled in her shoulders. This was the time when anticipation grew. Eyes trained on the alley's entrance, she fidgeted with the silvered knife in her hand, ignoring the cold, wet feel of the concrete ledge. Another kill would make the temporary discomfort worth the effort. Two even more.

Voices echoed in the darkness, and she checked her watch. Four a.m. That meant last call at Avalon, and a straggle of clubbers stumbling their way to the nearest subway. Unwitting bait for a perfect sting.

Footsteps too faint for human ears crept along the sidewalk almost as if on cue. Blair pursed her lips, listening. Witches were adept at magical camouflage, but she tightened the spell masking her scent and the sound of her heartbeat just in case.

Deepest night, the cold wind sighs,
Hide this witch from undead eyes.
Cord of strength and power twined,
Keep concealed all magic mine.

Satisfied, she sent her senses out to home in on their approach. Two youngbloods. She smirked to herself. It made sense. Clumsy attacks equaled vampires barely out of training fangs. A fact that made her job that much easier tonight.

A dirty yellow streetlight cast enough ambient light to give her far warning. Crouched on the balls of her feet, Blair jumped without a muffled thud, positioning herself for the kill.

Situating herself against a graduated stack of wood pallets, she hiked her skirt around torn panties. The last of the blood and vodka was smeared across the tops of her thigh-high boots to augment the scent already between her legs. She was ready.

"What did I tell you, man." Both youngbloods stole into the alley. "Easy pickings. Bitches always drink too much, and then some jackoff walks them half in the bag to a dark corner and wham, bam, thank you ma'am."

The other laughed, hovering as he sniffed the air above Blair's feigned slump. "Dude, you sure she's still alive? I don't hear no heartbeat." He inhaled again, cocking his head.

"Can't you smell the blood? It's all over her, man. Whoever did her, fucked her bloody."

The skeptical one straightened. "I don't know, dude. Doesn't feel right. She can't be much older than me."

"Yeah right." The brash one snorted. "You forget you stopped aging the minute you woke to darkness. Besides, who cares how old she is? She's a hot lunch. So, shut up already. Kick whatever moral has you by the balls and vamp up."

Blair tensed, ready to strike, but before she could send her blade home, the youngbloods wheeled in the dim light.

"Hey!" They took a step away from her toward the alley entrance. "Take a hike, loser. We were here first."

Blair cracked an eye open, but two youngbloods blocked her view. This was not good. Three vampires against one witch was a long shot at best, even with the witch-blood ace up her sleeve. She didn't dare send her senses out, or she'd really give her plan away.

"You deaf as well as stupid?" the youngblood tried again. "I said get lost."

Was the third vampire old enough to see through her glamour? She couldn't be sure. *Ugh.* Right now, she wished she'd listened to her horoscope when it said to stay in bed.

"You youngbloods really need to brush up on the rules around here." The vampire-come-lately was unfazed. "Avalon and the surrounding area belong to Carlos Salazar. It's off-limits. As are club patrons who are less than...aware."

The bigmouth vamp snorted. "Who are you? The undead gestapo? If Salazar wants his stupid rules enforced, then he shouldn't make them so easy to break."

"As far as you two are concerned, I'm fucking Batman. You have a choice. You can either leave the way you came,

intact, or you can stay as ashes. The last pair of youngbloods who decided to hunt our territory without consent ended with their hearts ripped out."

The tenor and cadence of his voice tingled over Blair's skin, and her pulse jumped. In that instant, the newcomer turned his attention to where she held still. She didn't need her eyes to sense the weight of his stare. The urge to open them and look nearly overwhelmed, though, almost as if the vampire cast his own compulsion.

Blair barely drew breath, resisting the press on her psyche. If he suspected anything, he didn't let on, and soon the force on her released. Witch blood was poisonous to most vampires but not all. It was a crap shoot most undead wouldn't bet on, but still.

"Fuck you and the horse you rode in on, asshole. The bitch is mine!" The brash youngblood lunged with a hiss, fangs fully descended.

Survival instinct kicked in, and Blair somersaulted out of his reach, landing in a defensive stance. The newcomer blurred past her, sending the loudmouth crashing against the closest wall. The force cracked both the cement and its cinderblock underlayer.

"Chip! Give it up." The other youngblood backed away from his unlucky friend. "Let him have her."

Nervous laughter bubbled in Blair's throat, and she snorted a stifled chuckle. "Chip? Where were you turned? The Westport Yacht Club?"

Even the newcomer's lip curled at that, but when the preppy vamp shook off the blow and straightened to attack, all humor left his face.

From his manner and speech, Blair guessed the stranger was older by at least a century. In the dim light he seemed dark haired and dark eyed, but when he moved

through the narrow swath of streetlight, she caught a glimpse of rich, hazel-green eyes in a chiseled face. Not that it mattered. There was nothing sexy about an undead leech.

Then why was her mouth dry and her limbs frozen, watching this older vampire teach the douchebag youngblood a lesson?

Every fiber screamed for her to run, but instead she stood mesmerized. Before she could second-guess herself again, the preppy vamp launched himself at the older vampire, but the elder moved with lightning grace, using the youngblood's momentum against him.

He flung the fool backward into his friend, and the two skidded across the dirty asphalt into a pile of broken pallets.

The force sent a jagged board through the other youngblood's chest, just missing his heart. A protracted hiss escaped Chip's mouth while the other shrank against the wall splattered with blood and vodka.

"I suppose there really is no cure for stupid."

The older vampire's statement was meant for the two youngbloods, but, as Blair stood transfixed, it could have easily applied to her as well.

This was the first time she'd witnessed vampire law in motion. Rules were broken. Exacting a penalty from the guilty was to be expected. Except one of the rules broken was tantamount to protecting the innocent.

Had she heard correctly?

This area belongs to Carlos Salazar. It's off-limits. As are club patrons who are less than…aware.

The concept floored Blair to her toes. Those were the older vampire's exact words. Did he mean just

unconscious victims, or anyone unaware they were being stalked?

Blair's first instinct was to dismiss the prospect as another guise. Yet, two youngblood vampires were now paying the price for an attempted attack on a perceived innocent.

No guise would go that far. Would it?

Spitting blood and teeth into his hand, the preppy youngblood shook off the second hit. "Look what you did, asshole!"

"Chip! Don't!"

With a snarl, she shoved his wounded friend to the ground when he tried to stop him from retaliating.

"I'm gonna rip your chest open and squeeze your heart like a pimple! Then I'm gonna suck that bitch dry, my fat meat buried in her bloody hole!"

Angry spittle spewed from the fool's mouth, but before he could make good on his threat, the elder whirled, slicing Chip's throat to his spine with his bare hand.

"Some vampires are too stupid to live." The older one wiped black blood from his hand, watching wide rivulets pour from the linear gash on Chip's throat.

He whirled again, and a spinning crescent kick finished the job. The preppy's head flew from his shoulders toward a pile of garbage stacked where his friend crouched.

The remaining youngblood sniveled as the elder approached, stepping over the headless body already flaking to ash. He vomited into the rubbish, not bothering to wipe his mouth before scuttling farther into the shadows.

"Count yourself lucky tonight, boy." The elder picked him up by his collar. The youngblood whimpered catlike,

tearing at the elder's jacket, drawing blood as he tried to get free.

If I catch you here again, nothing will help you. Tonight, you owe your pitiful escape to what's left of your moral compass. We're not animals without conscience, boy. Bide that well or suffer the same fate as your stupid friend."

The older vampire dropped the youngblood to the dirty asphalt. With a sucking sound, the shaken vampire scrambled to his feet and ran. The torn fabric from the elder's jacket fluttered to the ground behind him.

The older vampire turned slowly. His hazel eyes trained on Blair. He took a step toward her but then stopped, as if suspicious or curious.

"Why the hesitation? Surely, I'm no match for you." Blair raised her silvered blade.

"That's amusing, coming from someone holding a knife dipped in silver. Tell me, why didn't you run when you had the chance?"

She turned the knife so its silvered edge glinted in the dim. "I wanted to see what you would do."

"Really." He raised a dark eyebrow. "And the verdict?"

Sliding one foot back, she widened her defensive stance. "The jury's still out."

He took another step, and she held the knife out toward him. "Don't get cocky, old man. Three against one, the odds are in your favor. One on one, I can stand on my own."

"Old man? I'm twenty-two years old."

"Twenty-two?" She sidestepped pallet debris and slick, black blood that hadn't yet turned to ash. "How many birthdays ago, vamp boy?"

He inclined his head. "Touché."

The vampire's full mouth curved into an easy smile. Crooked, and a little teasing.

"Tell me, what's a pretty girl like you doing in a dirty alley at this time of night? Seems you should have a beau or at least an escort to see you home."

"Let me guess. You last saw twenty-two a hundred years ago because no one says beau anymore."

His teasing grin curled a little higher. "A little over a century, since you're so set on knowing."

Watching him speak mesmerized her nearly as much as watching his body move when he fought. Even with a hint of fang, his smile made her stomach jump. He was a filthy bloodsucker, but she had to admit he was charming. Not to mention easy on the eyes.

Thick dark hair curled to just below his ears. He wore it swept back, but the front of his hair fell into his eyes after the fight. She wanted to brush it away, just to see the green flecks in his hazel eyes.

Get a grip. He's glamouring you, stupid.

Staring him down, she lifted a hand and murmured under her breath, "*Revalabo stultitiam malefectum.*"

He met her gaze, humor flashing in his eyes. Had he heard the cast? She didn't know.

Guess he's not evil. Maybe it's okay to ogle a little more.

She shoved the thought away with a vengeance before she completely forgot herself and her reason for being here in the first place. He was the enemy, no matter how attractive.

"Well, then." She lifted her chin. "We seem to be at a stalemate. We both need to leave, but who first?"

"Ladies first, of course," he said with a slight bow. "After all, you said I was old-fashioned."

"I said you were old, not old-fashioned."

He laughed, and she licked her lips. God, undead or not, he was beautiful—if you could use the word to describe a man.

"Unless you're hesitating because you plan to pick up where your dead friend failed. I should warn you, I don't fight fair, and odds are stacked you'll end up ash on the asphalt just like preppy vamp boy." She tightened her grip on her blade.

"You're very sure of yourself, aren't you?" he asked, with a small appreciative grin. "What makes you think I have any interest in ravaging an unwilling woman?"

Taken aback by the question, she sputtered, "*Uhm,* because you're a vampire?"

She cringed inside. Like mall rat much? All she needed was a wad of chewing gum in her mouth and her hair twirled around her finger.

"Not to worry, sweetheart. I understood your subtext. Like totally."

"Very funny. Being nonplussed by your question makes me stupid? It only proves you're very good at what you are."

"And what's that, pray?"

She sniffed, lifting her chin. "You are deceit incarnate. Grief and death together, in an unfeeling, calculating predator."

All humor had gone out of the conversation, and the air was suddenly thick with uncertainty.

"That's quite an indictment."

Adrenaline rose in her blood, and she steeled herself as the clock ticked down. "I have cause in spades for my accusations."

"I see." He nodded." So, according to you, because I was unfortunate enough to *suffer* my fate, it then follows I am automatically inclined to inflict suffering *because* I am a vampire."

She kept her eyes on him but didn't reply.

"And that's your idea of how this works?" He actually laughed at her logic. "That suffering only begets more suffering. That no one can rise above circumstance and end a toxic cycle."

She opened her mouth but then shut it again. Why was he arguing the point? Who the hell did he think he was? Clarence Darrow? OJ's dream team?

Flecks of ash from the youngblood's decaying body crossed her peripheral vision, and she steeled herself again.

"A pig in a satin bonnet is still a pig, so don't try your double-talk with me. I know firsthand the harm vampires bring and the grief they leave in their wake."

He shook his head. "Why are you doing this? Anyone with sense would have run when they had the chance. Do you have a death wish?"

Spreading the neck of her blouse, she exposed her throat. "Not really. Do you?" The blade in her hand was not her only taunt.

"Go home, girl. You're in over your head, and I'm not interested in playing games with a Buffy wannabe."

With a quick flick of her hand, Blair sliced her palm with the tip of her blade. "You sure you're not interested?" Blood trickled over her palm to her fingers to drip onto the ash-coated asphalt.

His nostrils flared, and his eyes dilated red for a moment but then returned to their normal hazel. "Positive," he replied, digging in his pocket for a

handkerchief. "You may want to bind that wound, or someone else might take you up on your offer. I told you, I'm not interested in games. Especially not playing Russian roulette with witch blood."

Blair's jaw tightened. He'd resisted her cast before, but now she was going for the big guns.

Magic forces here and now,
Lend your sight, the truth allow.
Show this witch his evil heart,
His motives show, so there's no doubt.

She spoke the words loud and proud and threw her bloody hand up. Wind gusted in the alley, swirling ash and rubbish. White light surrounded the vampire, revealing his aura.

It showed dusky and wan, but the vampire's eyes stayed clear and hazel instead of turning black as she expected.

"My aura is no different than the others of my kind. It's misty and pale because I'm undead." Holding the handkerchief out, he took a step closer before blurring behind her, relieving her of her knife at the same time.

In that moment, their auras merged, and she gasped at the silken feel. The white light that encircled him drew power from her spell, and her aura illuminated his, lighting it until it glowed with gilt threads. Her breath caught in her throat as heat engulfed her head to toe. Carnal, yet pure and ethereal.

"Warmth and light." He rested his forehead on the back of her head, his body trembling. "Christ's wounds, it's been so long." A whispered prayer brushed her ear, and she glimpsed his mind. Gratitude. Peace. It was what he craved and what she inadvertently gave him.

She severed the spell's thrall. Cutting it cold. Why should he have peace? His kind didn't deserve it.

"Pity," she said, with a sniff. "And I thought you were daring, maybe even a little interesting. You sure you're not a bit curious? After all, I'm offering a willing taste. Who knows? You might be one of the lucky ones immune to the bane in my blood."

His breath kissed the edge of her ear, as it had earlier, and she braced herself against the sensual feel. He threw her at every turn, and, with his body molded to hers, she needed every bit of strength she could muster.

"I'm surprised there's no metallic tang of fear in your scent, though there is something unusual underlying." He gripped her wrists behind her back and went about the business of binding her cut. "That should hold your poison for now, but your wound may hinder your knife-wielding for a couple of days."

Spinning her around, he kept her locked tight in his arms. He inhaled the clean perfume of her hair. "Maybe I will help myself to you after all, witchling. A kiss in exchange for saving your life. Not much in terms of payment, don't you agree, little hellcat?"

"Hellcat?" Blair snorted. "You really know how to sweep a girl off her feet, old man. And I thought vampires were supposed to be sovereigns of seduction."

Hazel eyes darkened, and he let his lips brush hers with a feather's touch. Their breath mingled, and his clean, masculine scent filled her nose.

Every fiber came alive. Every synapse firing with anticipation. Her body hummed with the need to bare her flesh, her veins, anything he wanted.

His mouth took hers in a soft kiss, but as her lips parted to meet and demand more, he stepped away, breaking the spell.

"You aren't the only one who can weave a potent spell. Sovereigns of seduction, one. Witchling, zip." Touching two fingers to his brow, he bowed with another crooked grin and then turned for the shadows.

"Wait! What's your name?" Blair called after him, hating herself for asking. The breeze tickled her ear with his name even as it swirled the preppy vamp's ashes.

Eric.

Blair stood with her body still humming and her mind revolting against its betrayal. She reached behind her for an unbroken pallet and sank her ass to the flat wood.

Gulping in air, she swore under her breath. Eric, the centenarian vampire, had turned the tables and beaten her at her own game. Plus, the bastard still had her blade.

The same breeze swept up the torn piece of fabric the youngblood ripped from Eric's jacket and blew it toward her feet. She bent for it, lifting the material to her nose. God damn. Even muted, his scent electrified her body all over again.

She stuffed the scrap in her boot and then got up from the broken pallet. She'd find him again. Somehow, someway. There were too many questions that needed answering, including if he was truly as good as he tasted.

Chapter Two

*S*moke and the stench of spent gunpowder filled his nose. He stumbled, chasing long shadows. Felled bodies blocked his way as he searched. For what he didn't know. Panic squeezed his lungs, and a silent cry ripped from his chest in the lonely darkness.

He staggered toward a scorched cottage, cold and desolate. Following the chime of a grandfather clock, he pushed through the cottage's broken door. When he turned to mark time, the numbers melted from the clock's face.

Muscles tensed, he stood at the broken hearth as the clock's incessant chiming rang tandem with every breath. The cold feel of undead fingers gripped his shoulder, and the chiming ceased.

He was alone.

Smoke from the battlefield curled along the dirty cottage floor, even as moonlight winked through the crumbling roof. He turned for the door but stopped. A woman stood in the wisps and shadow. Face obscured, she walked toward him with an outstretched hand.

She whispered words unknown, and he pressed his lips to the tender flesh where her pulse beat. Blood burned on his tongue. Pleasure and pain scored his veins...

Eric landed on the floor with a thud. Jolting up, he cracked his head on the edge of the bed frame. "Ow! Fuck!"

"Mr. Eric. If the bed is too soft, we will get you a new one. There's no reason for you to sleep on the floor." Her heels clacked as she moved from window to window, opening the shutters to let sunset wink through the slats.

"Go away, Marta." Sucking a breath through his teeth, he probed the top of his head.

"But—"

He ignored her frown. "Enough fussing. And for the record, I did not sleep on the floor."

"Señor Salazar asked—"

Eric put up a staying hand. "Fine." Swiveling his legs around, he sat up on the floor beside the bed. "Leave me in peace and go tell Carlos I'll be downstairs as soon as I shower."

She went without another word, leaving Eric to climb into bed with a wince. He slumped onto his pillow, draping his arm over his eyes.

The wince wasn't for bumping his head. It was for the exhaustion he couldn't escape. The same dream had haunted him for years. Barren battlefield. Searching for the living but only finding death. Ruined lives. Undead thirst. Residual nightmares from both his human and undead existence. Night after night, the elements varied but not the theme.

"Eric Fraser, you are one fucked soul," he muttered beneath his forearm. "And the fates will never let you forget it."

He blew out a breath. Lately, the dream was unrelenting. Robbing him of what little rest he'd come to expect. This time the bastard fates decided on a twist. A faceless woman. Beguiling and soft, beckoning him with a glimmer of hope until he crumpled in pain.

Hope.

A word as alien to him as the word home. He pulled his arm back and sat up. Looking around, the bitter thought softened. Carlos Salazar took him in when he was cast off like yesterday's news. He and the others of this

unusual household gave him a place to settle. A place to call his own. A home. The only one he'd ever had. Living or undead.

If something else beckoned, it wouldn't be something to bring him to his knees. He'd had enough of that to last multiple lifetimes.

Another knock on his door told him he was taking too long, and a quick sniff let him know it was Marta still lurking in the hallway.

"I hear you, woman. I'm up, whether I want to be or not." Sunset winked through the slats as he yawned. "*Jeez.* Dracula never had to deal with this shit."

This shit, meaning a well-wishing family constantly poking their heads and two cents through the door. He'd always wished for a family, and now he had one, complete with opinions and attitude.

Guilt bit at him, and he swung his legs over the side of the bed. "Sorry, Marta," he called after, a small grin on his lips at the tap-tap of her heels as she hurried downstairs.

Marta was a good housekeeper, but she wasn't Rosa. No one would ever be. At least not to him. Rosa was *la Pequeña Madre.* She ran a tight ship for the household of vampires she affectionately called *her boys*, but she did so with quiet ease. A simple sniff spoke volumes, and they all toed the line.

It had been a little over a year since she died. More accurately, since the former Master Vampire of the New York took her life in a fit of pique, along with that of everyone else in that doomed shadow house.

Eric sighed, moving his hand to the tender spot on his head. Almost healed. Unlike the unlucky bastard who killed Rosa. Delivering final death to that pompous

undead ass should have been sweeter than warm blood, but it wasn't. It was hollow and empty.

He'd done the deed with enthusiasm, even reverence. Exacting justice for the mother figure he loved, so her death wasn't merely collateral blood from a tyrant gone mad.

Afterward, it took all his preternatural strength just to get out of bed and face the night. He knew it was the reason Carlos sent him to police their territories. Anything to give his rage and sadness a direction and outlet.

No doubt, Carlos sent Marta to rouse him to discuss the events of the night. Not that Eric could tell him anything he didn't already know. The Internet had nothing on the vampire underground when it came to spreading information.

He could hear Carlos now. *Hermano,* you'd be less likely to find trouble if you found a mate instead.

Hunting expeditions aside, Eric had to admit he'd grown tired of trolling for blood and sex. In the past, most of the women he allowed to get close showed themselves mercenary. They wanted the dark gift as much as they wanted him. He always refused. Even before meeting Carlos, he vowed he'd never curse anyone to his fate. Of course, that vow had yet to be tested as it had been with Carlos and his mate, Trina. Or Julian and Kat. Or even the oldest of their kind, Dominic De'Lessep and his mate, Belinda. He'd cross that bridge when the time came. In the meantime, he wasn't about to settle. He would wait for someone who stirred more than just his body and his thirst.

Like last night.

The intrusive thought pushed through his musings with the image of a certain headstrong witch whose kiss

tasted of sunshine and spring. *Do you have a death wish?* A half grin tugged at the memory, and how the little hellcat bared both her neck and her silvered blade.

His cock thickened at the thought of her curves, and their lush feel as he pressed himself to her back, binding her wound.

He shook his head, dismissing the errant thought even as his mouth watered. Carlos and his mate, Trina, would latch on to this tidbit and use it for sure.

Eric was the household's last holdout. A lone wolf, if you could call a member of the undead that and still live to see the next sunset.

Rosa had understood his foot-dragging. She'd known the deep cuts he carried, but even she held out hope he'd find someone to help heal past wounds. Still, she would've stood up to the family, in her quiet way, until he was ready.

He could picture her now. Cleaning cloth in hand as she wiped nonexistent dirt. A perfectly arched eyebrow spelling disappointment at any dissent. Total motherly guilt, in a four-foot-ten-inch powerhouse.

He pressed bare feet to the cold hardwood, savoring the feel of the grain through his soles. It was the one thing he relished about his undead state. The heightened senses. The faintest whispers heard. The infinitesimal movements caught. The scents on the breeze, and, of course, the smooth taste of copper on the tongue as it pulsed from an adrenaline-soaked vein.

Like the smooth scent of forbidden blood dripping from the witch's fingers? Or maybe it was the perfume of her skin lingering on your clothes after you left?

He scrubbed the heel of his hand into his eyes. Why was he so preoccupied with this woman? A witch, no less.

And, from the look of things, a vigilante. Two major strikes. Even if he was intrigued. It was thirst. That's all it was. The one thing no vampire could sleep or sequester away.

Are you, mijo? Just thirsty?

Rosa's voice stirred in his mind.

Eric padded into the bathroom. Preternatural sight made it unnecessary to turn on the lights, but he did anyway.

His reflection shocked him the same way it had when he first was turned to darkness. As a human, he was never what you would call drop-dead gorgeous. Who knew dropping dead at the hands of a vampire trolling the battlefields of northern France would make all the difference? To say he wore undead well was an understatement.

Eric turned on the tap, humming the ugly duckling theme song, but Rosa's deep-throated chuckle pricked the corners of his mind.

"*Ignore me all you want, papi. My words carry truth, and you know it. Like find likes, mijo. The brujita is as torn as you. Maybe you can help each other find what you both are searching for...*"

Water dripping from his chin, Eric stared at himself in the mirror. Was the pretty vigilante the faceless woman he'd been dreaming of for the past month?

What about that warmth and light?

He shook his head in the reflection. There was no way the witch couldn't have known her spell would cause their auras to merge. Closing his eyes, he still felt the warm, pure light permeating his entire being. His essence. It was unlike anything he'd ever experienced.

As tantalizing as the witch was, it was unlikely their paths would cross again. Not after last night. Witches had no real beef with the undead. If the girl truly was a vigilante, then she was rogue. No coven would go to war in such a stealthy way. A declaration would be required along with council parlay, with other supernatural species represented as mediators.

He stalked to his bedroom chair, grateful Marta hadn't taken his jacket to mend or throw out.

Sniffing the soft cotton, he inhaled deeper, holding his breath on his tongue to taste the different elements in her scent.

The tang of anger and deep-seated pain were there in spades but still no real fear. Puzzled, he dropped his jacket onto the chair again. What made this girl so angry and so soaked with guilt she risked hunting vampires alone? Yet she shared such an intimate encounter with him. The contradictions boggled.

He headed back to the bathroom and turned on the shower spray. Hot water cascaded over his skin, as his mind raced.

Of course. His head snapped up.

Survivor's guilt.

But the implications made no sense. What kind of vampire would be stupid enough to attack a coven of witches?

He smirked, soaping his body.

Youngbloods.

They were the only ones foolish and reckless enough to risk witch blood. The same kind of vampires she hunted last night.

He did a quick lather, rinse, and repeat and stepped out, reaching for a towel. If only he'd had the chance to

talk to her. Find out what happened for her to burn with such vehemence.

He shook his head. He wasn't about to ring the doorbell of every coven house in the city. She could be a solitary. In fact, that was the most likely scenario because if her Supreme ever found what she did in the dark, she'd be out on her gorgeous ass with her powers bound and gagged.

The Rosa in his head was right about one thing. The witch intrigued him more than just a bit. She was fiery and brave, despite her misguided sense of guilt fueling her crazy. Even if she'd like nothing more than to watch her blood scorch his veins.

Striding to the chair again, he grabbed his jacket and inhaled her scent once more, this time committing it to memory. Short of becoming a stalker, he'd find her again. If only to see if Rosa's advice to the lovelorn from beyond the grave held water. Could the witch be the one?

***

Eric paused at the kitchen door. Twilight was well past, and darkness shadowed the short hall leading from the foyer to the heart of the house.

He heard Marta hitch a ride with the rest of the staff to the main house in upstate New York, leaving the rest of the family to fend for themselves for the weekend. Not that vampires needed much in terms of help, especially not when the head of their house was just shy of a daywalker, courtesy of his advanced age.

At just over three hundred years old, Carlos could withstand much of the early morning and late afternoon sun, and all day if the weather was gray and overcast.

Late fall was usually cooperative on that score, with much of the month occupied with rain and wind to strip whatever leaves were left after Indian summer.

"Are you planning to join us, or lurk outside the door like a frightened human?" Julian joked, yanking the kitchen door open.

"Nice to see you, too, brother," Eric replied, pushing past him toward the table. "Kat give you the boot until you make up your mind, New York or Ireland?"

The sandy-haired British vampire took his thermal cup from the table and leaned against the granite counter. "Not on your undead life. We have decided to be bicontinental. I'm here to tie up loose ends before heading back, but I may stick around considering we have another vigilante on our hands."

"Another?" Eric hedged.

Carlos shot Julian a look. "Your brother is referring to Lily Saburi, the Alpha of the Brethren's mate, and her revenge tactics before she knew the HepZ virus was responsible for supernaturals killing so randomly. She was a hunter, and Central Park was her favorite place to stalk her prey. She took out a few undead rogues, but to be honest, they were attacking innocents, so the council never asked for reparation."

"You mean they were too afraid of Sean Leighton to do anything." Julian lifted his cup in salute. "Especially after Lily's blood turned out to be the seminal cure for the paranormal plague."

Eric kept a poker face, wanting to hear what they knew before tossing his info on the pile. "Why don't I know this, and why do you think we have another vigilante on our hands?"

Carlos poured a cup from the thermal carafe, holding it out for Eric. "Sustenance first. Your color tells me you haven't fed."

"Someone's been hunting youngbloods. Rémy Tessier has been keeping track through reports at the Red Veil," Julian interjected.

Eric sipped the warm crimson liquid. It was bagged blood, but it hit the spot after the previous evening's exertion. "He's our Adjudicator General now. Master Vampire of the New York Council, so who better to keep tabs, right?"

"Eric, my Spidey senses are on fire. What happened last night?" Julian asked, sparing a glance for Carlos.

Putting the warm mug on the table, Eric leaned on the kitchen bench. "I had to dispatch two youngbloods outside of Avalon. Their intent was clear. Rape and drain."

"Where?" Carlos asked.

"19th Street. In an alley."

Carlos eyed him, lacing his mug with a splash of rum. "Is that all?"

The head of their house was also a council adjudicator, so he already knew there was more to the story. Eric inhaled, draining his mug.

"That bad?" Julian raised an eyebrow. "I've never seen you down the crimson so fast."

Eric didn't reply, just kept his eyes on Carlos. "Their intended target was a snare."

"A snare? As in setup?" Julian put his cup down and moved to the table.

Nodding, Eric kept his face impassive. "The woman used herself as bait. She set the trap, but the youngbloods made it too easy. Like I said, their intent was clear."

"Screw their intent. They didn't get the chance to commit a crime. Last I checked it was innocent until proven guilty," Julian argued.

Carlos raised a hand stopping Julian's rant before it started. "*Mijo*, do you know who set this trap? Did you see?"

This was it. Carlos already knew about the youngbloods. Not just the two from last night, but all the others as well. He had no idea if the witchling had anything to do with the other attacks, but circumstantial evidence seemed to say otherwise. Carlos was looking to him to connect the dots.

Eric nodded as he met Carlos's eyes. "Yes. I even spoke with her."

"Her?" Julian stopped short. "A woman?"

"No, a cantaloupe," Eric shot back. "Of course a woman. Why are you so surprised? We just spoke of the Alpha's mate and her vigilante days. Is it such a shock another member of the fair sex would want to take action against a couple of douchebags?"

Julian frowned. "Lily is psychic. She could read the sins of the supernaturals she killed."

"Trust me. The girl in the alley could very well have the same talent." Eric leaned forward, elbows on the table.

"Boys, please. Try to stay in your lanes with this." Carlos's voice was calm, but the look on his face was anything but. "The last thing any of us want is to escalate an already toxic situation. You can't give the Alpha's mate a pass with one breath and then condemn the same type of crime in this situation with the next."

"Funny you should use the word toxic." Eric sat, toying with his cup.

"Stop hedging, *Mijo*. It's annoying. However distressing, just tell us facts."

"You're right." Eric spread his palms on the table. "It is distressing because the woman who sat in wait for the youngbloods was a witch. She used blood-laced vodka to lure the two idiots to the alley. I got there before she had the chance to use her silver."

"Silver." Julian tilted his head in obvious doubt. "She can't be much of a hunter, then. Silver only incapacitates. Like the net you used on Sebastién after what he did to Rosa?" Julian asked.

Eric got to his feet, knocking his empty cup over. "Say that bastard's name aloud again, and I'll rip your heart out!" The kneejerk reaction tightened his jaw, leaving his mouth twisted in anger. His eyes flamed hot as he stared at his brother.

"Enough!" Carlos banged a fist on the table. "With everything we've been through in the last year and a half, I can't have you two at odds." He pointed to Eric. "You. Sit and explain yourself—and, Julian, if you don't have anything productive to add, then keep quiet. You are not usually so unthinking, *mijo*. None of us need unhappy reminders. *Comprendes*? And for the record, a silver blade straight to the heart *can* kill a weakened vampire."

Eric sat without a word, grabbing a wad of napkins from the holder to mop up the splatters from his mug.

The harsh line of Julian's mouth softened, and he looked at his brother. "I'm sorry, Eric. I didn't mean anything by that. I loved Rosa, too."

Eric stopped what he was doing and met Julian's eyes. "I know, man, and I'm sorry for threatening you. You know I'd never really hurt you." He let a small smirk

tweak his lips. "Well, maybe a little, when you're being a tool."

Julian grinned, clasping his shoulder. "Back atcha, bro."

"Good. Now that you juveniles have sorted yourselves, we can settle this business." Carlos nodded to Eric.

"Right. As I was saying, the witch had a silver-edged knife. I didn't have to guess her plans. She projected her thoughts clearly enough. I couldn't read much more than that since I didn't sample her blood, but I saw enough to raise a question."

"I would think not," Carlos added.

"What I do know from her scent and from some of the things she said, it's clear she was a victim of a vampiric attack. She survived, obviously, but from what I gathered, her loved ones did not. It's the reason she hunts." Eric spared a look for Julian. "Much the same as with Lily."

"Eric—" Carlos cautioned.

"It's the truth, Carlos. Anyway, my guess is the witch pursues youngbloods because they are the most likely candidates for those responsible for what happened in her past. Youngbloods are the only ones reckless enough to risk witch blood."

"Any clue about her coven?" Carlos asked.

He shook his head. "Don't hold me to this, but I think she's acting alone. I spared one of the youngbloods last night, only because he showed conscience. He was very reluctant to go along with the other youngblood's unsavory plan.

"My sparing him seemed to throw the witch. After that, she was curious about me and my motives. Despite

her skepticism, she seemed truly rattled some of our kind actually have a moral compass."

Julian exhaled, crossing his arms. "There's likely no happy ending to this scenario. Carlos, you know if there are no mitigating circumstances, the Vampire Council will want her destroyed. Or at the very least, her coven notified so they can consequence her accordingly. We demanded as much from the Alpha of the Brethren when we found it was a Were that unleashed HepZ into our community. This witch will most likely end up with her heart in a box."

"Wow, Jules. When did you start taking an interest in our laws?"

His eyes moved to Eric. "When I nearly lost Kat to a psychopath, and *he* was one of our own. We shredded that rotting vampiric bag of bones for his crimes, so why wouldn't we go after an outsider making us her prey? I'm not saying the council will go that way, but you've got to admit it doesn't look good for the witch."

"Lily went all vigilante after a rabid Were killed her best friend. She took pot shots at vampires and Weres alike when she went target shooting in Central Park. Now she's the Alpha Female of the Brethren and mate to one of our strongest allies. Where were her mitigating reasons other than we needed her for the cure in her blood?"

"Your point?" Julian asked.

"Vampires aren't saints, Julian. We reap what we sow. Just because we choose to live by a moral code of conduct, doesn't mean the rest of our kind do. You said it yourself. Your mate was kidnapped and nearly killed by a vampire coloring outside the lines. Way outside the lines. Every day more of our kind evolve. The Red Veil and even the Vampire Council have come around to our way of

thinking, thanks to Carlos and Rémy. So mitigating circumstances aren't as hard to come by as once before."

"In certain instances, *mijo*," Carlos conceded. "Nonetheless, we still have laws to abide, and if this witch is motivated by hate, regardless of what caused that fury to take root and grow, she will have to be taken to task."

Julian nodded. "My beef with this witch isn't because I have a problem with her branch of our supernatural tree. It's because she's delivering final death to vampires who haven't directly wronged *her*."

"I know," Eric agreed. "Then again, don't you think we should learn the why behind her actions? Find out if there's basis for her motives? There's a reason behind her pain and her rage. Don't you think those ends should be heard before judgement is passed?" He shrugged. "You said it. Innocent until proven guilty."

Carlos stood, and they both shut up. "I need to discuss this with Rémy. Until we know more, I want everyone in this house to take extra care. I doubt this witch draws a line between true evil and what she perceives as such."

"My guess is she believes vampires are true evil," Eric added. "Or at least she did until last night. My saving her life gave her preconceptions a shakeup. She even let me kiss her. No glamour required."

Both sets of undead eyes turned.

"You got close to a silver-wielding witch just to steal a kiss?" Carlos raised an eyebrow. "*Dio.* I'd rather rub up against a cactus. Naked."

Eric laughed. "I'm not completely insane. I relieved her of the knife, first.

Julian raised a skeptical brow. "She must love you for that."

"Let's just say I left the witch speechless in more ways than one." Eric chuckled. "Sovereigns of seduction, one... Witchiepooh, zip."

"More likely she left vowing to cut your heart next chance she gets, Bro. If only to prove you wrong."

Carlos cocked his head. "I think you two just afforded us the perfect plan. Eric, I want you to tempt her out into the open. Get her to expose herself. See if you can find out what makes her tick before she realizes you're fishing."

"You want me to find her and then woo her?"

"Not to put too fine a point on it, but yes."

"And if she's as smart as I suspect?" Eric questioned.

Carlos's mouth quirked in a crooked grin. "Then finish what you started and seduce her to the darkness."

Eric raised an eyebrow. "We don't do that, Carlos. House rules, remember."

"I don't mean turn her. For God's sake, no. I meant make her see you for who you really are, *mijo*. You haven't said as much, but my gut tells me you made a connection with the witchy huntress. See where it takes you. I'll keep my own council about this until I hear otherwise from you. Rémy can wait. Like you said. We need to see if there are mitigating circumstances."

Eric didn't comment. He poured himself another mug from the carafe, nodding to Carlos and Julian as they left him to finish his second cup of crimson, alone.

He ran a hand through his hair, thinking. Carlos was three times his age, and usually right about most things. If he thought there was a link between him and the witch, then maybe what he'd felt since last night wasn't a one-off.

A connection. Hell, if that's what that touch of soul fire was when their auras merged, then he was in for one hell of a ride.

Chapter Three

"**M**om's calling you, weirdo. Better get going, or she'll come looking for you."

Blair stuck her tongue at her brother and gave his butt a whack with the narrow stick she'd found for the s'mores.

"Ow, quit it."

Their mother walked toward the edge of the clearing, shaking her head. "He's twelve, and you're seventeen. When are you going to learn?"

"I don't like when he calls me weirdo. I can't help it if I know things." Blair shrugged. "Maybe I'm psychic. Mikey's mad because I always know when he's planning stuff behind your back."

Her mother rolled her eyes. "You are not psychic, and no one likes a know-it-all or a tattletale. Go grab another bag of marshmallows from the tent. Get the jumbos. They're in the striped bag on top of the cooler."

"Okay, but this just proves I'm psychic, cuz I know you didn't bring the jumbos. You left them on the kitchen counter when you yelled for Dad to hurry up so we wouldn't hit rush hour traffic."

"Like I said. No one likes a know-it-all. Just get whatever I brought. Dad said the fire's just about perfect. Hurry up. It'll be dark soon."

Blair held her stick wand-like as her mother walked away to corral her brother. "If only," she mumbled.

Breathing ragged, Blair knotted the top sheet around her hand. She turned over but couldn't wake. She heard the screams coming. They always came…

The fire flickered, casting shadows along the ground. Dad sat on the center log, his face aglow from the firepit.

"Tonight's tale is about the vampire brothers of New Orleans and how they drained their victims and then disappeared."

Mikey groaned. "That's boring. Tell the one about the hitchhiker."

"Ssh. Let your dad tell the story." Mom winked, handing him another marshmallow.

"So, the story goes there was a pair of brothers. To their neighbors and the people on the street they seemed perfectly ordinary. It was the 1930s, and the depression hit Louisiana, like everywhere else. To make extra money, the brothers took in boarders, renting rooms in their house. No one thought it odd they worked only at night. Even when strange noises and crashing sounds woke their neighbors, no one said a word. Until, one night, a scream pierced the dead of night. Neighbors bolted from their beds only to see a woman running from the house, her wrists slit clean through...

The woman's eyes and hair were wild as though devils were on her heels. One neighbor grabbed her waist, forcing her to the ground so they could wrap her in a blanket. She fought. Screaming, "They're dead! They're dead! All dead!"

The neighbors tried to stop the bleeding, but it was too late. She slumped to the ground in a crimson pool. When the police came, they searched the house. They found two other boarders with their wrists torn, and over a dozen dead bodies drained of blood. The brothers tried to escape into the night, but eight police officers held them down.

They were arrested and eventually executed; their bodies interred in their family vault in Lafayette cemetery. A year later, floods overtook the cemetery, cracking the doors to the mausoleum. When the cemetery workers checked the next day,

the brothers' bodies were gone. It's said to this day, they still prowl, looking for new victims…

Dad snapped the marshmallow toasting stick in his hand, and Mikey jumped. "Pretty good, huh?"

Sweating, Blair's head thrashed on her pillow. They were here… They were always here.

"My compliments, sir. Exceptional, storytelling!"

Dad swiveled immediately as a man walked from the shadows into the firelight. He moved as though floating, and Mom immediately got up to stand between him and the kids.

"Can we help you?" Dad asked, getting up from his seat as well.

"I'm thrilled that story is still being told. I must admit, it has been a while. Though it wasn't eight police officers. It was twelve. Then again, I was still a youngblood…"

He inclined his head and then whistled, holding his hand toward the woods. "Speaking of youngbloods—" He grinned, letting two fangs glint in the orange light. You'll have to excuse his enthusiasm. He's very new…"

A wild man lunged from the shadows, knocking Mom to the ground. Her scream pierced the air but then died in a sickening gurgle. Blood splattered as he tore her throat, gorging on her pulsing jugular.

Eyes wild like in the story, Blair watched frozen in horror.

"Blair! For God's sake, run!" Dad grabbed Mikey, but it was too late. The vampire tore at them both.

He let their bodies slump to the ground, Blood-red eyes and stained teeth turned for her as she pivoted toward the camper.

"Run, little rabbit, but you can't hide." A cruel laugh broke the chilling silence. "Let's share the last one, eh?"

A snarl ripped from the older one's mouth, and he blurred to her side, knocking her to the ground. The other caught her leg and dragged her backward over her mother's lifeless legs.

Teeth pierced her flesh, but her scream drowned as agonized shrieks ripped from both monsters. Blood dripped from her legs and wrist as she scrambled to her feet. Their skin blackened and caved as they writhed. The younger one fell where he stood, his body imploding. The older one staggered toward her, one last word on his lips…Witch.

A strangled scream broke from Blair's mouth, and she bolted up in bed.

"Blair! For God's sake!" A slipper winged at her headboard. "What the hell is wrong with you!" Her cell phone alarm buzzed as if on cue, and Suzy threw her other slipper. "Are you deaf or just ignoring that goddamned foghorn?"

Blair blinked from her fog and fumbled to swipe dismiss on her phone's alarm. "Sorry, Suz. I had another bad dream."

Her roommate's reply muffled into her pillow before she pulled her comforter over her head. Something about bloody murder and cell phones."

"Been there done that, Suz ol' girl," Blair mumbled, throwing her covers off. Her body still hummed from the dream, and she half-yawned, half-shuddered as she got out of bed. Sparing a look at Suzy's comforter-covered lump, she grabbed her toiletry bag and headed for the common bathroom on their floor.

"Wow, not bothering with slippers or a robe this morning, eh, Care-Blair? Suzy's aim must be getting better."

"Shut up, Elizabeth."

Her friend held two mugs of steaming coffee. Lifting one, she let the aromatic steam waft. "I guess you don't want one of these, then."

"I take it back. You are a Cajun goddess." Blair accepted the mug and inhaled its chicory scent. Taking a taste, she groaned. "I owe you one, Lizzie Tish."

Lizzie chuckled. "Your New York-isms tickle me. What exactly is a *Tish*?" She followed Blair into the bathroom and leaned on one of the four sinks, sipping her coffee.

"I don't know, babe. It's something my mother used to call me. I think it's the name of a character from a radio program from the 1930s."

A character from the thirties. She cringed. Like the one with fangs and a major entitlement attitude that murdered her family and was now haunting her dreams.

Blair sucked in a breath, dismissing the thought. It was just a nightmare. "Anyway, the saying caught on and sort of stuck. At least around here."

"I heard you come in last night, *cher*. Or should I say this morning?"

Blair paused with her toothbrush. She closed her eyes and quickly finished brushing her teeth. She did the rinse and spit and then turned to face Lizzie's raised eyebrow.

"Does Tara know?" she asked, drying her mouth.

Lizzie shook her head. "I covered for you. Said you fell asleep in my room studying."

"Thank you. Now I really, really owe you." Blair's shoulders relaxed. She pinned her hair up, grabbing her things for the shower.

"It's not a hard fib to envision, though why someone would want a master's degree in the occult is beyond me. Talk about a yawn fest. We live it, *cher*. Every day. Why pile on when you could study art or literature or science. We don't have enough witchy women in the STEM field,

36

you know. Besides, your undergraduate degree is history. It doesn't mesh."

"It meshes fine. I'm right-brained, babe. Like most members of our talented troupe. Much of the occult is steeped in history, so it's a perfect fit. You know history is my jam, but this makes it creepy and cool." Blair turned on the spray, sticking her fingers under the water with a shiver. "Why does it take forever for hot water, every morning?"

"The coven house is old." Lizzie handed Blair her coffee again while she waited for steam. "Is it a guy?"

"Is what a guy?"

Lizzie cocked her head, giving her a dubious look. "I may speak with an accent, but that doesn't mean I think with one. If it's not a lover keeping you out until daybreak, then what? You know Tara's bound to find out."

"Trust me. It's better if you don't know."

"I don't like the sound of that, Blair Cabot. Does this have anything to do with the question you asked me yesterday?"

Blair shut the water off in the shower and then took Lizzie's mug from her hand and put it down on the white porcelain beside her cup.

"Not here." She motioned for Lizzie to follow.

They turned out of the bathroom and into the corridor. "What is this, Blair? We're a little old for hide-and-seek."

Blair took her friend's hand and tugged her toward the linen closet. Opening the door, she practically shoved Lizzie inside.

"Have you lost what little sense God gave you? Let me out of here!"

Blair put a finger to her lips and then looked over her shoulder before closing the door. "This is the only room in

Crow Haven House without a vent. You have no idea how voices carry on that gossip superhighway. I don't want anyone else knowing."

"Knowing what? You haven't told me anything."

"I know, and I apologize for that. I figured the less you knew the better. Especially with bloodhound Tara sniffing around."

"So?"

Blair looked at her friend. "I should have known you were too smart not to get suspicious, but before I tell you the truth, I have to be sure you won't snitch."

"Snitch?" Lizzie scoffed. "Girl, bless your *heart*. What are we, twelve?"

Blair's mouth dropped a little. "Listen, you raging Cajun, I know what that means. It's the same thing as me telling you to go scratch your ass. I'm serious, Lizzie. You have to give me your word."

"What do you expect when you basically said you *don't* trust me?" Lizzie crossed her arms. "Name one time I've broken your confidence."

"Never." Blair hesitated. "But this is different. This is dangerous."

"Dangerous!" Lizzie's whisper rose two octaves. "What the hell have you gotten yourself into? Yesterday you asked me if I ever heard of witches hooking up with vampires. Are you with a vampire? As in doing the nasty?"

Blair bit the inside of her cheek. Lizzie was still such a Southern belle. "The *nasty*? God, you kill me, Louisiana. *But* to answer your question, no. I am not fucking the enemy."

"Care-Blair, do you always have to be so crude? And vampires are not our enemies. They are *your* enemies. Like

I said yesterday, I have not heard of witches and vampires keeping company, but that doesn't mean it hasn't happened. There are obvious obstacles with our blood and all, but stranger things have happened. In *New Awlins*, you can't swing a cat without hitting a vampire or a witch. Especially in the Quarter. Proximity leads to strange bedfellows."

"I never understood that saying. Who in their right mind would swing a cat?"

Lizzie tightened her arms. "You are changing the subject again. And the saying comes from swinging a cat-o'-nine-tails. A vile historic kind of whip. Has something to do with the swing circumference. Now, what are you doing with vampires? Didn't your mama ever tell you not to touch dead things?"

"I'm killing them."

Lizzie's jaw fell at the matter-of-fact statement. "Blair Cabot! Why would you do such a horrendous thing? You are not a murderer."

"It's not murder if the thing you kill is already lifeless. And you know why I'm doing what I'm doing."

"Yes, I know…and I understand, or at least I'm trying to, but—" Lizzie's arms dropped to her sides, and she shook her head. "This is bad, Blair. Very bad. If Tara finds out…" Her eyes went wide. "Forget Tara. What if the Vampire Council finds out?"

Blair put her hand on Lizzie's arm. "They'll probably kill me. The undead are not the most forgiving bunch of walking corpses. They'll want their pound of living flesh in the form of my heart in a box."

"God, I don't even want to picture it."

Chuckling, Blair gave her friend's arm a squeeze. "I know, but I heard through the grapevine it's what they

demanded of the Alpha of the Brethren when they found who was responsible for the HepZ virus."

"Is this really how you want to get past what happened to your family? Revenge leads nowhere, *cher*. Certainly not to peace."

Blair threw her hands up. "Fuck that. I'm not ready to make peace. There's no kumbaya moment waiting for me in this, Lizzie. No matter what changes."

"That sounds an awful lot like a seed of doubt." She raised an eyebrow. "What changed, Blair?"

She met her friend's eyes. "Nothing. Not really."

"C'mon, *babe*." She mimicked Blair's New York accent. "I know you better than that, especially when you get that tiny crinkle between your eyes. You're not telling me everything."

"He kissed me."

"Wait. He who?"

Blair's brows knotted. "The vampire."

"Before or after you killed him."

"What? Oh God. Yuck! *Before*, dummy. After you stick them with silver, they sort of...disintegrate."

"Well, like the old boys at St. Louis Cathedral say, ashes to ashes." Lizzie winked.

"Ugh. I think I liked you better when your Southern sensibilities were shocked."

"I've been hanging around you too much." Lizzie smirked. "So, when he kissed you. Did you kiss him back? I hear the fanged ones are pretty fabulous when it comes to curling toes. Or so my shifter friends say."

"*Ew.* I thought their sniffing butts and rolling in foul scents was bad enough."

Lizzie pushed past her, reaching for the linen closet door. "You disappoint me, Blair. It's like you suddenly

hate all supernaturals. You never used to be this way, but this past year it's like you're possessed or something.

"We have a creed, or did you forget? Threefold. Remember? Barriers are breaking down between supernaturals all over the place. Friendships and alliances are being forged, and races are mixing. It's a beautiful thing, *cher*, but you can't see past your hate."

"The Red Veil never allowed witches on the premises. Now they do. I heard the Circle of the Raven had something to do with bringing that about. They had an issue with a rogue who abducted one of their coven sisters. The Master of the Vampire Council...Rémy Tessier, I think. He helped them rescue her, and he did so personally."

Blair snorted. "Probably his kind that abducted her in the first place. Ravens are Fae-kissed. Descended from the Shining Ones, or so they love to claim. Vampires can't resist Fae blood. It's their personal drug of choice."

"No, *cher*. It was a rogue Sidhe who abducted the Raven girl. The vampires helped rescue her because it was the right thing to do. This vampire that kissed you. Why?"

Blair blinked at Lizzie's gear shift. "Why what?"

"Why did he kiss you, especially if he knew what you were planning to do?"

Blair shrugged. "I don't know. Probably to make a point that he could. Sovereigns of seduction, and all that crap." She pursed her lips. "His words, actually."

"So, answer my question, then. Did you kiss him back?"

"No."

Lizzie cocked her head. "The lady doth protest too much, and too dang quickly. Plus, that crinkle between

your eyes just got deeper. You may not have kissed him, but you wanted to. Badly."

"What of it? Vampires are glamour and deceit rolled into one."

At another raised eyebrow, Blair exhaled hard. "Can you let the damn kiss go, and promise me you won't say anything to Tara?" Blair bounced on the balls of her feet. "C'mon, Lizzie. I really have to get in the shower and get to class, so please, promise me."

Inhaling a skeptical breath, her friend nodded. "On one condition. You promise *me* you won't hunt anymore."

Blair stuck her hand in her pajama pocket and crossed her fingers. "I promise."

"Nah, nah, lady." Lizzie crossed her arms at her chest. "I didn't just fall off a turnip truck. Show me both hands."

Rolling her eyes, Blair pulled her hand from her pocket and held both out straight.

"Good. Now swear."

Blair pecked on her friend's cheek. "Pinky promise."

Lizzie eyed her sideways. "I'm serious, Blair. You need to stay put. Odds are that kissing vampire knows your sins, and after last night he's got to know you're a witch. It's only a matter of time before he finds you."

She walked out of the linen closet, but Blair hung back. She lifted a finger to her mouth, the memory of Eric's kiss still on her lips. "Let's hope so, babe."

***

Blair stood eating a soft pretzel from a food cart across from the Raven motherhouse. By the time she got out of the shower and out the front door, it was too late to make it to class.

The library at Crow Haven House was small compared to the one at the Raven motherhouse. To be honest, Crow Haven was more dormitory than anything else. It had never bothered her before, but now she needed a true seat of learning.

She plopped a piece of salty pretzel into her mouth and chewed. It was funny, actually. Ironic. Crows and Ravens were kissing cousins in bird species as well as in the witching world. Fae blood notwithstanding. They were among the oldest recorded covens in the new world. They'd suffered their share of persecution over the centuries, including the infamous witch trials of 1692. Still, they survived. Thrived, even.

Blair washed down her mouthful of pretzel with the last of her coffee, hoping the Supreme of the Circle of the Raven was up for a little cousinly nepotism.

The motherhouse library was huge, and it came with its own archivist. Grania was as old as the hills, and when it came to lore, law, and legend, no one knew more. Somewhere in the Raven's coveted collection was a hint as to why she couldn't stop thinking about Eric.

Had the vampire glamoured her brain? Or was it something on a visceral level she didn't understand? Either way, she wanted it to stop. She wanted her body to stop betraying her every time she thought about him, his lips, or the amazing way he smelled. It was all a ruse, right? A ploy to lure in potential prey. It had to be.

She threw away her cup and what was left of her pretzel, fumbling in her pocket for a napkin or a tissue to wipe her mouth. Her fingers closed on something soft instead. It was the scrap from Eric's jacket.

Lifting it to her nose, she inhaled. Her stomach flip-flopped, not because the torn fabric belonged to a vampire, but because his scent made her knees weak.

"Get a grip, Blair. This is not playtime."

"*Playtime, cher?* Lizzie's soft chuckle feathered across her mind. *Who are you fooling? A tumble in the dark with that boy is just what you need. More, it's what you want.*"

With a guttural sniff, she dismissed the imagined chide and marched across the street. "Screw you, Louisiana. What I want is undead blood dripping from my silver." Blair exhaled. Her retort seemed full of piss and vinegar, but in truth it fell flat. She wanted to cross paths with Eric more than she let on, and for more reasons than she was comfortable even thinking about.

She stuffed the delicious scrap in her pocket again. A scrying session using his residual blood and a map of the city would give her a clue how to find him, but for now she had unnerving and conflicting reactions to explain, and the place for answers was dead ahead.

Blair stepped onto the curb and stood looking up at the historic structure. Raven house was huge. A park unto itself surrounded by tall trees and a wrought iron perimeter fence.

The place radiated wards and spelled sigils. She wasn't surprised. Not after what Lizzie said happened last spring.

Focusing her senses, Blair lifted a hand. "*Revalabo stultitiam.*" The air shimmered like gasoline on summer asphalt.

She smiled to herself. "I guess it does work." Eric's face danced through her mind from the last time she tried the spell.

It fell flatter than a pancake.

Yeah, but the next one worked. Deliciously, too. Who knew merging auras could be so silky and sexy?

Shut up.

Blair ignored her inner bicker and turned her attention to the wards at hand. The energy was thick, drawing power from natural ley lines crisscrossing the urban estate. Glowing at key points were protective sigils and runes cut into the energy. If an unwelcome visitor crossed one of them, they'd end up face-first in the dirt, counting their blessings it wasn't permanent.

Excited, Blair stepped over the crackling energy lines, careful not to trip the sigils. "Fae-kissed blood certainly packs a punch," she muttered, sliding past the last one.

"It certainly does, but you look adept enough."

Blair wheeled around, nearly smacking into an older woman with long, silvery pink hair. She was dressed in a gray velvet corset coat, trimmed with pink-and-yellow brocade. Pink kid boots and a long silky gray skirt peeked from below the coat's hem, and with her hair pulled into a curly top bun, she looked as though she'd just walked through time. The only giveaway she hadn't were the plastic supermarket bags in both hands.

"I'm sorry. I didn't mean… Wait, how did you get—" Blair blinked at the woman who'd appeared out of nowhere but then shut up, realizing she was making it worse.

The woman obviously belonged to the Raven motherhouse, and, as usual, her big mouth had set the tone before she even had the chance to introduce herself.

"Are you here to visit someone in particular?" She raised an eyebrow, reaching a gloved hand for the front door.

Blair glanced at her Converse and jeans, fidgeting with the string from her NYU hoodie under her rain jacket. "Uhm, no. Not really. I was hoping I'd be allowed to use your library for research."

The woman's eyes flicked to the collegiate letters on the sweatshirt. "Grad student, then?"

Blair blinked. "Master's program, but that's not why I'm here. I'm a Crow."

The pretty woman's eyebrow hiked higher.

"Sorry." Blair exhaled a nervous chuckle. "What I mean is I belong to Crow Haven House."

A smile spread across the woman's pretty face. "A sister witch, then." She nodded. "Come in. I'm sure we can accommodate you in whatever you need."

Blair wiped her feet on the welcome mat, impressed at how the tight weave sucked the wetness right from her sneakers. "Your wards are pretty strong. Are they to keep people out or keep members in?"

"Clever." The woman grinned, and the front door lock clicked open with barely a sound. "What's your name, child?"

"Blair Cabot."

She eyed Blair as she stepped through the entry. "A strong surname. Old, too. Like many of our kind," she replied. "I'm Caitlan. It's a pleasure to meet you."

Blair nearly fell over. The woman standing beside her at the motherhouse door was the Supreme of the Circle of the Ravens.

"I...I didn't mean anything about your wards," Blair stammered. "It wasn't a crack or anything. I'm not used to seeing that kind of protective power concentrated in one place."

Caitlan pushed the door wide and then stood to the side, letting Blair enter the foyer first. "I understand, dear."

"No, really. Crow Haven isn't like this..." Her voice trailed off as she walked into the old house's vestibule. Elegant didn't go far enough. If Caitlan looked as if she'd walked through time to get here, their home was beyond that.

"Are you sure you didn't spell this place to defy space and time? Your home looks as though it belongs to the Gilded Age with the Vanderbilts and the Astors."

Caitlan shut the door behind Blair. "Thank you, dear. We try." With a gentle wave, she lowered the foyer lighting to a muted glow. "Now. What can we help you with?"

This was the make-or-break moment. The ethereally elegant Raven would either escort her to the library or kick her to the curb.

"I am researching the undead and their relationship with witches. I'm particularly interested in the history surrounding how we became enemies."

"I see." Caitlan unbuttoned her coat before slipping it from slender shoulders. "Don't you think enemies is too strong a word? We have our obvious differences, and at times have been adversaries, but we come to each other's aid when necessary. In fact, we recently had a situation where the undead provided an invaluable service to this house."

"Of course. Bad choice of words." Blair gave what she hoped was a sheepish smile and crossed her fingers inside her coat pocket.

Hanging her coat on an ornate coatrack, Caitlan studied Blair for another moment before nodding. "Very

well. I'll let you use the library, but you will have to do so under the auspices of our archivist, Grania." She gestured to the rack. "You can hang your jacket on a lower rung."

"Of course. I've heard of Grania. Whatever help you can give is appreciated." Blair slid her backpack to the floor and shrugged out of her wet slicker.

Caitlan led the way to the back of the large house. Two double doors let into an anteroom of sorts. A mini library or reading room. From there, she slid aside a wide pocket door that opened into a room that rivaled the library from *Beauty and the Beast*, only rectangular.

"Grania, I've brought you a curious one. She's from Crow Haven House, and she's researching the undead." Caitlan cocked her head, giving Blair a quick study. "Though I'm not sure she really knows what she's looking for."

The old librarian wheezed a chuckle. "Who of the young ones do these days." She winked, flashing a bright smile. "I'll do what I can for you, dear. Even if the answers you receive aren't the ones you want or expect."

With a nod, Caitlan left them in awkward silence.

"I feel like I showed up for school naked," she joked, trying to shake off the feeling of being exposed.

"Ah, well. Then you must have things you want to keep hidden, sweetheart. Still, the wards allowed you through, even with your fancy footwork." She tapped the side of her nose. "Raven House is not the place to come if you have secrets you'd rather keep. Fae blood gives us sight, so tell me now if you wish to continue."

Blair nodded. "I think I have to, but you should know I've done things that perhaps you won't approve."

"No one here will sit in judgement of you. It's clear you're doing a fine job of that all on your own. My eyes

may be old, but I can see well enough the guilt and anger you carry. Perhaps what you find here will help."

Grania reached out a gnarled hand. Blair hesitated at first but then took the gesture. The moment her hand clasped the woman's papery skin, she knew Grania saw every act of revenge, every ounce of guilt and regret, and all her anger.

The old woman inhaled and then finally let go. "You have a lot of work ahead of you, my little Crow. Not so much searching my archive but searching your soul."

Seriously? She needed a lecture like she needed a hole in her head. "How long do you think this will take?"

Grania frowned, and her gimlet stare nearly rocked Blair to the door.

"It will take as long as it takes. You're not here to research the undead. You're here to search for freedom or forgiveness. Probably both. Buckle up, lovey. You're in for a bumpy ride."

Chapter Four

*T*emperatures plummeted as it neared midnight. Paths leading toward Central Park Lake and its wooded Rambles swirled with ground fog. Cool night air meeting warmed earth.

Eric moved through the ethereal scene, his long duster sweeping the vapor like Heathcliff walking the night-kissed moors. Chilled air never bothered him, even as a human, but the scent of fire and smoke in the distance and the swirl of ground fog made him shiver. It was only fog, but it was so like smoke in the way it wisped along the earth and hung in the air, it roused memories he'd rather forget.

Sad, angry musing could wait. He needed to feed. The park and its Rambles weren't usual places for youngbloods, so he didn't expect to run into the witch.

It perplexed him how much she'd occupied his mind since he walked away from that alley. Flashes from that night stirred him more ways than he'd like to admit. She'd asked his name but didn't offer hers. By that time, he was too far away for pleasantries and didn't trust himself to turn back. Their meeting wasn't exactly conducive to chat, not when she was more powerful a witch than he first thought.

Those moments of light and warmth still haunted him. If he closed his eyes, he could still feel the sensation. Like lifting your face to the summer sun.

His fangs tingled in his gums again. Anticipation. It wasn't the pull of his thirst. It was more than that. More than mere curiosity about the witch. He'd experienced a

glimpse of his own humanity again. More than just the small threads he'd managed to weave over the past century. His humanity the way it would have been. If...

He shook the feeling off. What-ifs were a game for children. For dreamers. And his dreams had been nightmares for a century. He didn't want games. Not anymore. Especially not the kind of game this witch played.

A small grin took his mouth. Hellcat. She was bold. Brave even, if somewhat misguided and full of piss and vinegar. Still, she had wit. *Where were you turned? The Westport Yacht Club?* He smirked at the memory. Under other circumstances, she might have been a fun friend.

Or more.

Her name. It was probably something charmed like Willow or Wren. Still, if *she* was as preoccupied with him as he was with her, then fate held nothing but disaster for them. If his past portended anything, they'd end up like Buffy and Angel. Drawn to one another but forever apart.

Again, what-ifs did no one any good.

"*Gah,* if Julian heard me now, he'd ask for my man card." The muttered reproach echoed in the stillness, and the overreaching hush piqued his senses.

The sprawling park was usually alive with...well, *life,* even in the dead of winter, but now it was quiet. Too quiet.

Vampires fed here. Generally, on the criminal element, but a few willing innocents did so for a price. He thought about Sam. A homeless vet who normally called the 68th Street subway, home. He made his position very clear when it came to supply and demand.

"Dude, even the Red Cross pays. Plasma earns me between twenty and fifty bucks. I get a cookie and orange juice before I hit the streets again, and, if I'm lucky, I even

score a sandwich. If you want the crimson, you gotta come up with the scratch."

Sam was quite the capitalist. Persuading his buddies into a round-robin service for certain vampires. Of course, no one believed the few who blabbed. Who would? Police and local psych wards chalked their blather up to forgotten meds. Still, their procurer kept things quiet. If humans knew what walked beside them in plain sight, it would be bad for business.

That tidbit would probably make the witch's mental hit list. A list of sins, he suspected, was very long and very detailed.

Eric scanned the entrance to the Rambles. The full moon hung high in the dark canvas, illuminating the thirty-eight acres of woods and rocky outcrops.

Weres raced the full moon in this section of the park, especially on a clear, cool night. If he was lucky, one of them would let him drink his fill. Shifter blood would slake his thirst for a month, but that wasn't his reason for seeking out a willing Were. He needed more than preternatural strength to stalk his witchling. Were blood would mask his undead pallor, making it easier to blend.

"Eric?"

The vampire turned, catching a refracted green glow peeking through the trees.

"Natasha?"

A lithe, feminine form uncoiled from all fours before walking with predatory grace from the scrub. The shifter was naked and glorious in the moonlight, and she moved with stealth even in human form.

"I was about to give chase when I caught your scent. What are you doing in the Rambles? Did you forget tonight is our Harvest Hunt?"

He smiled at the jaunty tilt to her head. Her question was rhetorical. One sniff told her everything she wanted to know.

"I was hoping to bump into you," he replied anyway, not owning he'd forgotten about their seasonal hunt.

The slant to her knowing grin matched her self-confident posture. "Bump me? Why, sir, whatever can you mean?" Her lips curled higher on one side, leaving no question about the smirk's invitation.

"Nat, don't tease. I've got a witch to find, and time is of the essence. However tempting your offer to play in the dark, I'll take a rain check."

"Essence is what you came looking for then, eh? My essence."

He nodded, keeping his eyes on the faint refracted glow still in her cat's eyes. "Unless you know a generous wolf who's willing to spare a pint or two."

She snorted. "Why would you want a smelly dog when you can have this?" She lifted her chin, letting the moonlight catch the sleek curve of her throat.

"Because you'd just as soon kill me as let me at your throat, and you know it. And you enjoy being an absolute tease."

"True enough."

"C'mon, Natasha. Be a pal. If I'm to find this witch and preserve my undead hide, I'll need every bit of *oomph* your shifter blood provides."

She flashed a small teasing grin, lifting her chin higher. "Nice try, Doughboy. I'm a Were, Eric. You can say whatever with your mouth, but your scent and your body language tell a different story. You've got the hots for this witch." One eyebrow arched. "And I thought you had enough of playing in the minefields."

"One, Doughboy was the term for American troops. I was Canadian forces. Two, I do not have the hots for the witch. I don't even know her name."

Natasha's eyebrow hiked higher. "You don't need to know someone's name to want to bump uglies with them. She got to you. Admit it, and then I'll give you my blood. Or you can deny it, as well as the chubby in your pants just talking about her, and I'll go join my hunt."

"A tease and a bitch." He exhaled, shaking his head. "God help me."

She glanced at the moon and her eyes glinted brighter before darkening to a deep forest green. "Ticktock, vampire. I've got people to meet and places to see, and my inner cougar wants raw earth under her paws."

"The witch intrigues me, okay? Satisfied?"

Natasha nodded. "It's a start. I don't know why you vampires need to make things so difficult. When shifters feel the heat, we simply raise ass and go to it. In human and animal form. Sex is a biological need. Like eating and sleeping."

"Vampires do neither, eat nor sleep. So, your point is?"

"Funny. I guess you *don't* need my blood, then."

He rolled his eyes. "Nat! *Jeez.* Are you this difficult with all your friends, or is it just me?"

"Just the ones who think too much." She beckoned him forward, and her eyes held his gaze as he approached. "Don't dwell so much, Doughboy. If the witch intrigues you, let her."

"Right now, the only thing intriguing is your blood."

She grinned. "You vampires are likes dogs with a bone. Seek her out, Eric. Times change. It wasn't so long ago my kind would sooner rip out your throat than ever consider offering you our necks. You want her? Go get her."

Eric's eyes burned, and he knew they flashed red in the darkness. His hand slid to the back of her neck beneath her pixie-styled hair. Whispering his thanks, he dipped his mouth to the pulsing vein beneath her jaw.

His fangs lengthened, but there was no surge of anticipation. No tingle. The vampiric equivalent to an adrenaline rush. Sharp tips penetrated the shifter's vein, and his mouth filled with rich Were blood. His body responded to the warm influx, stagnant cells swelling with supernatural life.

Natasha fit easily against him. From a distance, everything about their stance screamed sex, but it was the one element that didn't factor. Neither allowed it, keeping the lines between them clear and defined.

She sighed, opening her eyes. "I think we have a spectator."

Eric pulled his fangs from her throat, quickly sealing the wound. He licked her residual blood from his lips and then inhaled.

"Even I can smell it's a witch. The million-dollar question, is it your witch?" Nat asked, stepping away to let him scan the shadows.

He sniffed the cool air, but never sampling her blood made it hard to be sure. Closing his eyes, he inhaled deep, allowing the scents to separate. It was her.

"Come out, come out wherever you are, witchling," Eric called toward the shadows. "I can smell you, so don't bother running. You're a self-proclaimed hunter, but who would have guessed a voyeur as well? Tsk, tsk. I wonder what your coven would say?"

Natasha adjusted her collar, wiping her neck with the side of her hand. "Don't be a dick, Doughboy. Embarrassing her is not the fastest way into her pants."

"*Ssh.* That's not what I'm after."

Boots tapped on the pavement leading from the Lake. Blair stepped onto the moonlit path where Eric stood with Natasha.

"I am *not* a voyeur. I was out...out for—" She hesitated, pulling her coat tighter.

He crossed his arms, moving over to let Natasha slide in beside him. "Out for what? A run? If that's the case you're just in time to join the shifters on their Harvest Hunt."

"Eric—"

Natasha whispered a warning, but Blair lifted her chin. "No, it's okay, sweetheart. I wouldn't expect anything less from a filthy bloodsucker."

"*Jesus.* Can we stop with the name calling?" Eric shot back. "It's juvenile and it accomplishes nothing. Who are you? And why are you stalking my kind?"

He kept his face impassive, considering stalking *her* was the reason he came looking for Were blood. He had more than an inkling for why she was here, but if he meant what he said to Julian, he had to keep his cool or the witchling wouldn't stand a snowball's chance in hell of escaping vampiric retribution.

"Your being here is no coincidence, witch, so my impertinence is justified. Eric kept his poker face, even when the naked shifter elbowed the him. "Anyway, this is Natasha Wolfe. She's a cougar. I'd introduce *you*, but I haven't had the pleasure."

"And you never will, vampire."

Natasha raised an eyebrow. "Okay. Wow. I guess it's up to me to be the adult in the room. What Eric meant is I'm a Cougar, as in Were/shifter, not the middle-aged-prey-on-younger-men type."

Blair gave him a disgusted look which he ignored despite Nat's attempt at humor.

"Don't try to lighten the situation, Nat. Witchiepooh has ulterior motives for her presence tonight. I can smell the steel in her pocket. A blade with a silvered edge, just like the one I took from her the other night."

"I'm a woman alone in Central Park at night," she countered. "But I don't expect you'd understand, considering that makes me grade A prey for your kind."

Eric's irritation snapped. "Stop trying to turn this on me. I'm not the stalker here, Ms. Hide in the Shadows and Watch. Just how long were you crouched in the bushes, Witchiepooh?"

"Stop calling me that."

He shrugged. "I would, but you conveniently evade the question whenever I ask your identity."

"Why do you care who I am?"

Aggravated, Eric threw up a hand. "Oh, I don't know. Maybe so I can identify who's trying to kill me?"

"Ha. All the more reason for me to keep my identity quiet."

"Trust me, sweetheart. If I wanted to find you, I could. Unlike you, all I need is your scent. I could very easily read your thoughts or pick through your memories. But I won't."

She glanced at Natasha watching her with a frown. "Why not? It would give you the advantage."

"Because that's not who I am." He lifted one shoulder. "Just because you can, doesn't mean you should."

She blinked at his words. From the look on her face, he knew they threw her again, just like his questions had the other night. Was this progress, or was she too pigheaded to admit her own prejudice?

Ignoring him, she turned her attention to Nat. "And why is a shifter hanging around with the undead? It's as ironic as meeting a cat named Wolfe." Blair paused. "Still, I'm glad to meet you despite the circumstances. I'm Blair...Blair Cabot."

"Ironic?" Nat chuckled. "About as ironic as a witch named Blair. If I'm not mistaken, I think there's a movie in there somewhere."

Eric would have laughed at the clever quip, if not for the look on Blair's face. The witch had offered a tacit olive branch. Technically, she hadn't given her name to *him*. Her saving face in that way was almost comical, yet the subtext of it was significant.

"And I wasn't watching you." Blair sniffed. "I'm not a voyeur, though it was pretty obvious what you two were doing, or about to do when you sensed me. I can't help it if I interrupted your *whatever*, but it wasn't my intention."

Natasha laughed. "Nice try, Blair. You were standing there long enough. As to what we were doing or about to do, it's not what you think. What you witnessed was nothing more than me helping a friend. Like sharing half a candy bar with a coworker in an afternoon slump. Eric needed a boost, and I was happy to help. Truth is, you're curious about Eric, vampire or not. It's as saturated in your scent as the dirty-water hot dog you ate for lunch off that downtown food cart. You can't help yourself."

Blair opened her mouth to argue, but Natasha shut her down. "I'm a Were. So there's no arguing with the nose. The thing is, vamp boy is completely intrigued by you as well. He admitted it. So, as much as I relish sexually frustrated non-conversation, I'm going to leave you two to figure this out all on your own." She shrugged. "Or not. It's up to you. Either way, I have a hunt to get to."

She went up on tiptoe to peck Eric's cheek. "Call me if you change your mind about playing in the dark, Doughboy." With a nod to Blair, she took off for the woods.

Eric watched his friend disappear into the shadows, his close-lipped smile fading when he heard Blair walking in the opposite direction.

"Hey, where are you going?" He closed the distance between them, Natasha's blood heightening his speed along with everything else.

"Go away."

"Why? I thought we were making progress."

"Progress? Whatever your shifter friend thinks she sensed, there is no way you and I can be friends or anything else. Besides, I've never been so embarrassed in my life!"

He chuckled. "Wait until you're as old as I am. You'll stop counting the occasions."

"You were twenty-two." She sniffed. "How much embarrassment could you have before you were changed?"

He snorted. "You think the undead don't make gaffs? That a vampire can't stick his foot in his mouth, fangs and all, and then burn in self-conscious loathing afterward?"

"Wow. Dramatic much?" A reluctant smile tugged at the corner of her mouth. "Why did Natasha call you Doughboy? I'm assuming she didn't mean Pillsbury."

"So, you were spying on us the whole time."

Her jaw dropped, but she snapped it closed. "I was not, but I couldn't help overhearing some."

"Likely story."

"Well?"

Their footsteps fell into a rhythm on the empty path. In the distance were the sounds of the hunt under way, and the dual-natured racing the moon.

"No, definitely not Pillsbury. I may be fresh and hot, but she was referring to soldiers in World War I. The term was slang for American soldiers in the American Expeditionary Force. I'm Canadian, so it didn't apply."

Blair glanced across her shoulder at the tall, handsome vampire. "Are you saying you served in WWI?"

"I enlisted in 1916 when I turned twenty. I was lucky. I served two years without taking a bullet or mustard gas."

"Until?"

Eric glanced at the sky. An owl hooted in the distance, swooping from the trees toward an expanse of grass beside the lake. "Until the Battle of the Somme in 1916. I was wounded and somehow got left behind. I must have lost consciousness where I fell because, when I came to, the field was littered with bodies."

"France?"

He nodded. "Over five thousand Canadian troops lost their lives as we pushed back the Germans. I stumbled for days trying to get to my unit, dodging mortars and enemy fire, but a vampire found me first."

They walked to the edge of the lake. The moon illuminated the water and the surrounding landscape, turning everything a silvery gray, like an opulent black-and-white movie.

"My world has looked like this ever since. Shades of gray." With a sigh, he bent to pick up a handful of loose stones from the water's edge. "I miss the sun. The feel of it on my face. Its warmth on my skin."

Blair looked at him as he skipped stones across the lake's surface. "Were you cognizant of what was happening to you?"

"What do you mean?"

She looked away for a moment. "In the alley you spoke about rules. About people who were less than aware. You hinted they were off-limits, or something to that affect. Were you less than aware when you were turned?"

"I was badly wounded. Not quite gut shot but close. Somehow, I managed to get to my feet. Maybe it was the saturated blood on the battlefield, or maybe it was the scent of my blood since I was still alive. To this day, I'm not sure why I was singled out. I wasn't the only one wounded on that field in northern France. Perhaps it was because my unit left me for dead."

He threw another rock, watching it hop across the dark surface, leaving ripples behind.

"The vampire you mentioned in the alley. Carlos Salazar?" Blair asked, cautiously.

She was definitely a clever witch. "I'm impressed, Blair. What about him? If you're curious if he's the one who makes the rules you asked about, the answer is yes."

"No. I mean, that's great about the rules and all, and I want to know more about them, but what I was asking is if he was the one who found you in France."

Eric grunted. "I'm not that lucky. Not in my human life and certainly not since I woke to this existence. Carlos is the head of our family. There were five of us, originally. Carlos saved the other four from death or worse. As for me, he took me in when I had nowhere else to go.

"Carlos went through the same kind of raw turning. Being left to figure out his undead existence on his own. You see, in our world, if a vampire is created with

compassion and dignity, he or she retains the entire spectrum of human emotion. Everything from love and loyalty to jealousy and hate and all the shades of human feeling in between.

"If the opposite occurs, the youngblood vampire is left with only the self-serving vice and cruelty in which he was turned. It's all they retain. All they know."

She frowned, chewing her lip. "Your story sounds as though it falls into the cruel and self-serving category."

"I didn't know what had happened to me. I woke with a burning thirst nothing could quench. In my panic and fear, I did things I don't want to remember. Ever. I lost my soul in those early months, or whatever was left of it. I moved from place to place and enclave to enclave, finally finding myself in the sewers and catacombs of Paris. That's where Carlos found me trying to end my pitiful existence.

"Carlos took me in. Taught me what he was taught. Centuries earlier, an elder found *him* when he was mired in the same darkness of mind. He saved Carlos, and now Carlos pays it forward whenever he can. He saved me, as he was once saved, though I still struggle with inner demons." Eric shrugged. "I'm good with anger and retribution but not so much when it comes to other emotions."

"Sounds like you have commitment issues." She pursed her lips. "Like most men who equate a vow with forfeiting their youth."

His eyes stared at the water. "Come talk to me about forfeit when you've had your youth taken from you. With all the possibilities fate held in store and then be handed endless night and endless thirst instead." He turned to her. "And you wonder why some of my kind are the way they

are? Peel an onion, Blair. There are lots of layers on the way to reasons why."

"Eric, I—"

Surprised at the empathy on her face, he shrugged again. "Don't be sad for me, Blair. It was a long, long time ago. I'm one of the lucky ones. I've learned well how to walk the line between what's left of my humanity and what my nature insists. Especially since I've been a part of the Salazar household."

"You sound so…so…" She fumbled for the right word.

"Human?"

Nodding, she had to laugh. "I have my own sad tale, but I think we've had enough for one night."

"I'd like to hear your tale of woe some other time." He skipped the last rock in his hand and then wiped his palms on his pants. "If you'd let me."

She blinked up at him. "You would?"

"I know something bad happened to you. And I know vampires were responsible." He took her hand, turning her so she faced him. "I can't excuse what was done or what *you've* done in retaliation, but I hope you realize now, we're not all soulless predators." He smiled. "Even if the concept of undead souls is still up for debate."

"You sound like Angel from *Buffy the Vampire Slayer*."

"Funny. I had the same thought earlier tonight. Buffy slept with Angel, and it destroyed him." He forced his thoughts away from the parallels, even though it wasn't Buffy's blood that killed her vampire.

"Not the same, really. I mean, on the surface, yeah, but Buffy didn't want Angel to die.""

Eric took a deep breath. "You want me to die?"

She didn't reply, but she didn't pull away, either.

"Wow. Talk about a pregnant pause."

A scream pierced their awkward silence, and they both turned toward the sound.

Chapter Five

*A*t the pitiful scream, Eric lifted his head and inhaled, catching the mix of distress and resentment on Blair's face. "Blood. It's a vampire, maybe two."

He pivoted to race off, but Blair grabbed his arm.

"Wait, I'm going with you."

"Uh-uh." He shook his head. I won't be the one who puts you in danger. Anyway, unless you've got a broomstick hidden, you're not keeping up with me."

Before he could stop her, she clasped hold of his neck and hoisted herself onto his back. "I can keep up with you now, vamp boy."

"What are you doing?" He turned left and right to shake her off, but she wouldn't budge.

"Holding tight, what do you think? Way better than a pony ride. You've got a career ahead of you, cowboy."

He growled. "I'll ride *you* all kinds of ways, but this isn't a joke, Blair. Every second wasted could mean a life. It doesn't take that long for my kind to drain a victim."

"Then stop arguing, and giddyap." She rested her chin on his shoulder. "Or do I need to kick your flanks first?"

"*Ugh*, no respect." He rolled his eyes but didn't argue. Hooking his arms under her legs, he took off in a blur toward the trees.

Slowing, he stopped at a heavy thicket and let Blair slide from her perch. "Stay here until I assess the situation." He eyed her hard. "No arguments."

"Nice try, Eric, but this isn't my first rodeo," she whispered straightening her coat. "There's more to me than just my silver, but go ahead and take the lead." She

pulled her blade from its hiding place and then slid one foot into defensive stance.

"Generosity incarnate," he muttered, stepping to the front.

"Hey!" She frowned at him.

He shrugged. "You called me deceit incarnate. What's good for the goose, eh?"

She let out a huff but didn't reply.

"Okay, witchling. Tell me you have a hex ready. Something that can stun, or else you are staying put."

Blair slipped to his side with a grin. "Now that's more like it." Pausing, she cocked her head to peer at him sideways. "Innocents take precedence, right?"

"If you're asking will I change sides and join my comrades once I smell blood, the answer is no. I don't kill for sport."

"Never?"

Taken aback, he stiffened. "Never. Sustenance is another story, but even then, I haven't inadvertently taken a life in a very long time."

"How do you survive otherwise?" She paused. "When there's no willing Were to lend a vein?"

The question was honest. There was no pretense or mocking in her scent, so he answered. "Contrary to what you think, vampires don't have to kill in order to feed."

"So, it's a matter of choice, then." Her voice was barely a whisper as if a realization hit her square in the face. "Like you said. For sport."

Now was not the time for this conversation, so he didn't reply. "C'mon, Blair. Let's do this." He waited until she looked at him again. "Together."

With a nod, she let Eric move first. He blurred past her into the small clearing. Two youngbloods had what

looked to be a homeless woman bound at the wrists and blindfolded.

The two were obviously too drunk on blood and power to notice she and Eric had joined the party. The homeless woman was quiet but terrified. They had her stripped naked from the waist up and dripping blood from her throat and her breasts.

"Come on, baby, give us some sugar," one of the youngbloods taunted, making kissing sounds. "Blood like candy from all that cheap bourbon."

The other grabbed his crotch, with a laugh. "This way, honey. I've got something sweet for you right here."

"How about this instead, you fucking leeches!" The two turned, and Blair flung her hand out. "*Stuporem Omnino!*"

A flash of white light blinded them, and they staggered backward. She hit them again. "*Debilito!*"

Her last spell ricocheted, hitting only one of the two. One fell to his knees, but the other lunged fully fanged for Eric.

"Don't be stupid, boy." Eric pivoted, sending the bungling youngblood into the dirt. "You don't stand a chance against me. Let the woman go. We don't hunt innocents in this park."

"Fuck you, asshole." The youngblood's words slurred through stained fangs. He clamored to his feet again, not listening to reason. "You wanna come to the party? There's a price, and it's coming out of your ass."

"Some people want to do things the hard way." Eric backhanded the bastard, sending him flying into a rocky outcrop. The force hit with a deafening crack, crumbling stone from the rock's face. The youngblood slumped

forward, impaled on a short, sharp branch growing between the rocks.

The homeless woman whimpered choked sobs where she fell. Blair knelt beside her, sparing a glance for Eric before murmuring a temporary spell to ease her.

"Cruel memories seen and heard, mute her senses, make them blurred. Let sleep come 'til all is done, my magic spent, its power run."

Blair removed the woman's blindfold and then untied her wrists. She eased her to the base of a tree and watched her sink into a quiet sleep, away from what she and Eric had to finish.

"One down, one to go," Eric said stalking to where the other youngblood crouched, blinking off Blair's double stun.

"Fucking A, dude. What gives?" No need to go all turf king. Ever hear of the undead bro code?" The youngblood shook his head to clear the stupor. "I can't hear outta one ear, man." He touched the side of his head with a wince, pulling his fingers back covered in black blood. "What the hell!"

Scrambling to his feet, he whirled in Blair's direction as she walked from settling his victim. "What did you do to me, witch!"

"That's Ms. Witch to you, asshole." Blair flung the debilitation spell at him again and again, hitting him point-blank. "Keep coming, and I'll stun you straight to hell."

His breath rushed from his chest, and he stumbled back. Blood ran from his other ear, but he kept his feet. "Not if I kill you first!"

"Give it up, *bro*," Eric mimicked the youngblood's slang. "My witch will force-feed you her blood and then

dance on your ashes. And there is *no* undead bro code. Unless you count the one where I rip your fangs out and feed them to you for messing with an innocent."

Blair blinked, taken aback. *My witch.* The words startled but not in a bad way.

"Vamps don't scam on their own kind, bro. That raggedy bitch is mine! Bought and paid for with a cheap bottle of Four Roses." The youngblood scowled, flinging a dirty hand to Blair. "You got your own spicy snack. Why are you being be a tool about ours?"

"You really are dumber than you look, youngblood." Eric exhaled a disgusted breath. "You think because you have a set of fangs and a dick it gives you carte blanche to do whatever you want? We have laws for a reason, boy."

"We're the top of the food chain, baby." The youngblood straightened a little more as the effects of Blair's spell waned. "Central Park is anything goes. It's BYOB. Bring your own blood." The youngblood snorted at his own stupid joke.

Shaking his head, Eric frowned. "You are sorely mistaken. Don't be as stubborn as your unfortunate friend. Listen to me. Central Park is shared territory with other supernaturals. Hunting here is off-limits except for the criminal element. Though from your nasty pong, it's obvious you've been feeding in the sewers."

The youngblood sniffed, raising his chin. "Who cares where I feed? And where the hell is Munch?"

"Munch? You're kidding, right? First a preppy, and now one of Robin Hood's Merry Men?" Blair laughed, catching Eric stifling a chuckle. "Let me guess." She gave the youngblood a cursory once-over. "Based on that *teeny tiny* bulge in your pants, I'm guessing you're Little John, right?"

The youngblood's eyes flared red. "You won't think you're so clever when Munch drains you, witch. How do you think he got his nickname? He's immune to your poison."

Eric swung a hand toward the rocky outcrop. "Maybe, but he's not immune to a short, sharp branch through his heart. He'll be a flakey pile of ash by the time we're done with you. It's clear now, you're a lost cause."

"Think again, bro. You and your hex pet." With a snarl, the youngblood lunged for Blair's throat.

With a fluid pivot, Blair threw her blade at the youngblood's chest. He twisted at the last second, taking the silver deep in his shoulder.

"*Aaargh!*" he shrieked as the blade's silver edge scorched his flesh inside and out. He fell to his knees, crumpling into himself in pain. "Bitch! I'll rip your throat out!"

Hands shaking, he reached for the hilt, but before he could pull it loose, Blair grabbed a second blade from her boot.

"How about a little Chinese water torture, witchy style?" She stood over him and fisted his hair. "Drip, drip, drip."

"Blair, no."

She blinked, holding the point of the second blade to the underside of her forearm, directly above the youngblood's face.

"Why not? You said let's do this together, right? Or are you backpedaling now?"

"I'm not backpedaling, but you can't be the one, Blair. I've scanned his thoughts, and I know what he's done. Not just to that poor woman but so many others. He's a disease. A disgrace to my kind just like his flaking friend.

If you killed him when he attacked, it would be self-defense. But now?" He shook his head. "You need to let go."

"It would be so easy, Eric. His veins would sizzle, and he'd self-combust, turning to ash from the inside out. So satisfying."

Stunned and impressed, Eric shook his head. "You are one scary wicked witch."

"Well, at least I'm not green."

The youngblood wrenched his head from Blair's grip with a snarl, freeing himself. He knocked her away and then rolled to the side. "Fuck you, witch!" Scrambling to his feet, he took off in a blur.

"Eric!"

"Stay here!"

He launched himself toward the sky, somersaulting to cut the youngblood off before he disappeared into the maze of trees. The bastard stumbled, trying to pivot direction, but Eric was too fast.

Cocking his hand, he sliced the youngblood's throat to his spine, the same as he had the preppy vamp in the alley. The vampire slumped to the ground, his head hanging by skin and a little muscle.

Eric turned, watching Blair puff as she came up to the scene. "I was right about the broomstick, huh."

She chuckled, catching her breath. "I guess so."

"You wouldn't happen to have a spell to conjure flame?"

With a grin, Blair twirled a hand over a small pile of leaves. Levitating a few of the smaller ones, she whispered one word.

"Incendo."

The dead leaves flamed brilliant orange as she floated them toward the vampire's lifeless form. His black blood ignited and then was gone in a flash of ash.

She winced at a bloody slash on her arm. "Courtesy of our friend's fingernails when he knocked me down."

"I can fix that for you if you want," he said, handing her a handkerchief from his pocket.

She chuckled. "Do you always carry one of these, or only when you run into me?"

"Old-fashioned, remember?"

"I thought it was just old." She knotted the soft cotton around the wound, wincing. "I don't suppose you have a tube of Neosporin with you, too? That youngblood's fingernails were bacteria encrusted. I see a course of antibiotics in my future."

They left the youngblood's ashes and headed to the narrow clearing. "You won't need antibiotics if you let me help you."

"Why? You have some magical healing spells I don't know about?"

He shrugged. "My blood. Yours might be poisonous to me, but mine heals. Ironic, isn't it?"

Blair hesitated, mid-step. "I'm not drinking your blood, Eric."

"I didn't offer," he laughed.

She blinked. "Oh, I thought—" She shook her head. "Forget it."

"You don't have to consume my blood for it to mend your wound. A little dripped on the slash, and it's easy peasy lemon squeezy."

She laughed. "Easy peasy? That's up there with oops-a-daisies."

"Fine. Make fun. Do you want me to mend that slash or not?"

They got to the edge of the clearing. "Before we take care of me, what are we going to do about her? I muted her senses and put her to sleep, but—" She gestured to the woman still by the tree.

"I'll have to wipe her memory," Eric replied.

"You can do that? Alter memories?"

He shook his head. "Not alter, remove. It's akin to glamouring but mostly for protection. The undead developed the skill back when people still believed we roamed the streets at night." He paused. "I could do the same for you, if you want."

"Wipe my memory." It was her turn to shake her head. "Of what? You? The vampires I executed? My family and what happened to them? All those things make me, *me*, Eric. I wouldn't want to lose who I am simply because it's painful. Plus, I don't want to forget you. At least not yet."

Blair watched him heal the wounds the youngbloods had inflicted on the poor woman, both physically and mentally. The ragged soul took the handful of money Eric offered and then vanished into the shadows as though she were a supernatural herself.

"Done and done," he said, returning.

Holding her arm out, Blair nodded. "Okay, Doctor Death, you can mend me."

"Just like that, eh?"

She nodded. "You were gentle with that poor woman, so I trust you."

He took her hand and held it tight. "You trust me, but you don't hate me, do you?"

"I don't know what I feel." Her face was conflicted. "What your friend Natasha said earlier—" She tilted her head as if tempting a kiss, but he knew better. "Is it true?"

"That you want me?"

"No...I mean, you know." She exhaled, clearly trying to deal with competing emotions straining her mind. "All of it. Is it true?"

At the small fluster, high color stained her cheeks. Blair's breath puffed in small white clouds, and it mixed with the sudden rush in her blood, adding to her unbelievable scent. His fangs tingled inside his gums. Anticipation. Foreplay. Want.

"Yes, Blair." He angled his head opposite hers. "It's all true."

Sliding his hand behind her head, Eric leaned in, stealing a quick kiss. She froze for an instant but then lifted her face to meet his demand.

Breath mingled and tongues danced, wrestling as his hands slid through her hair, loosening the long braid that fell past her shoulders.

His body hardened, and his cock thickened at the taste of her mouth. One hand snuck from her hair to rest at her collarbone, and the feel of her pulse beneath her soft skin nearly sent him over the edge.

Blair's body responded, and she groaned. The sound was almost pained, as if fighting against a betrayal she had no hope of winning. Her blood coursed with need and sex-laced adrenaline. The scent of her arousal filled his nose, and his fangs pierced his gums.

He jerked back, breaking their kiss. The last thing he wanted was for Blair to think his story and its telling was a ploy. She already believed vampires to be deceit incarnate. If their time together had given her prejudice

pause, then sharp fangs mid-kiss would shrivel that hope as quickly as a withering glance would shrivel his erection.

Not to mention, unconsciously grazing her tongue or her lips was a risk. A hint of blood in a kiss would normally heighten his expectation, but Blair's blood was potentially crimson death.

She stood catching her breath, her inner turmoil now dealing with rejection on top of everything else.

"Why did you pull away? Do you know how hard that was for me?" she demanded, tugging at his arm.

Clenching his jaw, he willed his fangs to recede. Only then did he turn. "I'm sorry, Blair. I know the leap of faith that kiss represented. It's not you. You have no idea how badly I want you, but I'm not sure you want to go where I think we were headed."

She let go of his arm with a shaky exhale. "I appreciate the chivalry, Eric. Every time I'm with you, you surprise me. One by one, you are singlehandedly dismantling my biases."

"I'm just being me, but if changing your mind about my kind is a biproduct of you spending time with me, then so be it. I'll take that as a win."

"Normally, if a guy decided for me either way about sex, I have my feminist hat on so tight it would change my eye color. I'm perfectly able to judge for myself how far I want this or anything else to go."

"Blair—"

"Let me finish. You know by now I'm a strong woman, with strong passions. With my past, I can't get a grip on what I feel for you. Do I want to wrap my legs around your hips and ride you into the sunset? Yes. Am I afraid that if

I do, I'll want to plunge my blade into your heart and then slit my throat for betraying my family? Also, yes."

The sincerity of her voice cut through him, and he reached for her hand.

"Eric, my passion for you is way up there, and from the hard bar pressed against my hip earlier, I'd say you're *up* for me as well."

He couldn't help but smirk. "You had to go for the penis joke, wow."

"Well, if the erection fits." She stepped in closer, going up on tiptoe to brush her lips to his. "Perhaps at some point we'll get to see if it fits other places as well."

Eric untangled himself from her and stepped away. "Blair." He held her hands at an arm's distance again. "Natasha was right, earlier. She smelled more than just intrigue on me. I've wanted you since I tasted your lips in that godforsaken alley. But there's more to sex with a vampire than friction and moving parts."

"More how?" Her brows knit for a moment, and then both rose in understanding. "Oh, *more.*"

She swallowed, and a flash of revulsion shadowed her face before she squelched it.

"Exactly. Being up for a roll in the grass is one thing, but I don't know if I could keep my other appetites under control. I'd never hurt you, that I can promise, but sharing blood is part of sex for the undead, and I know you are not ready for that. You're just getting comfortable with walking and talking with me." He shrugged. "And the occasional curious kiss."

"You're being polite, but there's also the other elephant between us."

"Besides your predisposition to cut my heart from my chest?"

The breeze brushed strands of loose hair from her braid. "The fact my blood kills."

"Not always, and not every vampire, but often enough we should take this slowly, for now. We barely know each other. So maybe it's a good thing we have all these—"

"Obstacles?"

He ran a hand over her cheek, pushing her hair behind her ear. "I was going to say, variables."

Blair pulled her hands from his and stepped back from him even farther. "You're right. I'm not ready. Even if my blood was no different than Natasha's or some random human's, I still wouldn't be ready. To be honest, I can't believe I'm standing here having a conversation with you, let alone contemplating sex. If I'm even more honest, I'd admit I didn't come here to kill you tonight. Knife in my pocket notwithstanding."

She picked up her blade from the ground by the youngblood's ashes, and the silvered edge glinted in the full moonlight. "I put the edge on it myself this afternoon. Even then, I knew it was just bravado. I forgot about the second one in my boot. Truth is, I haven't stopped thinking about you since the alley, either."

"I'm not a youngblood, so maybe that has something to do with why you're lusting for my dick and not my blood."

A laugh snorted from her nose. "I can't believe you thought that word, let alone spoke it. So much for old-fashioned."

"I was a soldier, Blair." He shrugged, grinning. "Still, the term is slightly less crass than *cock* but only by a pubic hair."

"Ugh, stop."

"That's the problem. With you, I don't want to stop."

Blair glanced at the ground and then up at him. "I have a lot to think about, Eric. A lot to reconcile." She tapped the side of her head. "In here…" She tapped her chest next. "And in here."

"I know. And if spending time with me is too much, I understand. It's hard to face any kind of crossroads, but when that crossroads shakes your values to their core?"

She nodded. "You don't need to spell it out. I'm living it in my head right now. Maybe we meet and I can tell you my history? How about tomorrow?"

"I can't tomorrow, but what about this weekend? I have a place we can go where won't be interrupted. We can talk all you want."

She exhaled, and it tasted a little of relief. "Sounds like a date."

"Date." Eric had to laugh. "I haven't dated since women's ankles were considered provocative."

An owl hooted again, and Blair shivered. "Did the temperature drop again? I'm suddenly chilled to the bone."

Slipping his arms from his jacket, he wrapped the soft wool around her shoulders.

"It's warm." She pulled his jacket closer over her light coat. "I thought vampires didn't generate body heat."

"Trade secrets, Blair. We've got a lot to talk about, but for now let's grab a cab so I can get you home. That way, I'll have your address."

She laughed this time. "Wow. You really haven't dated in decades. How about I give you my cell phone number instead? That way you can text or even leave me a voice mail if you prefer voice chat."

"Text? Voice chat?" He shook his head. "Millennials really know nothing about romance. Swipe left. Swipe

right. And they call mine the Lost Generation." He snorted. "Bugger that. Even with the horrors of war, we still knew how to court a woman."

He took Blair's hand and spun her in a circle until she fell into his arms, dizzy. "So, Blair Witch, prepare to be swept off your feet."

"Promise?" she asked, breathless.

"Soldier's swear."

Chapter Six

Blair blew off class again, rushing to the Raven motherhouse for her daily meeting with Grania. She stood on the front stoop, bouncing on the balls of her feet while waiting for someone to answer the bell.

Now more than ever, she needed to find something in their vast library to give her hope. Something she could hold onto that proved she and Eric weren't doomed to spend their lives like Buffy and Angel.

That Eric knew the show's characters by name as well as the plot still made her chuckle. A vampire who watched a vampire romantic suspense. Who would have thought?

The day was overcast, and a cold drizzle matted her hair to her head, but she didn't care. The adventure had begun a new chapter, and maybe this time she could ride the roller coaster and still look at herself in the mirror.

"Blair. So, you're back again." Caitlan answered the door with a raised eyebrow. "Is Grania expecting you, or is this a social visit?"

She walked into the sumptuous foyer and shrugged out of her wet raincoat, handing it to Caitlan to hang on the rack with the other coats.

"She's expecting me. I hope that's all right."

Caitlan nodded. "Of course. I wasn't sure after your first two meetings with her whether or not you'd want to continue. She said you didn't discover much more than we already know."

The *tap-tap* of a cane along the hardwood drew their attention. Grania stood hunched in the hallway beside the main steps.

"I found something, girl. It's not much yet, but I think it will give us a clue where to look for more."

Blair tamped down on her urge to squeal and followed Grania's slow progress toward the library. She slid open the wide pocket door, waiting for the old woman to pass before gliding it shut behind them.

Every eye in the anteroom salon peeked from their books, obviously curious about the visiting Crow.

"Looks like Old Grania's got a new BFF," one giggled, earning a gimlet stare from the old woman.

The poor girl nearly swallowed her tongue, and Blair had to bite hers not to laugh. She didn't need to give Caitlan reason to send her packing for disrespect. She wasn't a Raven, and the others made that clear.

Grania hoisted herself into her chair at the desk, resting her walking stick against the window.

"Don't pay that lot any mind. They think I don't know what they whisper about me." She tapped the side of her nose. "Sad, really. They don't grasp how much weight an elder's opinion carries when Caitlan chooses who is to be initiated. Having Fae-kissed blood gets you through those doors, but it doesn't make you a Raven."

She patted Blair's hand. "You've shown more interest in our common history than that lot has in years."

"Does that mean I can be a Raven?" Blair teased.

"Sweet girl, if I could bend the rules, I would. Right now, all the girls in this house are newcomers with Fae-kissed blood. After what happened last spring when a rogue Sidhe set his sights on us, we decided it was time to close ranks. Poor Caitlan was so rattled, I had to come out of retirement. You are the first non-Fae-kissed witch she's allowed through the doors since." Grania nodded. "Caitlan must have seen something special in you. If I

could convince our Supreme otherwise, I would have you here permanently."

"I didn't know non-Fae-kissed blood had been admitted in the past. I would have come here had I known. Not that I'm unhappy at Crow Haven House. Tara's great, but we don't have anything like this." Blair gestured toward the immense shelves.

"Indeed."

"What happened to the pledges who weren't Fae-kissed?"

Grania opened the top drawer to her desk. "The girls were referred to other coven houses across the city and state. Some chose to go home." She sighed. "It's a sad state of affairs, but we nearly lost an initiate and a halfling Sidhe in a power struggle not of our making. Other covens think Fae-kissed blood is something special. It is. But it also comes with a price."

She pulled a book from the drawer and handed it to Blair. "This is what I've found. I've marked the page so you can read for yourself."

Blair slid her finger into the top of the volume where Grania had placed the marker. The inside pages were handwritten, and when she turned the book over to the cover, she realized it was a diary of sorts.

"What is this?" She held the book up to catch Grania's attention from what she read at the desk.

"What does it look like to you?"

"A diary."

"Exactly."

Blair looked at the old woman, confused. "Grania, what could someone's personal diary tell me that reference books couldn't?"

Grania pulled her glasses from her nose. Her watery blue eyes considered Blair where she sat at the study table. "And where do you think reference books come from? We may be Fae-kissed, but there are no sea-monks scribing the edges of books or Google goblins cataloguing our history. No, child. Reference books start with people's written recollections. From their experiences and experiments. There is no better way to search for answers, especially when one is trying to find a way to justify their actions."

The old woman's words hit home, and Blair's throat tightened. She knew Grania had keen powers of observation from when she held her hand at their initial meeting. She assumed the woman read her body language. Now she realized she must have seen her thoughts and deeds for real.

"*Uhm*, maybe I should get going. I appreciate your help, Grania, but I don't think I'm going to find what I'm looking for in your library. Diaries are great, but I'm looking for something more jurisdictive. Besides, I need to figure things out on my own. Wasn't that what you said? Experience and experimentation?" Blair's words rushed from her mouth as she gathered her bag and notebooks.

Grania watched her shuffle and knock papers off the study table before rapping her gnarled knuckles on the desk. "Blair, calm yourself and sit."

The young witch perched on the end of one of the chairs but kept her bag close. Uncomfortable didn't go far enough to describe the embarrassed pit knotting in her stomach.

"You think I can read minds?" The old witch chuckled. "Fae-blood gives us sight, but even that's limited. I can cast a spell with my eyes closed to get people to spill their inner secrets, but that's as close as I get to being Carnac the

Magnificent." Her wheezy chuckle made Blair wince. "You're too young to know who that is, but I think you get my drift. When you first came here, I told you this house isn't the place to keep secrets. Old witches need a little fun in our prehistoric lives, so I tell youngsters that to scare the bejesus out of you."

The old woman was batshit crazy. Blair smiled politely, lifting her backpack onto her shoulder. "If it's all the same, I still think I'd better go. Whether you can read minds, or you're simply adept at reading people in general, I'm not up to facing what I think you know about me."

"You wouldn't be so quick to run if your past actions were truly reconciled in your heart. Great evil has been done by people who believed they had right on their side, vindicating their actions. History proves it time and time again, yet we continue to make the same human mistakes."

Suddenly, the large library seemed smaller and tighter, and though Grania's words weren't addressed to anything specific, Blair's chest squeezed.

"Revenge is not a balm, Blair. You've clung to its coldness like a life raft since you came into your own as a witch. Your experiences are written all over you. You are a walking, talking diary."

Blair's eyes widened. "You spoke to Tara."

"I didn't have to." Grania shook her head. "I knew your mother. Not your adopted mother, but your birth mother."

Blair went from perching on the edge of her chair to standing. "How? When?"

"A very long time ago. When your mother was younger than you. She was an outcast. Belonging to no one

and nowhere. Her parentage was such a question mark. So much so, that acceptance was never in the cards for her. I tried to be a bridge for her, but even then my hands were tied. So many layers of hate and distrust. Your poor mother suffered, never fully fitting anywhere."

"You make it sound as if my mother was a half-cast of some kind."

Grania nodded. "She was, in a way. Supernatural sets didn't mix back then. Rival covens. Intra-species relations. On paper, it didn't happen. Ever. But in reality?" She spread her hands. "Not like today."

She got up from her chair and hobbled without her cane to where Blair stood. Pulling the page-marker from the diary still on the table, she crumpled the scrap in her hand.

"Instead of one passage, I think it best if you read the diary in full. It might clarify things for you in a way no reference book could."

Blair lifted the book, turning it over in her hand. "Are you telling me this is my mother's diary?"

Grania shook her head. "No, like it says on the cover, it belonged to our Supreme at the time. She wrote of events you might find pertinent, and her opinions about matters and what transpired after the fact. I'll leave the rest for you, but—"

She turned with a soft grunt, holding onto one of the sturdy chairs as she worked her way to a short bookshelf tucked into a window alcove. The wooden shelves were covered in dust. The books, plain bound, with no titles on the spines.

Grania bent for something, and Blair rushed to catch her arm. "Careful! Just tell me what you're looking for,

and I'll get it." The last thing she wanted was for the old woman to fall and break a hip.

Dust left the old witch coughing enough for Blair to grab a bottle of water from her backpack. Grania took a sip.

"Thank you, honey," she said taking in a clear breath. "Old books don't go along with old lungs."

"What are you looking for that can't wait? Reading your Supreme's tight scrawl is going to be hard enough." Blair gestured to the diary with the cap to the water bottle.

"Because, dear girl, you asked if that was your mother's diary." She handed Blair the water bottle, and then bent for three black leather-bound volumes from the bottommost shelf.

Slipping them from their place, she held out a hand for Blair to help her up. "*That* diary belonged to our Supreme, but *these* belonged to your mother. This bookcase is mine. It holds precious cargo. I personally warded the shelves/ so no one touches the books but me." She paused. "Or, in this case, someone with a blood link to the author."

Speechless, Blair's mouth went dry. "How? No one has ever been able to tell me anything about my birth mother. Not even her name."

She glanced from the slim leather volumes in Grania's gnarled hand to the old woman's face. "Even Tara doesn't know my origins, and she's the head of my coven. She found me after I took an Ancestry DNA test. I don't know how, but I think she gets some sort of alert whenever someone is a match for certain bloodlines."

Grania gestured to her desk, and Blair helped her walk to her chair. The old woman sat, but instead of looking exhausted or overwhelmed, her eyes were bright.

Blair's mind raced. Could this be true? Or was this a delusion of an old witch past her prime? Grania admitted to pranking initiates into thinking she could read minds. What if Caitlan only brought the old woman home because she felt bad for her? What if all her research help was simply a way to keep old Grania out of everyone's hair?

Blair reached for the box of tissues on the desk. She had chewed the inside of her lip so hard she tasted blood. Eric's words flashed through her mind at the metallic tang. Could she kill him with a kiss? Even if drawing blood was an accident?

That was a conversation for this weekend. Right now, she had other concerns. Like her true identity. If her mother was a half-cast, then what did that make her?

"Grania, please. Everything else aside. You have to tell me how you knew me for who I am. Without a word or a sign or a goddamned birth certificate! The only one I have is from my adoptive parents. Even then there were blanks where biological data should have been registered."

"Blair, I knew you for your mother's daughter because you look just like her. Same beautiful chestnut hair. Same cat's-eye slant to your amber eyes. However, it's the birthmark at the top of your left breast that told me your parentage without a doubt. I noticed it the second time you came to see me.

"You were wearing that pretty, persimmon-colored camisole under your cardigan. When it got warm, you took your sweater off. It wasn't until you bent to dig in your backpack for something that I noticed the mark. I knew then.

"I did a lot of soul-searching after that, and it was then I called your Supreme. To connect the dots, I needed to

know the rest of your story, so I asked Tara. I'm not a mind reader, honey. I'm simply trying to help you put the pieces of your puzzle together. I think these diaries are the final pieces."

Grania gestured for Blair to take the volumes. "Read them. Or not. It's up to you. I'll be here if you have questions."

Blair took the diaries from the old woman's hand and placed them side by side on the desk. They were ordinary leather-bound journals. The kind you'd find in any stationary store. Roman numerals I, II, and III, written in silver ink on each cover delineated the diaries' reading order.

"I'm afraid to open them," Blair whispered more to herself than Grania. "What if they disintegrate at my touch, or the moment the air hits the pages?"

The old witch chuckled. "They're old, honey. Not ancient." She pushed the first volume closer. "Go on. Open the cover to the flyleaf."

Blair ran her hand over the silver ink. Her fingers traced the cracks in the old leather for traces of magic. Signs or images. Anything really. Slipping her fingers under the cover's lip, she opened it to the inside page. There, in the same silver lettering, was the date and her mother's name.

She looked up from the pages with her brow in a knot. "Are you sure these are my mother's diaries? The name and date say, Geneviève Cabot - December 1942. The time frame is off by decades. The date is more in line with a grandmother, rather than my mother."

Grania's gaze didn't flinch. "These are your mother's diaries. She was eighteen when she penned the first, and

one year older with every subsequent volume. In fact, your birth is recorded at the end of the third diary."

The date on the third volume read 1945. Blair shook her head, stepping from the desk. "I'm only twenty-four years old. Even if my adopted birth certificate is off by a year or two, there's no way."

With elbows on the librarian's desk, Grania templed her fingers as she looked at Blair's shocked face. "I'm much older than I appear, dear. As are you. Read your mother's diaries. They will tell you most of what you need to know. Then, and only then, will I fill in the rest."

Stunned speechless for real, Blair could only nod. She took her mother's diaries and that of the Supreme and stuffed them into her backpack with her notebooks. She didn't bother with the water bottle she gave Grania, leaving it on the table with the cap.

She walked out of the library without a word. Barely mumbling a goodbye as she took her raincoat from the hall rack. Not bothering to put it on, she made it down the stairs and to the gate before she stood, zombie-like, at the curb.

"I'm a fucking old lady." Laughter burst at knowing she sounded like a complete nut. Still, who cared? This was lower Manhattan. Everyone here was already halfway round the bend.

Blair walked at a fast clip to the subway and hopped the first train heading uptown. She needed a drink before anything else.

Shoving her backpack to the side, she sat on the hard, molded plastic seat and closed her eyes. D-Day and Normandy Beach. The end of the second World War and the famous Times Square kiss that went round the world.

Images from every History Channel special she ever watched on the subject flew through her mind. There was no way. If she was born at the end of WWII, then she would have been nineteen when the Beatles took America by storm. She would have been part of Woodstock, civil rights protests, the sexual revolution.

She had no memory of any of it, other than what she read in books and saw on TV. With an exhale, she opened her eyes and pulled her bag around to her lap. Even if there was some weird time-bending magic afoot, those diaries couldn't explain what happened to her adopted family or how she came to live with them. Or could they?

She felt for the books inside her pack. There was only one way to find out. She had to read the diaries. All of them. How was she to do so at Crow Haven House, with Suzy snoring in the next bed? Or with Lizzie's well-meaning prying over her shoulder? Ugh, and Tara. After Grania's call, the Supreme was bound to crawl up her butt the minute she got the chance.

Chewing on her lip, she winced at the spot she'd gnawed earlier. She needed to hole up somewhere and read. Alone. A hotel room was the perfect answer. Reaching into her pocket, she pulled out her phone and scrolled for Eric's number. She blinked, staring at the waiting call button on her screen.

Eric. Hi. Yeah, it's Blair… Listen, I know my blood might kill you, but can you rent a hotel room for me? No, not so we can get nasty, but so I can hole up and read my dead mother's diaries. Oh, and room service would be great. Kiss-kiss…

"Ugh. You can't call him for this." Locking her phone, Blair shoved it into her pocket.

The train slowed, and the telltale screech of brakes as it pulled into the station made her teeth hurt even more

than the tight clench she'd had since she left the Raven house.

This wasn't her stop, but she didn't care. She needed to walk and to think. Maybe she'd trip over a miracle. One in the shape of a wallet stuffed with cash, in front of a hotel that still accepted green.

"Fat chance, Witchiepooh. You'd do better finding out your mother was a Faerie, and that's why you don't age"—

She froze mid-step leading up to street level from the subway. Ravens were Fae-kissed. Was that why Grania knew her mother?

Turning on her heel, she ran down the steps and over to the downtown platform for the Number 6 train to West Fourth Street-Washington Square Station. She needed to get to the NYU library, specifically the occult section.

She stopped mid-step again.

Witches were matriarchal by nature. Power was inherited through the mother. Period. Blair ignored the commuters rushing past, bumping her left and right for blocking the platform.

Damn.

It would have been so cool to be a Sidhe. That would explain a lot. Why she never had a problem attracting the opposite sex, supernatural or otherwise. It would also explain why she was so successful hunting vampires. Fae blood was something they couldn't resist.

Frowning, she found a relatively clean bench across from the tracks and sat. Something vampires couldn't resist. Yet, Eric resisted. She pursed her lips. Then again, Eric wasn't like other undead. From what he said, his entire family was atypical of the lot.

Her witchy abilities were the one immutable fact she couldn't contradict. It was in her DNA. That meant her mother *had* to be the witch in her biological parentage.

The downtown train squealed into the station, and she looked up from her musing. At eighteen, her mother would have already come into her abilities. Longevity wasn't a white witch ability, so unless her mother was a dark practitioner, it followed that her extreme longevity had to come from her biological father. That's if Grania wasn't completely delusional.

The door chimes binged, and she slipped into the closest car before they shut. The library at school would have the answer. She hoped. A Sidhe father was still a possibility, but the Fae weren't the only supernaturals with extreme longevity.

Her phone dinged in her pocket. Whoever texted her could wait, but she peeked at the notification anyway.

Eric.

I know we said the weekend, but I can't stop thinking about you. We're still on for our book of revelations talk, but I thought maybe you'd like to hang out tonight. Watch a movie. Talking optional. Wine for certain. Pizza?

He texted in full sentences. So not a millennial.

She smiled. Funny how he said book of revelations. Her thumb hovered over the reply button. It had to be a coincidence, right? There was no way he knew about Grania and the diaries. Hell, the information hadn't had a chance to gel in her mind, let alone be cohesive enough for someone to cherry-pick from her thoughts.

Even if Eric's claim was true, and he could read her mind or pick through her memories, he said he wouldn't.

She believed him.

In fact, she believed a lot more of him than that.

Eric affected her on a visceral level. Not just a physical attraction, but a connection that went deeper. Almost subliminal. It wasn't glamour, either. It felt…spiritual.

Gah, she nearly made herself gag, yet it was undeniable.

Eric made her feel safe. Centered. Especially since he proved himself at the park. Not that it was a test. God, no. If she could go back in time and stop that poor woman from enduring that torture, she would. Still, she wasn't sorry those youngbloods were dead.

She'd come to grips with her conflicting feelings after he dropped her home. The entire time he walked with her, and when they stood by the lake, she was calm. Even as they fought side by side. It was a strange kind of peace. Sense of belonging.

The sensation was odd and had no footing in reason, yet there it was, living alongside her loathing and anger for others of his kind.

She might not have an explanation for what she felt, but right now she didn't care. A bottle of wine with the man who occupied her thoughts was just what she needed.

She hit reply.
No talking sounds perfect.
Wine even better.
Red if you've got.
And Chinese. Not pizza.
Noodles.

Her phone dinged a second later with his address and a huge smile emoji. The train rattled and the interior lights flickered as it gathered speed toward the next stop. With a grin, she got up to stand by the car doors. She needed to make another U-turn and jump on the next uptown train to the east side.

Chapter Seven

*E*ric answered the bell before it even rang. He stood in the backlit hall wearing light denim jeans and a black sweater. He looked amazing, and the genuine smile on his face made every argument she had with herself after they texted, disappear.

She'd never been indecisive. For her to waffle between loathing vampires for what they did, and wanting Eric, for what she *wanted* him to do, left her head spinning.

Looking at him in the doorway now, she needed to turn off the inner monologue and just let go and let God. She wanted to be here, or she wouldn't be standing on his front stoop.

"You look as if you've been arguing with the devil." He bent to peck her cheek. "But you're here, so I guess win-win."

She laughed, stepping past him as he moved aside to let her through the door. "And you sound as though you've been inside my head."

"Not a chance." He crossed his heart. "Tempting, but no. I told you last night, I don't trespass. I've had it done to me, and it's not a comfortable feeling."

She followed him through the polished foyer, taking in the rich Aubusson carpets and the mahogany railings that led to the second floor. There was a wrought iron chandelier with gold accents hanging mid-hall, and she stared at it thinking she'd seen something like it before.

Grania's revelations were making her second-guess her own mind. Mentally dismissing the possibilities, she turned off that part of her brain to concentrate instead on

her senses. Sight, smell, hearing, taste, touch, and the sixth…whatever made her witchy side shiver.

"In my day we called this the parlor." He motioned for Blair to sit on the couch. "Make yourself at home. You didn't specify what kind of red, so I guessed and uncorked a really good Shiraz."

She nodded. "Love it. I'd ask what you like to drink, but I think that's obvious."

"I like good wine, but I prefer a good Irish whiskey. Jameson's is my favorite, but Glen Scotia from Scotland will do me just fine."

"You can drink?"

He raised an eyebrow.

"Don't be a smart-ass. You know what I mean.

He laughed, pouring two glasses of the Shiraz. "As long as it's naturally brewed or distilled, we can drink what we like. But no chemicals. Nothing processed."

"The rest of us should follow that example. Half the health problems we have are a direct result of processed foods and the additives used since the end of the second World War. At least that's what I think."

"One of the many perks of being undead." He winked. "No illness."

"Don't get cute. What about food? Can you eat what you like as well?"

"Define can?"

She rolled her eyes. "Will it kill you?"

"If you're asking if I can physically consume human food, then the answer is yes. Can I digest it and glean nutrients the way you do? No. Will I be sick? Most likely, but I won't die."

He handed her one of the wineglasses then held his out for a quick clink. "Say something. I can't tell if you're fascinated or appalled."

"Believe me. I'm completely fascinated. Especially as a master's student of the occult. One conversation and you would blow the lid off the department at NYU, as well as some of the pompous windbag academics who think they know everything because they can read ancient texts. You'd probably give my history professors a run for their money, too. Firsthand accounts, up close and personal, you know?"

Eric took his wine and sat beside her. "You sound as though you've gone toe-to-toe with that lot. It must be hard."

"Listening to them drone on? Yep."

"No, I meant being a blood witch and having to hide your light under a bushel."

She smirked, angling her head. "I'm often tempted to curse a few of those bores with body lice, but our rule of three keeps getting in the way."

He took a sip from his drink but didn't comment.

"I know what you're thinking." She gestured with her glass. "You're wondering why my rule of three didn't stop me from hunting youngbloods."

They were side by side on the couch, but Eric's gaze took on a million-mile stare.

"Earth to Eric. Have I blown it before the food even arrives?"

He put his glass down and shifted to face her on the couch. "Perhaps your rule of three is a conversation best left for our weekend chat. I invited you tonight with no strings attached. Just two people spending time together."

She ran a finger over the rim of her glass and was about to press the issue when the doorbell rang.

"That'll be the food."

Getting up from the sofa, he went to answer the door. A minute or so of muffled conversation and he was back with a Chinese take-out bag.

"I ordered chicken lo mein, vegetable dumplings, and fried rice. I figured those were a safe bet." He placed the cartons on the coffee table, reaching into the accompanying bag for paper plates and napkins. "Please, help yourself. I already…had dinner."

Now it was her turn to raise an eyebrow, not knowing if he was serious or just teasing again.

"I wasn't sure what kind of movies you like, so I figured we'd do Netflix or Amazon Prime. We have both."

Blair helped herself to a skosh of each. Picking at the noodles, she plopped a finger full into her mouth and chewed.

"I like rom coms and romantic suspense, but I also like dramas and classic movies," she replied, swallowing.

"When you say classics, do you mean Bronte and Austin, or do you mean *Casablanca*?" he asked queuing up the correct remote.

"Here's looking at you, kid." She grinned. "I like them all, especially film noir. If you're talking classic romance, my favorites are *Pride and Prejudice* and *Wuthering Heights*. For me it's a tossup between Mr. Darcy and Heathcliff."

"For what?"

"For most tormented lover of the year."

Eric lifted his glass in salute. "*He shall never know I love him: and that, not because he's handsome, but because he's more myself than I am. Whatever our souls are made out of, his and mine are the same.*"

"Catherine Earnshaw." Blair gave him a soft, close-lipped smile. "That's who gets your vote. The most insipid heroine in all literature."

"You said most tormented. In *Wuthering Heights*, Cathy is Heathcliff's counterpart, just as Elizabeth Bennet is Mr. Darcy's in *Pride and Prejudice*. Cathy's reluctance to admit she loves Heathcliff stems from her fear. Fear her passion for him will consume her. It's—"

"Cowardly," she finished his sentence.

"No. It's beautiful and tragic."

"Maybe." Blair paused, thinking. "When you put it that way, I guess, in some miniscule way, I identify with her."

"How?" Eric asked.

"*Terror made me cruel...*" she answered his question with another quote.

"That sounds like a topic for our chat weekend."

She nodded, with a tired laugh. "We may have to spread that weekend over a month of Sundays to get through my demons."

"I'm game if you are, but for now I'd like you to answer my question. Why do you identify with Cathy Earnshaw if you think her character weak? You're anything *but* weak."

"It has to do with you."

"Me?" Surprise was all over his face. "I make you feel weak?"

Blair shook her head. "You make me feel things I'd rather not feel. Emotions I'm having a hard time reconciling."

"Reconciling how?"

"How I feel about you." She paused, putting her plate and her wineglass on the coffee table. "I'm going to trust you with something I hope you won't use against me."

He took both her hands, and she visibly shivered. "Please don't. After what happened in the park, the less I know about your nightly doings, the better."

"Eric, I'm not about to incriminate myself. I'm not stupid enough to put either of us in that position."

Her fingers curled with his against his chest. His flesh wasn't cold, but there was no natural rise and fall. No breath. No soft thrum beneath their hands.

"You're undead, and despite my obvious disdain for your kind, I'm drawn to *you*. I can't help it. Being with you lifts my heart. For some reason, I feel safe and at peace."

She glanced away.

"Blair—" He pulled his hand from their combined grip. "Look at me."

"Eric, don't. You'll only make things worse."

He cupped her chin. "No. I'm glad you told me. Why on earth would I use something like that against you? I'm as drawn to you as you are to me. In fact, it's maddening."

"I know!" She laughed, turning to meet his hazel gaze.

"What do you want, Blair?"

"Are you talking movies, or—"

"What do you want from *me*? That's what I'm asking."

She bit the corner of her lip. "I'm not sure. Too many variables."

Eric couldn't stop a small chuckle. "Not to mention I still think you're pretty scary."

"Me? You severed heads with a single blow. Twice!"

"Not my finest moments, to be sure." He angled his head, watching her face. "There's something you're not asking me. What is it?"

"Can I kill you with a kiss?"

The puzzled smirk on his face said it all. "You're going to have to qualify that one, love."

"Just before you texted, I got some pretty upsetting news. World-rocking kind of news. So much so, I gnawed the inside of my cheek until I drew blood. What if that happens when we're, you know. Theoretically, I could kill you with a kiss."

"Blair, you could do that even without the taste of crimson."

She shoved his shoulder. "I'm serious, Eric. How are we to get around this? Against my better judgement. Like it or not. I'm attracted to you. *More* than attracted."

"Now you sound like Mr. Darcy."

Blair rolled her eyes. "Will you stop? I'm serious. I mean, if I *knew* my blood wouldn't harm you, we'd already be—"

"Giving my mattress a workout."

Heat tickled her cheeks, and she gave him a sheepish smile. "Not exactly how I'd put it but yes."

"What if we mitigated the risk."

"How so?"

He lifted his glass, swirling the ruby liquid. "A drop. Not straight but mixed with something to lessen any possible effect."

"A drop of my blood in a glass of wine is your solution."

"Or whiskey." He nodded. "Perhaps more than a single drop but yes. If our worst fears transpire, then my reaction to the tiny amount of witch blood might not be so bad. It might make me ill or burn a bit, but it won't kill me. I hope."

The clocked ticked on the fireplace mantel as she watched his enthused face. He was serious.

"Well?"

Blair blinked at him, shaking her head. "I am not taking that chance with you."

"Why not?" Sitting up, he shifted on the sofa to face her. "We'll never get past where we are now if we don't try. I'm willing to take the chance. After all, *I'm* the one playing with fire. What did you call it in the park? Chinese water torture, witchy style?"

"That was *not* the same thing, and you know it."

He shrugged. "Think of it this way, then. Perhaps we'll uncover something for future witch/vamp couples. A way to build up a tolerance."

"We're just getting to know each other, Eric. I'm not ready for that kind of risk. I *am* ready to take things to the next level physically, if you get my meaning, but we have to do so *á la Pretty Woman*."

He frowned, puzzle again. "I don't follow."

"The eighties classic. Prostitute meets rich playboy. Hires her for a night of fun. She agrees but just one rule. No kissing."

"You're kidding."

"Apparently it's a thing. A kiss is considered too personal. Your breath mingles, and with it a bit of your soul."

"Oh, c'mon." Eric scoffed. "The dude can have her any way he wants, put other things in her mouth, bigger things, and *that's* not personal?"

She laughed out loud, snorting a little. "Well, that's one opinion."

"I'm right though."

"Yes, but in our case, I think *á la Pretty Woman* is the way to go. You won't have to worry about scraping my tongue or my lips, and as long as you keep your sharp, pointy bits to yourself, we'll be fine."

He chuckled, shaking his head. "Why do I feel like we need to sign on the dotted line somewhere?" A roguish smile took his lips. "Still, if I can't kiss your mouth, then I can't kiss other parts of you, either."

He lifted his hand, letting his thumb trail the swell of her breast to circle her nipple. "Such a shame, really. Vampires have very specific talents." Cupping her breast through her blouse, he bent to nip her nipple through the soft fabric.

"Eric—"

"So much to taste and be tasted, Blair." The wet fabric molded her hard bud, increasing the friction until she arched her back with a quick gasp.

His hand dropped from her other breast, drifting over her waist to the top of her black leggings. "You're wet for me already, Blair. Your scent clings to the air and makes my mouth water."

Slipping his fingers below the elastic waistband, he trailed lower until the tips grazed soft fluff. His voice thickened as he dipped his hand farther to spread her slick folds.

"Close your eyes, Blair. Feel my fingers slipping deep into your wet cleft. My mouth through the thin fabric of your blouse."

Her hips raised to meet his hand, and her head dropped against the arm of the couch. Eric curled his hand to her slit, his thumb ringing her nub with a soft, smooth rhythm.

"What do you want, Blair? More?"

She cried out as his fingers drove deeper, circling her inner spot. Preternatural speed drove her higher. "Fuck! Eric! You're a human vibrator!"

He smiled against her wet breast, nipping her nipple again before he knelt between her knees. "Oh, love, you're close. I can smell your blood swelling your sex. Your nub is hard and throbbing but not as hard and throbbing as my cock."

She groaned loud and breathless, grinding her hips against his hand.

"Think, Blair. My hard flesh filling your tight channel. Spreading you wet and wide. Hot friction, fast and deep. My rigid length feeding you inches over and over..."

Crying out, she arched her body. Spasms shook her to her core as her walls squeezed his hand. "Let it flood you, Blair. Fill you and then ebb because I'm not done with you tonight, love."

Pulling his hand from her sex, he stroked the swollen flesh through her dampened leggings. He slid his thumbs beneath the Lycra band and slipped them from her hips before dragging them down to her ankles and then to the floor.

"Open your eyes, Blair."

She did, expecting to see his face contorted and grotesque. The vampiric feeding face, but instead Eric looked as he usually did. Gorgeous. Beautiful. If you could use the word to describe a man. He stroked her wet flesh, dipping his fingers into her slick pool again, and then lifted them to his mouth.

He licked them one at a time, with only a hint of fang showing. The way his eyes locked with hers, and the slow lap of his tongue was the most erotic thing she'd ever seen.

"I want to taste you fully, Blair. To lick your sex and tease your nub, but I can wait." He licked his thumb last and moaned. He pulled his sweater from his shoulders and then unbuttoned his jeans, one button at a time.

"Your scent haunts me, and now your sweet flavor tantalizes..." One hand trailed his smooth chest, his fingers passing lean, defined muscles cut along his torso. They dipped to the deep vee of his hips and the hint of dark hair and what waited beyond.

Blair licked her lips, watching as he pushed the denim the rest of the way past his hips, taking his boxer briefs with them.

"Oh, Eric. You are definitely not related to the little Pillsbury dude. You are every inch a soldier...Doughboy. Every hard, long, muscled inch."

With a grin, he fisted his hard length, and then beckoned her closer. "Your *Pretty Woman* style said nothing about *your* mouth."

Blair sat up and covered his hand with her own. Together they worked his shaft in long, slow strokes. Pressing his ridged head to her lips, she licked the swollen flesh before taking him deep.

She swallowed his full length, working the corded mass with the flat of her tongue. She drew back, curling around the engorged ridge.

Eric's hazel eyes darkened. "Close your eyes, Blair."

She did, and he pulled from her hand and mouth. Gritting his teeth, he forced his fangs to retract, cutting his bottom lip. The blood on his tongue forced a snarl from his throat, and he turned his head.

"Eric—"

Blair reached for him. "Let me see you."

He turned, and his face had changed. Not to the extent she expected but enough to notice. His lips were red, and she saw the small puncture on his bottom lip.

Reaching up, she caught a tiny drop on her thumb and brought it to her mouth. She circled the pad the same way she had his swollen head, sucking her thumb deep.

The moment his blood hit her tongue, she gasped. Heat coursed through her body, and wetness pooled between her legs.

"Fuck me, Eric! Fuck me now!"

With a muffled groan, he pushed her knees wide and plunged his cock through her slick folds. He thrust hard and fast, driving his full length balls deep.

Blair cried out, her legs shaking as he rode her toward climax. Her hips met his thrust for thrust. Every muscle tensed as he held himself buried inside her walls. His head burst, pulsing in time with her spasms as they climaxed together.

Panting, he slumped to her damp shirt, his head on her breasts. "Not bad for no kissing, eh, pretty woman?"

She smacked the back of his head. "Why didn't you tell me your blood was so fucking amazing. I've never climaxed like that in my life."

"What a gyp." He grinned, resting his chin on her chest. "Your blood could kill me, and mine sends you rocketing into ultimate ecstasy. I'd say we need to fix this, don't you, Witchiepooh?"

She laughed, straining to kiss his nose. "I'll see what I can do."

"Otherwise, are you okay?" he asked, the humor fading a bit from his face. "I mean, with me. With this."

"Eric, I've never been more okay in my life, and that's not the drop of vampire blood talking. I mean it. I don't

want us to be Buffy and Angel. I want us to be...I don't know. Some other epic supernatural couple."

He kissed her breast through her shirt. "Why can't we be Eric and Blair, and be our own epic supernatural couple?"

She smiled. "That's the best idea you've had yet."

"Oh really?" He pushed his still-hard member deep again. "You think?"

Blair sucked in a breath "Well, maybe second best."

Chapter Eight

*S*he sat across from Eric in a smoke-filled room. It wasn't cigarette smoke, or even cigar. It was incense. Coven members watched the game, ringing her back in a semicircle, while shadowed vampires watched from behind Eric.

Elbows on the polished wood, she laced her fingers together. Six shot glasses waited on the table's surface, each filled with a crimson liquid.

"Place your bets," a disembodied voice called, and witches and vampires alike tossed money on the table.

Pulling a card from her sleeve, she placed it on the table facing outward. Wheel of Fortune. She rested her hand beside the card.

Eric flipped his card as well. The Lovers.

She raised an eyebrow at the telling cards. "Happiness and peace for me. Love for you."

"For us..."

He reached for her, but she pulled her hand away.

"Perhaps."

"Choose," the voice ordered.

She scanned the six identical shot glasses. Sour wine, sweet wine, vampire blood, or witch blood. Scents masked. It was anyone's guess.

She selected one and then waited for Eric to make his pick.

"Drink."

Eyes on him, she lifted her glass but waited. "You take the lead, again." Her voice reverberated, as if in an echo.

"Here's looking at you, kid." He downed the shot.

She flinched, waiting for the worst until Eric banged the glass upside down on the table.

It was her turn.

Lifting the glass, she shot the liquid back. Sweet wine. "So far, so good." She licked her lips and then turned the glass over as well.

"Round two. Draw again."

She picked a card from thin air.

Three of Swords.

Bad card. She stared at it. Whispers taunted her ear. Their dull hum drifting past like ghosts. The desolate figure on her card turned with one word. Heartache.

Eric drew his card.

"Death," he murmured, dropping it on the table.

Her eyes found his, and they held a darkness she never saw before.

"Tides are changing, Blair. What's a witch to do?"

She blinked at him not understanding.

"Choose," the voice ordered once more.

They each picked a shot glass.

"Bottoms up." She drained the glass and coughed. Sour wine.

Eric lifted his shot to his lips, keeping his eyes on her. "There's no escaping one's nature, Blair." He threw the crimson back in one go, putting the glass on the table.

She reached for him this time, but it was too late. His hazel eyes dripped blood from the corners as her witch blood spread. Eric's mouth worked, but only one word escaped his lips. Betrayed.

"Eric!"

He screamed, his body writhing as his blood boiled beneath his skin. Black scorch lines traced every vein and artery until he burst into flame.

Blair bolted up in bed with a gasp. Disoriented, she scanned the room until she realized she was in her advisor's side office at the NYU library.

Slumping on the daybed, she scrubbed her eyes with the palm of her hand. "I must be certifiable."

What the hell kind of dream was that? A warped version of the scene with Christopher Walken from *The Deerhunter*. Russian Roulette Witchy Style. *Gah*, she had joked about that one too many times it was making her nuttier than usual.

No escaping one's nature.

That's what she always thought. What she preached. That was, until Eric. He changed everything in a week's time. Of course, if not for the fact she panted after him like a bitch in heat, she might not have given his words or actions a second thought. Still, it was because of him she had no desire to hunt. Not without reason, and not without him. Otherwise, she was no better than those she hunted. A vigilante.

He was right. So was Grania. Evil executed under the pretext of virtue was still evil.

It seemed only hours since she woke in Eric's bed with the sun blinking through his shutters. Its warmth waking her to the fact he was gone. A calculated plan, since the blackout curtains were still pinned to either side of the window.

That was two days ago.

He left a note on his pillow saying he'd gone to his rest just before dawn, and he would meet her on Saturday. His place. Sunset. The note didn't say where he was or what he'd be up to in the meantime, but Blair wasn't worried. She had other fish to fry, and the time apart would give her a chance to process.

She was a vampire hunter, falling in love with a vampire. The fact was both surreal and ridiculous, making her a walking-talking contradiction.

Eric had made love to her body, but he'd also seduced her mind. Not a glamour or a ruse. But a true seduction. Every sense was set ablaze when he spoke. When they touched.

Instincts told her he mirrored her feelings in every way and was just as thrown by their unnerving connection. Since leaving his place, she hadn't slept. Mostly because her brain worked overtime trying to make sense of the past week.

Every time she closed her eyes, her mind skipped. Jumping broken-record style from past to present to future. At least she didn't have to ride her emotional roller coaster in front of her coven sisters. Normally, she was the one with the popcorn as coven drama unfolded. Staying at Eric's was not an option. Not that he'd say no. Still, waking up in his bed rather than doing the walk of shame at dawn was one thing. Becoming a fixture for days was quite another.

NYUs library was open twenty-four hours. She could have hunkered down in the stacks if she had to, but thanks to her degree advisor, she had another choice. Dr. Lynetta Wells was the head of Mythological Studies and taught most classes on the occult. The university was on fall break, so she offered her side office for a few days in exchange for help grading undergraduate term papers.

"Make yourself comfortable, Blair, but don't give the city's rats any help. The rodent population doesn't care this is a seat of higher learning. Take out the trash." Lynetta winked, packing her briefcase for the break. "I'll be in and out, but you've got my email if you need me."

Blair hadn't seen Dr. Wells since. Good thing, since she'd raided her stash of Diet Coke and dark chocolate.

Exhausted, she stretched, stifling a yawn. She'd been staring at books and manuscripts for over twenty-four hours. From the drool marks on her notes, she must have passed out. Thank God it was on the daybed in the side office, and not at her cubby in the stacks, or someone might have hit her with Narcan.

She sat up against a cushion and picked up one of her legal pads. Sheets and sheets filled with scribbled notes on entities and longevity. The clock on Dr. Wells' desk chimed eight bells.

Eight p.m.

Swinging her legs over the side of the daybed, she ran her fingers through her snarled hair and then walked to peek out the window. The city had slowed, thanks to a chilly rain. Washington Square Park was in shadow across the street, with just the yellow glow from the streetlights to illuminate the trees.

How many undead prowled the darkness not one hundred meters from where she sat? Maybe Eric was one of them. Washington Square wasn't as big or as wooded as Central Park, but it had lots of dark corners.

She hated the reality of Eric's undead needs. Whatever their connection, he was still a vampire, and that meant blood. He certainly didn't get any from her the other night. Eric was still a predator by definition, even if she knew she wasn't his mark.

Her hand rose instinctively to the spot above her left breast. She had a different kind of mark to worry about than whether or not she was vampire bait. She turned for the daybed and her notes, scribbling a thought in the corner.

"Sigils and Demon marks. Interesting."

Blair jumped with an abrupt breath. "Dr. Wells! *Jesus.* You startled me."

"One of my more refined teacher tricks." She winked, putting her purse on the rumpled daybed. "Works like a charm, especially during exams."

"Remind me to get you a bell for your neck." Blair chuckled, still a little taken aback.

The professor gestured to her scattered notes and the various books on the study desk beneath the window. "Horror myths? Is this why you're squirreled away in the stacks when you should be enjoying a break from this place? That's not part of your degree plan."

What could she say to the woman? Sorry, Doc, but I'm a blood witch and I just learned my biological father is either fury, fanged, immortal, or demonic? Yeah, right. Not a chance.

Blair lifted one shoulder, letting it drop nonchalantly. "It's a hobby of mine. No big."

"Hobby? At a study desk past the stacks, you've got papers and books strewn across a table meant for six people. I've seen panicked thesis students less manic."

Blair grabbed her notebooks, stuffing them into the center zip of her backpack. "You know me when something piques my imagination. I'm not as frenzied or disorganized as this looks. I'll straighten that table outside the stacks, tonight. I promise. The side office, too."

Why was the woman poking around? It was her office and all, but damn. If she wanted prying eyes, she would have stayed at Crow Haven House.

The professor considered her the way she would an old text. "Your tenacity is what makes you a good teaching

assistant, Blair, but—" Her words clipped when she caught sight one of Grania's diaries on the study desk.

"Now that looks intriguing." She reached for it, but Blair picked it up before she could.

"Why are you so tense? Don't tell me one of my students asked you to finish *their* work over break?"

Blair shook her head. "No, it's my own personal project." She swallowed, thinking fast. "A gothic romance. Silly, I know."

A wide smile spread on Lynetta's face. "Gothic romance." She nodded. "I'm a big fan. The good ones always research their facts, even if they end up fictionized." She looked at the number of books piled on the desk with an impressed nod. "Still, it's an awful lot of material for a novel."

She picked up Blair's sketchbook, scanning the detailed drawings, page by page. Inside were comprehensive illustrations of vampires and other supernaturals.

The outer office door opened and closed, and the muffled approach of footsteps scuffed along the carpet, getting closer. Was this Grand Central? She had work to do.

"Damn, girl. When did you decide to go from student to raggedy hermit over night? Just look at you, *cher*."

"Lizzie. What are you doing here? Did Tara send you to find me?" Blair asked, surprised to see her friend.

"Of course not. I'm no spy." Liz put her purse down on the desk and then shrugged out of her jacket. "Suzy gloated about having your room to herself, so I got suspicious." She waited for Blair to introduce her to the older woman, but no. "I beg your pardon, but if we wait for Blair to make the introductions, we'll both be old and

grizzled. Truth is, she isn't usually this rude. I'm Elizabeth Gaudet."

Lynetta turned, sketches still in hand. "Dr. Lynetta Wells. Pleasure to meet one of Blair's friends. Are you at NYU as well?"

"No, I leave that to the clever witches of the world."

"Clever witches." She looked at Blair with a raised brow. "That's an unusual turn of phrase."

Lizzie looked at the book in Dr. Wells' hand. "These are really good, Blair. I didn't realize you were so talented."

"How do you know they're my drawings?"

Lizzie smirked, giving her friend a look. "The handwriting." She tapped one of the pages. "I'd recognize your chicken scratch anywhere." She waited for her to elaborate, but when she didn't, she moved to smooth the daybed before plopping down on the end.

"Your friend is being rather cagey, Elizabeth. Though I have to say I'm impressed with these as well." Dr. Wells lifted the sketchbook before putting it on the desk. "The notes on abilities and longevity next to each drawing are especially detailed, though you've got some of the information on Incubi and Succubi wrong.

"They are both immortal but only so because they feed off soul energy. Mostly from humans, but on the rare occasion, they find themselves drawn to certain supernaturals. They do so by arousing sexual passion. They syphon soul energy when their victim reaches orgasm. Usually they hypnotize a victim into compliance by looking in their eyes, but older, more experienced demons can do so from say, across a room."

"That kind of manipulation is despicable," Liz replied. "Talk about a predatory race. Sounds like a giant

inferiority complex that needs feeding. Not their immortality."

Lynetta stared at Lizzie, steady and unblinking. The poor girl looked everywhere else, fidgeting with the buttons on her cardigan before finally taking it from her shoulders. "Is it hot in here, or is it just me?"

"You'll have to forgive Lizzie, Dr. Wells. She's a demure kind. Overt talk gives her hives."

Dr. Wells broke eye contact with a laugh. "So it would seem. You need to relax, love. I wouldn't worry about demonic lovers. You'd barely be a snack, unless, of course, they end up owning you, body and soul. If that were the case, you'd be helpless to resist." She clicked the inside of her cheek. "Death by sex. Unless they knock you up first."

Blair felt the color drain from her face. Could Lynetta have inadvertently given her the answer about her parentage? It made sense. Every bit. She needed to get rid of Lizzie and Dr. Wells and hit the books.

"Well, ladies. It was a pleasure and very enlightening, if not entertaining." She picked up her purse, letting her fingers trail Lizzie's arm.

The girl flinched, and Lynetta chuckled. "You're in New York now, love. Lighten up." Her gaze considered Liz more closely. "So artless yet so much beneath the surface. What fun it would be to awaken all that sleeping passion and free your vagina."

Lizzie's mouth dropped open, earning a smirk from the professor. Sparing a wink for Blair, Lynetta left the way she came in, with barely a sound.

Blair waited for the telltale snick that the door closed before turning to Lizzie's stunned face.

"What's with that woman?" Liz asked, blowing out a breath. "She and her awakened vagina can kiss my Cajun

butt. There may be a lid on this pot, but that doesn't mean there's no spice simmering."

"Forget Dr. Wells and her woke vagina. Why are you here, Liz? For real this time. If I had wanted a parade of people interrupting my work, I would have stayed home."

"Stop being so...so...*you!*" Lizzie threw a hand up. "I don't need a reason to check on my best friend. I called four fucking morgues, Blair! After your linen closet confession, what the hell was I supposed to think when you disappeared for days? I was out of my mind thinking some vampire finally got the better of you. I nearly broke my promise and told Tara!" She sniffed. "Though I'm glad I didn't. It's obvious you've been here the whole time."

With a guilty exhale, Blair pursed her lips. "Well, not the whole time."

"Blair Cabot! You promised." Liz smacked her palms down on her thighs. "At least tell me you didn't kill anyone this time."

"Well technically, no—"

"If it wasn't a goddamned death sentence, I'd report you to the Vampire Council myself, you lying little witch."

Blair burst out laughing. "Whoa! Listen to all that colorful language, N'awlins. Did you just forfeit your debutante card, or is there a demerit system?"

"Bless your Yankee heart, but it's pronounced New Awlins." An annoyed grin pursed Lizzie's mouth. "Stop wriggling on the line and tell me the truth. Did you go hunting again?"

Blair traced a crisscross over her heart. "Not since we last spoke. Though happening upon a situation doesn't technically count as hunting, right?"

"Blair, what am I gonna do with you? Did this happening involve killing?"

"In self-defense and the defense of an innocent woman."

Lizzie answered with an unladylike grumble. "You could have told me in the first place instead of making me cuss like a gutter rat."

"It was worth seeing you break a sweat. Still, I may have bent my promise a bit."

"Blair!"

"No, no. I told you the truth about hunting and all."

"But?"

"But I did go out with the intent of finding."

Lizzie's brows knotted. "If this is another game of semantics—"

"It's not. I swear," Blair replied quickly. "I went looking for someone, Liz." She angled her head, intentionally.

Blair's meaning dawned, and a smile spread across Liz's pink lips. "Well?"

"Well what?"

"Did you find him?"

"Him who?"

"Red beans and rice, Blair! The kissing vampire?"

Blair chuckled. "Eric would get a kick out of you and that nickname. Like the kissing bandit."

"Your vampire's name is Eric? Not a very inspired name."

Blair laughed. "What did you expect? Vlad or Bram?"

Lizzie shrugged. "Maybe." Leaning forward, she grinned. "So?"

"Sew buttons," Blair replied, fishing in a near-empty bag of chips she left on the desk.

"Ugh. I want details, Blair."

"Eric's different." She shrugged. "I don't know what else to tell you."

"I swear, Blair. You give me play-by-plays when you sleep with guys you pick up at Starbucks. Why not now? How is this vampire different? Is he European, or maybe Asian? Or do you mean different as in a forked tongue, or a penis with teeth, or something weird like that?"

"*Jesus*, Liz. What's the temperature of crazy inside your head?" Blair snorted a laugh. "Where do you come up with this stuff?"

"At least I don't entertain guests with ink all over my face."

Blair grabbed her cell phone and reversed the camera to check. "I look like a pen ejaculated all over my face."

She wet a napkin with her tongue and scrubbed the side of her cheek. Lizzie sat on the daybed with a face that looked like she'd sucked on a lemon.

"Stop sulking," Blair said, crumpling the napkin. She felt bad teasing her friend. "You want details, I'll give you details. But whatever I tell you falls under the same promise you made in the linen closet. You cannot tell Tara or anyone else. It's not safe. Not for me or for Eric."

"Well, I've kept your secrets so far." Lizzie got up to pluck a stray potato chip from her friend's hair. "Does this crash pad have a shower?"

"Yes, and it even has soap." She swung an arm around her friend's shoulders.

"Good. Use it. I'll straighten up in here and then you can tell me all about your kissing vampire."

Chapter Nine

*E*ric sat in the living room, nursing a thermal mug of crimson. The townhouse was quiet. Marta and the other staff were still upstate with the family. Carlos was the only one who stayed behind besides him, so there was really no one to disturb his rest this evening. Still, his mind wouldn't allow a lie-in, and he rose before sunset.

Carlos was at the council for their weekly meeting with the Weres. The head of their house would keep his word and not tell the council about the witch. Yet. It was just as well Carlos wasn't home. Eric wasn't in the mood to talk. Or argue.

He hadn't told Carlos, or anyone, he'd spent time with Blair. Intimate time. Technically, he did what the head of their house requested. He'd found the witch. More to the point, she found him.

Eric smiled to himself. If nothing else, Blair was relentless and resourceful. That she used that stupid scrap of fabric from his jacket to scry for him was genius.

Sighing low, he rested his head on the couch. Blair's scent still lingered, teasing his senses. If Carlos noticed, he didn't say. It was only a matter of time before the head of their house figured it out, or Eric had no choice but to tell him the truth.

He knew what the council would demand, and he wasn't willing to give them what they'd need to launch an inquiry.

Would he lie for Blair? In a heartbeat. Did the vampires she ended deserve to die? Of that he had no doubt. The same way he knew the two in the park were beyond hope.

Blair would hate him if she knew, but he'd given her thoughts a cursory scan that night in the alley. It was before he told her he wouldn't, and it wasn't as though he took a walk through private memories. There was enough of her blood-trace in the air that night, he didn't need to taste her to make the connection. Every youngblood she targeted was guilty as hell. Not only marking innocents as prey but taking pleasure in torture for sport.

He exhaled, raking a hand through his hair. As for the rest, he'd know more once he and Blair spoke this weekend. Right now, it was all he could do to keep the last few nights from driving him mad.

Talking about his past was never easy, but with Blair it seemed effortless. Perhaps he wanted to change her mind so badly. To let her see vampires were no different from humans. They were good and evil, and suffered as well as brought suffering.

With one leg draped over the edge of a living room chair, he sat in the dark. A low fire burned in the hearth, so he didn't turn on the lights. To be honest, he preferred the solitude of the shadows. It matched his thoughts.

He sighed and went to the tray on the side credenza where Carlos kept his rum and lifted the bottle of Jameson's Black Label. Unscrewing the cap, he poured a generous helping into what was left of his crimson and then put the bottle back.

It was going to be one of those nights.

Carrying his drink up the steps to his bedroom, he took every stair with care. Not because he felt weak, but because the staircase held so many memories.

The first day he came to live with Carlos and his family and could barely tolerate the human staff without salivating for their blood. The first time he was strong

enough to come down from his bedroom to join the others as his brother Miguel played the guitar. Or when he was strong enough to let Rosa fuss over him, eventually letting the little madre into his room and then into his heart.

The natural comings and goings of this house ticked like a metronome, steady and constant, and eventually its unvarying cadence became the heartbeat in his chest. Now Blair was part of that natural, living tempo, adding her scent and images to the tapestry in his mind.

Evening had waxed into night. He was supposed to meet Carlos after the council meeting and go over plans for renovations at Club Avalon. Something Julian was supposed to handle but couldn't since Kat needed him to catch a plane to Dublin. That was the loose end he had to tie up.

Eric put his drink down on his night table. Eleven p.m. An hour and a half until he had to head downtown. The last thing he wanted was to run into Rémy. Carlos he could handle, but Rémy would give him that unnerving stare, the ruined side of his once-beautiful face, making it hard to evade answering questions.

Still, Rémy wasn't a hard-ass. He would want to see if there were mitigating reasons for Blair's actions as well. He wasn't as patient as Carlos, but he understood to what lengths pain could push an individual. He'd suffered himself, but his mate Jenya and her past had taught him the value of the full story.

He took a deep gulp of his drink, letting the Jameson's burn on the way down. Carlos drank rum for the scent and the flavor, but he was too much an elder for the effects of the alcohol. Eric was still young enough in his undead life to experience a bit of the tipsy. The burn reminded him of that and of times long gone.

He looked to the window as a streak of light from passing headlights caught his eye. He walked to the curtains and pushed them aside. Streetlights and passing cars gleamed on the wet streets, but the city was quieter than usual. He smiled to himself. Once, it was the steady rumble of carriage wheels that would bring you to the window, not the flash of a headlamp as they were once called.

Glancing at the clock again, Eric quickly finished his drink and walked into the bathroom. He turned on the shower and waited as the room filled with steam before stepping into the spray to ease the tension from his shoulders. It cascaded over his body, the feel casting his mind to Blair's warm skin and the warmth that rocked him to the core when their auras merged. It was magic. There was no other way to describe it. If he could combine the two, he'd never pine for the sun again.

Closing his eyes, he imagined what it would be like. Their bodies entwined. His full length deep within her as her scent and the lure of her forbidden blood tantalized him. The tingle of magic as she whispered her spell, and then the heady rush of their merge making his cock swell and hers crest to climax.

He groaned, wrapping his hand around his shaft. He kept the image clear in his mind as he worked his cock. Jolts shivered from his spine into his groin as his hand moved in time with the vision in his head.

"Blair," he murmured, as water pounded his shoulders and he worked his member in his palm. He pictured her face as she came, and the feel of her walls squeezing his length. His palm cured over his head, faster and faster until he exploded in his own hand.

With his forehead on the warm tile, he caught his breath before turning to lean his shoulders against the marble. He'd self-satisfied before, usually when he took blood without a sexual release. Now, the thought of sharing either with anyone but Blair left him hollow, and the idea shook him harder than his climax. He was falling for the witch. Falling, as in head over heels.

Eric stood in the shower letting the water beat on his head. There was no way he'd let the Vampire Council have her no matter what her crimes. He'd walk into the sun first, and he knew Carlos would never let that happen. He had to find an extenuating reason for her actions, either that or fabricate one.

White lies were something he'd learned early in his human life. It was a matter of survival then, and if it came to that, it would be a matter of survival now. Not physical survival but certainly mental and emotional. For the first time since he was turned, he felt as though he could be whole again. As whole as a vampire could be. For the first time in a century, he wanted a future and what it held. He wanted to hope.

Rinsing off, Eric got out of the shower. He towel-dried his hair and then wrapped the soft terry around his hips. He sat on the bed, turning on the television for background noise. Nothing ever held his interest but the History Channel, and tonight was no different. As if by fate, an upcoming program flashed on the television screen. *The Great War, Secrets of WWI.*

Canadian or not, he'd certainly served in the heat of it, enough to deserve any kind of accolade, even if he wasn't technically killed in the line of duty. He'd checked the official record once he'd settled in New York. It read: Eric

Michael Fraser. Missing in Action. Presumed Dead. August 30, 1918.

Ironic really. Considering the Armistice came just two months later, ending the war on November 11th. He'd survived the battlefield, only to meet death on the way home.

Doughboy.

With all the sadness implicated in that word, he couldn't help the close-lipped smile that tugged at his mouth. *You are definitely not related to the little Pillsbury dude. You are every inch a soldier...Doughboy. Every hard, long, muscled inch.* Natasha may have started it, but now and forever that nickname belonged exclusively to Blair for him.

Eric stacked three pillows against the headboard and turned the volume up on the TV. He reached for a chain hanging from the side of his headboard. Attached were his army dog tags and a small compass. He rolled the compass across his palm, feeling the grooves from its looping inscription against his fingers. He didn't need to look at the aged metal to know what it said. *History is philosophy—teaching by example and also by warning.*

The quote was from 17th century political philosopher, Henry St. John. But wasn't St. John or what he believed that mattered. It was the words themselves and how their meaning tethered Eric to his past, present, and future.

Carlos had gifted him the compass after he joined their family in New York in 1928. Ten years after he'd been turned to darkness.

The gesture was simple. A gift to mark his path and remind him there was always a way home.

His words to Blair were the truth. He was better with anger and retribution than other, gentler emotions. The

feelings Blair stirred were certainly putting him to the test. The sins of his past were best left in the past, but tonight, that was easier said than done. For the first time in a century, there was so much at stake.

The television flickered in the background, and he closed his eyes against its violent scenes and droning narration and let the memories flood once more.

Chapter Ten

Pre-dawn hours
Northern France
Western Front
September 2ⁿᵈ, 1918

An elbow hit Eric in the arm. "You look like you're about to heave, boyo. Take a swig o' this. It'll help."

A bottle was held out, and in the dim light he saw it was Glen Scotia whiskey. He turned to Duncan, surprised.

"How did you come by this? The rest of us have been making do with rot gut." Eric took the bottle, running a finger over the label to clear the soot.

"Maisie. She hid it in my kit after me last leave, darlin' girl." Duncan clicked his cheek.

Eric wiped the top and swallowed a deep gulp.

He coughed, and Duncan chuckled. "Brings ya right home, even in this godforsaken place.

They were on the front lines of the Western Front at the basin of the River Somme in Northern France.

Sitting with Duncan in the trenches, he glanced at the soldiers that made up their line. Ced, Wesley, and all the others. Tired and scared, they sat out a lull in the shelling on wooden boards that kept their arses out of the muck and mud, or at least that was the theory. Eighteen miles of trenches were dug. Seven feet deep and six feet wide, with a thick line of sandbags to absorb any bullets and shell fragments. Dug with their hands, dodging and digging while mortars exploded on the battlefield above.

The battle lines along the Somme were dubbed Death's Anteroom, complete with a barbed wire and wooden spiked maze he and his line had to run while dodging machine gun fire.

"Think mebbe they're done for the night?" Eric coughed and then took another swig. "I don't know about you, but I could use a little shut-eye."

Duncan winced, lifting his feet out of the mud to rest on a fallen sandbag. "And I want a fire with wiener roast and a cold beer, but right now I'd settle for dry socks and boots that don't leak."

"I've got an extra pair in my kit. They've been darned, but they're okay. You're welcome to them." He lifted the bottle for another mouthful and then handed the whiskey back to his friend. "For sharing your Scotia."

"Ach, you're a good egg, Eric Fraser. May we both live to see twenty-one." He saluted his friend with the neck of the bottle.

Eric leaned his head against the sandbag wall to stare at the starless sky. Smoke hung in the air like a permanent pong, burning the inside of his nose and tightening his lungs. Still, at least it wasn't gas.

How many times had they heard the panicked shout, *Gas, Gas, Gas!* He and Duncan had taken masks off two dead Jerrys on their last rush to push the Germans back. Whether they worked or not, he didn't know.

"I've got you beat there, my friend. If it's past midnight, then I'm twenty-two today."

Duncan grinned, his teeth flashing white in the moonlight. "Happy Birthday, boyo. Twenty-two. How long have you been fighting this godless, pointless war? Hell, you must have been in from the start in '14."

"Just two years. To be honest, I'm still surprised I haven't bayonetted myself. I chalk it up to our commander. He's not a toff. Started as an enlisted gunner and worked his way up." Eric nodded. "He doesn't make stupid ego-driven decisions designed by committee. He knows what it's like to be in our boots. Literally."

Ced chuckled. "Jeez, Fraser, tell us how you really feel."

"What I want to know is how you managed to ditch conscription for two years," Duncan raised a brow."

"I'm no coward, if that's what you're implying."

"I know that up close and personal, but I got called up practically the day after I turned eighteen. What did you do? Disappear?"

Eric shrugged. "It's not hard to do in a city like Halifax, but no. My guess is the War Office had no idea how to locate me. It's the only good thing about being an orphan with no real address to your name. If the War Office can't find you, they can't take you. I saw returning soldiers at the docks. Most were on stretchers. Broken in spirit and in body. No thanks. I tramped from place to place. A dayworker for the war effort, here, a farm migrant during the summer months, there. I did everything I could to keep myself fed and warm."

"You're a home child?" Wesley asked, surprised.

Eric dismissed him. "You say it as if I've got a communicable disease. I had parents until I was seven, but they both died of influenza only months apart." He shrugged. "Can't cry over it forever. Except for the headmaster and his stick, Halifax Protestant was pretty decent. At least I had Mrs. Beech."

"Patroness or bedmate?" Ced joked, grabbing his crotch. "Or mebbe both, eh?"

Eric threw a handful of muck at him.

"What the fuck, Fraser?" Ced went to get up, but Duncan pushed him down.

"If you're going to think like a pig, then you should look like a pig. Mrs. Beech was the home's cook and housekeeper," Eric replied. "She was like a mother to us boys. She stood between me and the headmaster's stick more times than I can count."

"So, answer the question, then, Fraser. How'd you dodge the draft?" Wesley cocked his head.

"I didn't," Eric replied matter-of-factly. "I was given a choice. Jail time or enlist."

Duncan's mouth dropped. "A home child and a felon? Boyo, that whistle blows, and it's you who's first up and over and into the fray. You've got some atoning to do."

"Like hell I do." Eric snorted. "I've been on the short end of the stick since my parents died."

Ced scraped at the mud on his boots. "Do tell."

"Here's one for the books. Our headmaster called me to his office the day before my eighteenth birthday. He told me by law I had to leave by the weekend, but that it was my lucky day. He'd arranged for me to take a position with the local smithy."

"What's wrong with that? He sounds like a decent enough chap," Wesley replied.

Eric shook his head. "Neither were decent. Smedley, or Smelly as the boys called him, was on the take from a known sexual deviant. The smithy liked his boys young, usually ten or twelve, but, for some reason, he took a fancy to me. I refused the position, and Smedley went apoplectic.

"He raised his stick to cane me plenty, but, this last time, I grabbed it and sent it clattering across the room."

All eyes were on Eric now. "Lord, boyo. What happened next?" Duncan asked.

"Smedley wasn't a very big man, but to a little boy he'd seemed monstrous. I wasn't a boy anymore, so I saw him for what he was. A fat, greedy son of a bitch who sold the orphans in his care for profit. If I close my eyes, I can still hear the argument."

"Ah, Fraser. Good. Come in and sit down." Mr. Smedley waved him to a chair. "I have some news for you."

Eric sat on the edge of the wooden chair, not wanting to get too comfortable. Not that he could in the same office that saw both his palms and his backside caned.

"As you'll be eighteen in a matter of days, it's my duty to inform you that you will be leaving Halifax Protestant at that time. You have a relatively good record, so I was able to secure a position for you with Mr. Carnes."

"The blacksmith?"

Smedley nodded. "Indeed. He's looking for a young lad with a strong back, so I struck a bargain with him and secured you the spot. He wanted a younger boy, but he set eyes on you and agreed on the spot." He considered Eric over the top of his square spectacles. "You must have made a good impression."

"I've never met the man, let alone spoken with him. How could I have made an impression?"

Smedley cleaned his specs before putting them on his nose. "Maybe he liked the look of you. You're not handsome, but you're strong. Well-made."

"Headmaster...everyone knows Mr. Carnes is...is...." Eric's words cut short when Smedley lifted his caning stick onto his desk.

"Is what, Fraser?"

Eric tightened his jaw and sat up straight. "He's a prig, sir. And I've heard he uses the boys in his employ for other things.

Unnatural things. Especially the young ones. A young boy can hardly lift a heavy pail, let alone smithy tools. Carnes wants them young because they can't fight back, and no one will believe them if they talk."

The stick came down on the desk with a whack. "For shame! I will not have a good man's name besmirched by the likes of you. You're nobody, Fraser. Nothing! You've got no name, no people, and no prospects. Your time here taught you to read and write, boy, and you know your way around the tool shed, but don't you realize this is your chance to learn a trade?"

"If learning to bend over and say more please, like I'm some buggered Oliver Twist, is what you consider learning a trade, then I'll take my chances with hammer and nail!" Eric pointed his finger at Smedley. "It's you should be ashamed, hawking the boys from this house to a deviant."

The headmaster stood, his round face red. "Get out! I don't want to see your face or hear your name again! You will leave this house tonight!" He raised his cane, but before he could strike, Eric grabbed it from his hand and threw it across the room.

"You can't make me do anything anymore, and if you get the constable, I'll tell him about your arrangement with Mr. Carnes. They know all about him, Mr. Smedley, and I'm sure they'd be right interested to learn the details of your bargain."

The headmaster's eyes bulged, and his normally red face went purple. He tugged on his stiff detachable collar, white spittle at the corners of his mouth. He fell into his chair, choking.

Eric pushed from him, staring. "Mrs. Beech! Help!" He ran for the door and clattered down the first few steps. "Someone! Come quick!"

A clamor of boys ran up the stairs with Mrs. B in tow, but by the time they got there, Mr. Smedley had slumped over the desk with his tongue out.

"Lordy! What happened?" Mrs. Beech asked, crossing herself.

Eric shook his head. "I don't know. One minute he was talking, the next it looked like he choked on his own tongue."

Mrs. Beech crossed herself again and then shooed the boys out, sending one for the doctor and the other for the constable.

"The constable! They're gonna think I had something to do with him offing," Eric said, holding the older woman's sleeve.

"Tosh. I'll not let them say a blessed thing against ye. Yer the best lad in this house."

"But I turn eighteen on Saturday." Eric looked at her, wringing her hands. "I didn't do anything wrong, Mrs. Beech. I swear. It was Smedley. He wanted to put me with the smithy."

"Wi' Carnes?" Mrs. B's knuckles turned white. Her lips pressed in a thin line. "Then I hope his carcass is burnin' wi' the other devils of his ilk!" She took Eric's arms, tugged him into the office, and closed the door. "Ye have to walk a straight line, lad. Ya ken me clear enough? We had a wee Christmas miracle today, so don't be wastin' it." She kept her voice low. "It could take the board a month or more to appoint a new man. Yer stayin' put 'til then. Hear? I'll see what I can do fer ye after that."

"Jesus H. Christ," Duncan crossed himself. "So, did you get to stay?"

Eric shook his head, pulling his uniform tunic tighter around his chest against the damp. "So much for the kindness of strangers and all the candles Mrs. Beech lit for me. It took the board two weeks to find a new headmaster and that new headmaster a day to finish the job Smedley began. I refused the position with Mr. Carnes and was shown the door that same hour.

"Mrs. Beech's hands were tied. She couldn't do more than offer me the odd meal when rations allowed. Besides, the younger boys needed her. She was the only mother

most of them had, and I wouldn't take that from them. Not when I had a strong back and the will to survive."

Duncan scratched his head, stunned. "Lordy, Fraser. You make me want to write me ma and tell her how much I love her."

"You should, Dunc. If you've got a loving ma, never take her for granted. Still, the plot thickens, if you're interested."

"More? Hells bells." Dunc whistled low. "If you were a lass, you'd be a regular Jane Eyre."

Ced laughed, giving Duncan's shoulder a shove. "So hoity toity wi' your book learning. If Fraser's tale is too much for your delicate ears, you can always sit in the mud by yourself."

"Go on, Eric. Finish the story." Wesley nodded. "It's not like the wonderous Theda Bara is showing up to entertain us otherwise."

Eric shrugged. "It's just my sad tale, lads. Nothing to write home about. I was tossed out of the Halifax Protestant with two crisp dollar bills, courtesy of Mrs. Beech and the Bank of Nova Scotia, and a single set of clean clothes. That's all I had to my name. That and Mrs. B's tears.

"The money she gave me should've lasted, but I made the stupid mistake of taking it out of my pocket to pay for my lodgings that night, only to find myself on the floor, beaten about the head. When I came to, the money and everything else was gone.

"That's when I moved from place to place and job to job. No real address for the War Office, or anyone else, to find me. Work was hard to come by, and eventually I ended up sleeping in the park. Something the local constabulary wasn't too keen on."

"Move along, bucko. You can't sleep here."

Eric sat up and rubbed one eye. "And where do you suppose I go, Constable? Perhaps the Ritz, eh?"

A beefy arm yanked him up, giving him a shove. "I don't care where you go, as long as it ain't here."

"What about your house? You seem well fed. In fact, big enough to keep an elephant on his toes. Tell me, does the circus spotlight fat pirouetting police constables for entertainment these days?"

Eric twirled ballerina-style, knowing it might earn him a cracked skull, but he was hoping for a night in the clink. Someplace warm with a hot meal.

"Okay, wiseacre. You just earned yourself a night behind bars." The constable's beefy arm was attached to an even beefier hand, and it clamped over Eric's shoulder.

Eric smirked at the memory. "I shared a cell for the night with another bloke. He was a local gang member. Petty crimes, mostly. Nothing too bad. That night we got to talking, and he offered me a place to stay in exchange for a white lie. Beggars can't be choosers, so I agreed. I stayed with him until I saved enough money to head for the States. I set my sights on Boston. I had skills, and there was work to be had. I would have made it, too, if it wasn't for my gang.

"Looks like I got myself company for the night."

Eric didn't reply, simply took his bunk and stretched out, grateful for the cot and the thin blanket.

"Shut up, Everts." The beefy constable pointed at him. "You'll cool your heels in here until you tell the judge the truth."

A second constable stopped at the entrance with two trays. "Food, gentlemen." He dropped Eric's tray on the bed. Green peas rolled onto the thin blanket.

"It's not the Ritz, like you asked," the beefy constable taunted. "So maybe I should take it back to the kitchen. Tell cookie it's not up to your liking."

Eric snatched the plate and spoon before the constable could take it away, earning a snide laugh for the effort.

"Nighty night, gents."

Everts watched Eric eat. "Lemme guess. No place to go, so you got yourself arrested."

Eric paused, spoon to mouth, but didn't reply.

"Not to worry, boyo. The coppers aren't going to charge you for nothing. Vagrancy isn't a real crime. They lock up the likes of us in case we've been at the drink. Says it's to protect you and me. Me? I'm thinking it's them we need protecting from, eh?"

Eric blinked at him.

"You are a quiet one."

"I talk when I've got something to say, and I ain't got nothing to say to you," Eric replied, still chewing.

Everts shrugged. "Suit yourself." He held out his roll to Eric, gesturing for him to take it. "Go on. I ain't gonna bite, and I don't want nothing for it, neither."

Eric snatched it from his hand and bit into it as if starving.

"When's the last time you et, eh, boyo?"

Swallowing, Eric gulped half his water. "You've got a lot of questions, don'tcha?"

"Mebbe."

"Well, if you want answers, then stop calling me boyo. You can't be more than one or two years older than me."

"True enough." Everts chuckled. "But I make up for that with street smarts." He tapped the side of his head.

"Yeah?"

"Yeah."

Eric considered the young man. "If you've got so much street starts, who protects you, then? You're in here with me, so they must not do a grand job of it."

Everts grinned. "They do a fine job. I'm bench warming for one of the boys."

"Bench warming?"

The other boy nodded. "I took a fall for one of my brothers. He would have been caged for a long haul, but I told the coppers he was with me, sleeping in the park. Same as you." He tapped the side of his nose. "Listen, if you want to earn yourself a little street sway, you could always back up me story. Say you saw us across the green."

"But I didn't see you."

"You could say you did." Everts got up from his bunk and moved to sit beside Eric. "Who's to know? It's just a harmless lie. My people will spring us both, then, and I can introduce you to Mickey and the boys." He bumped Eric's arm with the side of his fist. "Tell them you did me good."

"Mickey?" Eric asked.

"He runs our cooperative, so to speak." The boy grinned, flashing brownish teeth. "He's not one to let a favor go by. If you play your cards right, he might let you stay with us. Warm bed. Square meals."

"He sounds like Fagan."

The other boy's eyes narrowed. "I don't know no Fagan. Is he from the Saddle Street boys?"

Eric grinned, chuckling. "No, from **Oliver Twist**. The book? Charles Dickens?"

The boy shrugged. "I ain't been schooled much, so I'll have to take your word for it."

Eric wiped his mouth on the side of his hand. The other lad was just as scruffy as him, but his clothes were in good condition and his shoes looked newish.

"What would Mickey have me do if he let me stay?"

"You might have to help on a caper or two. Nothing fancy. Maybe be a lookout for—" He gave a chin pop toward the cell bars.

"You're a gang, then?"

The young man sat up straight and sniffed. "Better known as the Tower Boys." He gave Eric a proud wink. "Mebbe you heard of us."

Eric didn't comment.

"Trust me, boyo, with this war, there's opportunity for everyone who wants it. Why not take a bite from the apple when it's there for the taking?"

"You mean greasy thieving and whatnot."

He laughed. "For someone so book smart, you really are right thick. Opportunity is opportunity. What has this world shown you, boyo? If you don't do you first, it'll be done to you. Listen, if you want to get in with us, I told you how. We take care of our own." The young man sniffed, running a finger across his nose. "You do this, and I'll vouch for you with Mickey afterward. At least you'll get a supper into you. You look like a right skeleton."

"What's your name, anyway?" Eric asked.

The boy smiled. "Tommy Everts."

"Eric Fraser."

Tommy grinned. "Well, Eric Fraser. Do we have a deal, then?"

Eric paused, looking around the cell. This was his present, but he'd be damned if it was to be his future. He needed a breather to find his feet, and the Tower Boys sounded like just the ticket.

"Yeah, I'm in."

Tommy spit in his palm and held it out, gesturing for Eric to do the same.

"That was the beginning of how I ended up in this trench. The clincher happened about six months later. Tommy woke me up in the middle of the night. I'd never seen him so scared.

"What the hell, Tommy?" Eric bolted up in his bed.

"It's bad, boyo. Everything went wrong. I know you're leaving for Boston in the morning, but you gotta help me. Help us."

"Slow down and tell me what happened."

"I killed the night guard at the docks. I didn't mean to, but he wouldn't shut up."

"What the hell, Tommy! And you come here? Are you daft? This is the first place they'll look for you."

"You mean look for YOU." Tommy shoved a finger in Eric's chest.

"Oh no," Eric said, shoving Tommy's hand away. "I'm done with all this. I told you last week."

Tommy shrugged. "We've given you a roof over your head, a bed to sleep in, and three squares a day, Eric. We even let you keep a share of whatever we take in for being our eyes and ears. So you're gonna do this, or Mickey and me won't be happy about it."

"I'm not going to jail for something I didn't do."

Putting his hand on his hip, Tommy flashed his pistol, letting Eric know it wasn't a choice.

"You're the newest in, boyo. Newest in does the dirty work, and you're gonna bench warm for me, same as I did for Mickey the night you and I met..."

Slack-jawed, Duncan handed the bottle of Glen Scotia to Eric again. "Wet your whistle, my friend, because you gotta finish this tale."

Eric watched the sandbags leak slow trickles of grainy silt into the mud. "I already told you what happened next. I kept my trap shut when the coppers showed up. I could've run, but I didn't need a wanted poster following me to Boston. The coppers hauled every one of the Tower Boys. Mickey and Tommy pinned it on me, as I suspected. They left me holding the bag. Alone.

"How old are you, son?"

"I'm twenty, your honor."

"Twenty years old and standing before me for manslaughter." The magistrate rubbed his chin. *"Problem is, I don't believe you're the guilty party. The facts don't add up. I think you're shackling yourself to the yoke against your will."*

The magistrate nodded slowly. *"I think, yes, young man. You see, I know all about the Tower Boys, and I know how Mickey Mulvaney runs his…business. So, I'm going to give you a choice, lad. You can do time for something we both know you didn't do, or you can enlist. As it stands, your path will surely show you the gallows, so why not make something of your life instead?"*

Eric didn't reply, but he angled his head slightly, listening to the option.

"I'd rather see you throw yourself on a sword for God and Country than be the fall guy for a greasy harbor rat like Mulvaney. The choice is yours."

The magistrate closed the file on his judicial bench then looked at Eric again. *"Before you make your choice, I want you to do one thing first. Look around you. Look at the gallery here today. Are any of your boys in attendance? The empty chairs speak volumes, eh?"* He raised an eyebrow. *"Something to think on, son, eh?*

Eric toyed with the nearly empty bottle of whiskey. "If I went to jail, my life would've been over for something I didn't do. Dead wasted. No odds." He exhaled, draining the dregs. "But, if I signed on the dotted line for a round-trip ticket to the front, then at least I had a fighting chance. A clean slate with an honorable discharge in my pocket once the war was over."

"Fighting chance, indeed." Duncan snorted. "After all that, it's no wonder you're such a son of a bitch."

Eric rolled his aching neck. "I have my moments. God and I aren't on great terms much of the time. Especially these days. Every time we gain a few godforsaken yards, my blood boils when I see how many didn't make it. Broken and bloody where they fell."

"We all feel that. And even if your ma and pa had lived, you would have ended up here anyway. Just from a different path." Duncan eyed his mate. "What now? You got anything to go back to? Me, I've got Maisie waiting. Keepin' my bed warm for me."

Eric shrugged. "Doesn't matter. I had nothing when I left, and I've got nothing now. It's either life or death."

"Damn, Fraser. You're more miserable than the war." Ced shook his head. "Don'tcha have friends waiting at home? What about that housekeep, Mrs. Beech? Bet she'd be glad you made it back in one piece."

Eric lifted one shoulder. "Mebbe, but I don't want to think about it. I hold my breath each time a mortar hits close enough to feel the dirt spray my face. I pray to a God I'm not even sure is listening, whenever I climb that ladder up and over to run the next barbed wire maze. It's been two years since I got here, and we've pushed the Germans way back. If I can hold out a little more, I just might make it home to find out what matters. We all might."

A high-pitched whistle had them all on their feet. The mortar exploded at the mouth of their section, shaking Eric's diaphragm and squeezing his guts. Duncan fell forward, landing at his feet, motionless. His friend's spine split down to organs and bone. Ces and Wesley were closer to the blast, taking even more of the impact.

"Gas, Gas, Gas!"

Eric scrambled as far as he could, yanking the mask he took from the fallen German over his face as the yellow cloud engulfed the entire line. The trench filled, and boys fell, crawling through the mud, gasping for clean air like fish on the bow of a boat.

Bleeding from shrapnel, he grabbed his rifle and ran. Clambering over bodies for a ladder to the surface. Smoke from the shelling was thick, cut only by the pulsing flash and staccato *ratatatatat* of machine gun fire.

The offensive had begun. Like the rest of his life, he was alone. He held his rifle cocked and ready, his bayonet aimed for the whites of enemy eyes. Crouching, he ran, twisting and pivoting to avoid barbed wire and the *chevaux de frise* spiked barricades set in a defensive line.

His line was decimated. Gone. He needed to find the rest of his battalion and let his commanding officer know.

Another mortar shrilled the air, and Eric threw himself to the ground, rolling for cover as best he could. The shell hit, exploding ten feet from where he ducked.

Searing pain ripped through his side and down his spine. He cried out, but his shouts were drowned by more mortar fire. Blood soaked through his uniform shirt straight to his jacket. Its warmth was comforting at first, like a blanket against the pervasive damp. Pressing his hand to the damage, he tried to focus as his sight dimmed, until he slumped forward into blackness.

Chapter Eleven

Twilight
Deserted battlefield
Northern France

Eric's eyes fluttered open. For a moment, he thought he might be dead, but the sharp jutting pain in his side told him otherwise.

The trenches and the adjacent no-man's-land were dim and eerily quiet. No men shouting. No men running. No screams and no gunfire. Just smoke, silence, and a pervasive chill.

Gritting his teeth, Eric got to his knees and nearly vomited from the pain. "Medic!" he croaked, wincing. "Medic! Stretcher bearer!" Stillness was all that replied.

With a raw breath, he slumped against the base of the spiked barricade again. Where was everyone? Command must have pushed back, but by now they should have sent a squad for rescue and recovery. A cold realization dawned, and the understanding froze the breath in his chest. Command thought him dead where he fell. Either that or they thought him too far gone to save.

Closing his eyes, he shifted against the barricade's rough cross-beamed base to assess his state. He counted each breath. In. Out. In. Out. Time ticked until he found a small reserve of strength.

He squinted into the twilight for any sign of life but quickly lost count of the lifeless bodies around him. Some were twisted on barbed wire, machine gunned where they

stood. Others were facedown in the mud. The worst were the ones staring with dead eyes toward the sky.

An angry cry broke from his throat, ragged and dry. Breathless, he allowed himself that one moment, and then steeled his heart. He could either lie in the mud and die or swallow the pain and find what remained of his battalion.

The sky was bleak. Even the weak glow from the setting sun offered no comfort. Just residual smoke and soul-numbing despair cast over the landscape.

With his forearm pressed across his belly, Eric forced himself to his knees again. Holding his breath, he fisted his shredded tunic, keeping pressure on his wound.

Teeth clenched, he got to his feet. The sound of his racked grunt strange in the eerie quiet. Panting, he squeezed his eyes closed and waited to catch his breath before taking his first step.

"*Arrgh,* Jesus Fucking *Christ!*" His knees nearly buckling in pain.

He held tight to the barricade and kept his feet before staggering forward, his steps short and faltering. He needed a medic to bind his wound.

Squinting, he caught a flash of white by one of the ladders leading up from the trenches. He shuffled faster, every breath a prayer. As he got closer, his steps slowed.

"Fuck me." He exhaled against his disappointment.

The glimpse of white was nothing but a Red Cross symbol on a medic's bag. A bag still attached to what remained of its owner.

Not having the strength to wallow or rail, Eric gathered himself and wrestled the bag from the dead medic's arm.

"Okay, my friend. Let's see what you've got for me."

Opening the flap, he rummaged through a bite stick, tourniquets, adhesive plaster, safety pins, individual dressing packets, aromatic spirits of ammonia, and, finally, rolls of antiseptic gauze.

"Bingo." He took two of the antiseptic rolls, tucking the rest with the other supplies. "Here goes nothing." Using his teeth, Eric tore open the wrappers, careful not to drop the gauze.

Shoving the bite stick between his teeth, he held his breath as he twined the sterile dressing around his waist, layering it tight over his wound. Blood seeped through the white bandage, but at least the pressure was steady and even.

"Not quite Florence Nightingale but good enough."

Wincing, he slung the medic's bag over his shoulder, and then reached for a rifle-bayonet stuck on one of the sandbags. He emptied the gun's chamber, pocketing the ammunition before disengaging the seventeen-inch blade and stowing it in his boot.

Leaning on the long gun for support, he shuffled past the dead medic, stopping only for another abandoned rifle to keep as a weapon.

Darkness was falling fast, so he glanced at the trees that followed the river. He was bound to find someone along the makeshift road, or, more likely, they would find him.

"Up and over, boys," he mumbled into the gloom and set off.

Eric made slow, light-headed progress, following the sound of the water in the distance. By now, the smoke had cleared enough for the moon to offer some light.

His mouth was parched and his tongue like sandpaper. After two years in the trenches, he'd seen and heard

enough to know it was from blood loss. If he was going to survive, he needed water.

The river was his only option, even if it meant veering into the trees. Putting one foot in front of the other, he made his way through the scrub. He followed a deer path, heeding the sound of the water growing louder.

"Am I the only living thing left on this godforsaken planet?" He looked up at the moon and exhaled. "Mighty quiet for an all-knowing and *supposedly* all-caring being, *eh*, God? If you're listening with even half an ear, how about a little help?"

Eric walked on, finally getting far enough into the woods there was barely a reminder the world was at war. Water flowed serenely, lapping at a low, mossy bank. The eerie quiet of the battlefield had given way to ordinary night sounds, and he took his first clear breath since setting off.

Placing his weapons by the water's edge, he sank to his knees to rummage in the medic's bag for something to scoop the cool liquid. Finding a hipflask in a side pocket, he uncapped the top and inhaled. The flagon was almost empty, but the oaky scent of whiskey filled his nose just the same.

"To numb the pain, soldier." He tipped the flask to his lips, taking a small swig. Tempted as he was to drain the rest, he needed water, not whiskey. What was left in the flask would be enough to kill whatever germs lurked in the river water. He held his side tight and leaned with the flask to the water's edge, only to jerk up startled.

"Excuse the intrusion, soldier," the stranger said. "I didn't mean to alarm you. Especially not when I see you're so badly wounded." The man stood to the side, behind Eric's shoulder.

Eric exhaled his relief. "I didn't hear you approach. In fact, I had begun to fear I was the last surviving man on Earth. Can you help me get to my battalion? They can't be far, but I won't make it walking."

The man's nostrils flared, and he cocked his head oddly. "I daresay, not. You're bleeding far too much."

Eric stared at the man, perplexed. The stranger hadn't offered aid or even a hand to help him to his feet.

"Won't you help me, sir? I'm sure my commanding officer will be grateful for your assistance." Eric held out his hand, hoping the stranger wasn't a German sympathizer.

The man slipped his fingers around Eric's wrist. "Your pulse is still strong," he said, with an impressed look. "You're a spirited one. Clutching to life despite all odds."

Eric's hackles rose at the unusual remark and the cool, delicate feel of the man's fingers. Was he a doctor? He'd noted his wounds. Wouldn't his manner be more concerned if he was a medic?

The man's face was odd as well. The longer Eric looked up at him, the more his features seemed to change. They appeared to grow coarser. Broader. Verging on ugly. And his eyes...they were almost reddish in the dim light. Maybe the deep wound had made him feverish, and he imagined it.

Pulling his hand from the stranger's grip, Eric reached for his rifle, holding the bayonet level with the man's gut. "If you're not going to help me, then I suggest you move along. There's been enough wasted blood this day."

"I couldn't agree more."

Before Eric could cock the trigger, his gun went flying. Rotating in the air until it came down to pierce the soft ground fifty yards from the riverbank.

The strange man grabbed Eric by the throat, lifting him feather-like off the bank. He held him aloft until the soldier's bloody gauze was level with his face.

Eric's pain vanished as his fight-or-flight instincts took over, and he struggled to free himself from the stranger's grip. The man inhaled, reaching the tip of his tongue toward the blood-soaked bandage.

"Blood is so intoxicating when mixed with fear and anger, but even more so when adrenaline is laced with courage and self-preservation. It makes the copper tang even sweeter on the tongue."

Eric's scream died in his throat as the man's grip tightened. "Such spirit. Even now, as I squeeze the life from your body, your eyes fight to live." The stranger tsked. "Such a waste."

The man dropped Eric to the ground with a muffled thud. He coughed, dragging in a ragged breath, even as fresh blood seeped from his wound. There was no mistaking the color of the man's eyes now. They flashed deep red. Blood red. As red as the blood soaking the gauze at his side.

"Who are you?" Eric choked out, somehow finding his feet again. "What are you?"

"No fear. Even now, eh?" A slow, appreciative smile spread on his pale face. "I can't decide if that makes you extraordinarily stupid or just extraordinary. Either way, you intrigue me."

Eric lifted his hands in defense, backing up one step. "What do you want of me?"

"I am death, boy." The man gave a curt bow. "But tonight, I think perhaps not. I overheard you in the trenches. How your blood boils at God himself for his lack

of interest and disdain. Even a little while ago, you mocked him for his continued silence."

He grinned at Eric's shocked face, flashing a hint of fang. "I thought it would be fun to answer, since he refuses."

"Answer what? If you're the reaper, then get on with it, man. If not, be gone with you!"

The stranger laughed; his red eyes deadly but amused. "You don't fear the reaper, but you should fear me."

"Who are you?" Eric asked, stumbling back, his feet slipping on the riverbank.

The man's amused grin widened. With a hiss, fangs descended from his gums, razor sharp and as long as the man's little finger.

Eric's mouth dropped in stunned silence, and he tripped, falling on his ass in the water.

"God is the ultimate absentee landlord, boy. He doesn't care as long as the rent is paid." The stranger blurred with a splash, yanking Eric's head to one side.

He struggled, but the man's grip was like iron. The stranger bent his lips to the soldier's throat but jerked with a hiss the moment his chin brushed the silver chain around Eric's neck.

Eric lurched away. His wound painless with adrenaline as he ran. He'd dodged shells and bullets for two years, but this was truly a race for his life.

He tore through the woods, ignoring the sting from twigs and leaves whipping his face. One word banged on his brain.

Vampire.

But how? They were just fright night stories for Halloween. Campfire tales like the "Headless Horseman" and "Bloody Mary."

As surreal the possibility, Eric didn't dare look behind. Every story he'd ever heard as a child ran through his mind. Holy water, crucifixes, wooden stakes, silver.

His eyes jerked for the road.

Sanctified ground.

Vampires and all manner of devils couldn't set foot on holy soil. A small stone church stood not far from where they'd dug the trenches. German mortars had destroyed most of the structure, but it sat on sanctified earth until the Vatican said otherwise.

Running, Eric held his side until he spotted the scorched stones. Letting go, he sprinted the last few meters and crossed the threshold, stumbling to his knees in front of the ruined altar.

"Fancy meeting you here, lone wolf," the man said, stepping out from the shadows. "The better to eat you with, I think."

A cruel smile peeled over his fangs. Lifting his hand, the vampire pointed to the silver chain and the St. Christopher medal at Eric's throat.

"You might want to take that off and stow it someplace safe." He stalked closer. "Trust me. When you wake, it will burn your flesh like the fires of Hell."

"Wake? If this is a nightmare, then I will myself to wake up now!"

The vampire closed the distance between them. "This is no dream, my boy. This is where your true life begins." He cocked his head. "Everyone's experience is different, so, my intriguing friend, we will see how it is for you."

"How what is? Stay away from me!"

Eric picked up a large wooden cross and swung it in front of him.

"This is holy ground! Begone, devil!"

The vampire actually laughed. "So brave yet so very foolish. Silver is one thing, but the rest is fodder for penny dreadful novellas."

He lunged, yanking the large wooden cross from the soldier's hand. "Yet I am *very* real." He flung the cross toward the altar. It landed upside down with a crash as he fisted Eric's hair.

Lip curled, he wrenched Eric's neck and ripped the chain from his neck. He threw it across the ruined church, ignoring the burn. "And you, my brave soldier, are mine."

The vampire plunged his fangs deep into Eric's throat. He took long, sloppy pulls, letting blood drip from his chin.

Eric struggled, even as the stranger pulled his fangs from his vein, smacking his lips. "Your blood is sweet, even if meager from all you spilled. It sets my own aflame."

Sliding his hand from Eric's throat, his fingers glided past his bandages. He shredded them with a single finger before toying over the waistband to his uniform pants.

"Don't fight it, boy. Your swelling manhood tells me your body understands, even if your mind doesn't. Soon you'll see, sex and blood are one and the same for us, and we take what we want from all. A vampire's pull is fatal but so irresistible." The vampire laughed, reaching for the soldier's crotch.

Eric's mind rebelled, fighting every second of the vampire's assault. He shoved him away with his last bit of strength. "No! Get away from me!"

"Even now your body betrays you. Why are you fighting the inevitable?"

"You'll have to kill me first, you bastard!"

The predator's eyes flashed, both surprised and impressed at the show of muscle, and his lip curled. "As you wish."

Cringing at the vampire's grotesque face, he knew then he hadn't imagined the facial changes. It was true.

All of it.

The vampire reached for the deep gash at Eric's side, and plunged his hand into the tender, ripped flesh.

"Your blood is mine. Your body is mine." He twisted Eric's wound like so much raw meat.

Eric screamed, his eyes rolling back in his head. Whatever blood remained dripped to the scorched slate, and he slumped to the floor.

"Not so fast, boy. The reaper can't have you and neither can God. Not yet."

The vampire slashed a vein in his wrist and shoved the welling black blood to Eric's lips. "Let's see if you truly are as extraordinary as you seem."

Eric's eyes flew open at the pungent taste. He tore from the vampire's hold, twisting his head away, but the vampire tightened the grip on his hair to punishing.

"Don't fight me! I will know you, and I will have you. You are mine until I release you."

The vampire's blood filled his mouth, and he gagged, finally swallowing the viscous fluid. It churned in Eric's stomach and his veins. Pain sluiced through his limbs, scorching his organs and forcing the breath from his lungs. It raced wildfire-like, leaving his flesh tingling and icy hot, burning every molecule, muscle, and nerve in its path.

The will to live warred with nausea and scorching pain, but even that small amount gave him the strength to fight. He would not be owned.

Self-preservation kicked in the way it had his entire life. *If you can't lick 'em at their own game, cheat.* Eric clutched the vampire's wrist, drawing deep gulps. With a revulsed cry, he ripped his mouth away and flung the vampire across the room.

Chest heaving, he knelt in front of the broken altar. What had he done? He'd blasphemed in a holy place, baptizing himself in black blood from the devil himself.

Gone was the pain from the mortar shell. Gone, the light-headed weakness and his need for clean, clear water. Instead, his throat burned as though nothing on earth could quench his thirst.

His eyes darted to his chain plainly hidden in the rubble, yet somehow it gleamed like a beacon. He blinked, confused. His nose wrinkled from the acrid smell clinging to the burnt stones, yet his nostrils flared from the residual scent of his own human blood.

Dumbfounded, the vampire laughed. Shaking off the broken bits of char, he stared at Eric with a stunned grin.

"I said you were either extraordinarily stupid or simply extraordinary, and now I see my gamble paid off handsomely." His face was both perplexed and amused. "How fast your body took to the black blood. Clearly an undead nature suits you very well."

Eric watched him from a natural crouch as his eyes darted from place to place and thing to thing, his mind and senses bombarded like the worst kind of mortar shells.

"What have you done to me? You fed me ichor from Hell, now you've made me Tantalus."

The vampire shook his head with another laugh. "No, boy. Though I'm impressed a soldier knows Greek mythology. Tantalus was made to stand in a pool and never drink. You, my brave progeny, will drink your fill.

The undead walk this earth as gods. Our black blood isn't ichor from Olympus, but it has made you immortal, and human blood is your ambrosia. Your nectar."

Eric glanced at his blood-soaked bandages still sitting in a puddle of his human blood. His mouth watered, and he knew the vampire spoke truth. He was a monster. A soulless creature banned from the light of God.

Anger burned hotter than the vampire's blood in his veins, and an anguished cry ripped from his throat.

"Careful, boy. Your senses will bewilder and overwhelm until you can sort the scents and sensations."

"What is your name, vampire?"

He smirked. "That tone is a bit of the pot calling the kettle black. You are as much a predator as me, my boy."

"I'm not your boy."

Pushing through the broken wood, the vampire's lips curled. "Oh, but you are. I own you now. Body and soul."

Eric remembered the bayonet in his boot. With a snarl, he reached for the steel blade, sending it torpedo-like toward the vampire's chest. The force flung him backward into the scorched stone, the sharp steel pinning him to the wall. Eric lunged, reaching the vampire before he could break free.

"You want strong, eh? Be careful what you wish for because now you've got it in spades."

His hands wrapped around the vampire's head, his thumbs pressing at his eyes. "No one owns me. No. One."

With a crack and a pop, Eric crushed the vampire's skull, his thumbs gouging his eyes from their sockets. He yanked his limp form from the wall and flung him toward the front of the church. The vampire landed on the upturned cross, the burnt wood staking him through the heart.

Eric watched the vampire's limp form flake to white ash, his remnants mixing with the charred ash from the church fire. Poetic justice.

"Huh. Silver and wooden stakes. Good to know. I guess God was listening after all."

He walked out of the church and into the night. If silver and stakes were true, what about the coming dawn? He glanced at the sky and instinctively he knew.

He had to find shelter.

And blood.

Chapter Twelve

Avalon was crowded as usual. Eric walked through the main level, spotting Carlos nursing his rum at the bar.

"You know, *mijo*. This is where I first saw Trina." He turned as Eric approached. "She stood outside that alcove and saw right through my wards. She intrigued me then, and she continues to every day."

"I know, Carlos. I've been happy for you since you first brought her to me, to all of us." He wanted to ask about the meeting, but he didn't want to tip the elder to his anxiety. He would raise too many questions. That's if Carlos didn't already sense it.

"Come, then. Have a drink. Or have you forgotten the date?"

Eric's brows pulled together. "Date? Was I supposed to do something, and this is your buildup for ripping out my fangs for dropping the ball?"

"It's one hundred years since you joined our family. One hundred and one since you first set foot in New York."

Carlos's face was both nostalgic and serene. He was a man who walked through fire and darkness to come out the other side happy and fulfilled. Well, as much as a vampire could be in this world.

Trina was a youngblood yet, so it would be centuries before she and Carlos could walk in the sun together. That would make things complete. At least in Eric's eyes. To walk in the sun with love and happiness would be more than he could hope for.

He watched the head of their house order a shot of Glen Scotia, urging him to sit. What would Carlos say if he told him how it felt to merge auras with a witch? How the high lingered like being sun-kissed. Would he understand then why Blair had captured his mind so?

"Drink with me, *mijo*. Today is a good day. There have been no new cases of HepZ for over a month. I think we have finally turned a corner, and our shadow houses can return to full capacity. We begin canvasing for donors this week." He nodded. "Rémy and I are changing the rules. No one will have to suffer under the thumb of one master.

"The council was too content to let Sebastién have his head, and Rémy and I were guilty of that complacency. No more. I know it's unheard of, but we are implementing a new system of checks and balances, and that includes monthly meetings with the Alpha of the Brethren, Caitlan Ahern, the Supreme of the Circle of the Raven, and Gareth Fairfax, Fae-halfling and representative of the Seelie Court. We haven't been able to convince the Unseelie to join us yet, but we're working on it."

Eric took his whiskey neat and shot it back. Maybe this was his chance. "Sean Leighton and the Weres, I get, but why are you and Rémy including witches and the Fae?"

"Because, my youngblood friend, after what happened in the spring, when three vampires were compelled to murder an innocent Were in order to kidnap a Raven/Fae halfling, we need to do whatever it takes to avoid that from happening again. Open communication is the answer. It will help prevent rogues from going off on their own without fear of consequence."

Eric didn't answer. He simply nodded and then tapped the bar for another shot.

"Speaking of rogues…" Carlos hesitated, ordering another drink for himself as well.

This was it. Eric could already guess Carlos wanted an update. He had to play it cool or he'd blow it before ever getting the chance to have that in-depth talk with Blair. He knew in his gut she'd lead him to the vindicating reasons he needed to save her skin.

"I'm sorry, *mijo*, but I wanted to catch the bartender's attention before he walked away. Avalon is my territory, but that and a buck fifty will get you on the bus, as Trina likes to say." He chuckled. "I still haven't gotten used to her New York-isms, especially since bus fare is much more than that now."

"I think maybe you need to go pay your lady a visit. You have Trina on the brain tonight. At this time of night, you could make Verplanck from here in an hour and a half. I bet she'd be thrilled, too."

Carlos flashed a lopsided grin that said he was stupid in love with his lady. "She's working on controlling her thirst, so it's best I'm not there to distract her. Still, I plan to go up this weekend, but first we have to deal with your rogue witch. It's what I was starting to say before I caught the bartender's eye."

"I haven't found anything much, yet."

Carlos eyed him. "Either this rogue is worrying you to the point your scent has changed, or you know more than you let on. Which is it, *mijo*? I told you I wouldn't mention the situation to Rémy, and I haven't. However, if you keep things from me, I won't have a choice, and it will be you who suffers."

"Goddamn that nose of yours. You're getting as bad as the wolves." Eric exhaled, raking a hand through his hair. "Yes, I have information, but I'm not comfortable telling

you about it because it's incomplete. I found her a couple of nights ago, or more to the point, she found me. I gate crashed the Harvest Hunt in Central Park to fuel up for the search, but she beat me to it. Blair is a pretty formidable practitioner."

Carlos raised an eyebrow, waiting for the bartender to refill both their drinks. He nodded his thanks, sliding a twenty his way before turning to Eric.

"Central Park? Rémy had reports of two more dead youngbloods. Are you telling me you were there when she killed them, and you didn't stop her?"

"I delivered final death. They died by my hand, not hers. In fact, she hasn't hunted since that night in the alley. I know there's more to her story than what's on the surface. Like Lily."

Carlos paused, lifting his tumbler of rum. "Don't go there, Eric. That argument will only hold so much water."

"I know, and that's why I need more time. I'm seeing her again this weekend. She's coming to the house." He hesitated. "Again."

"Again? It was her scent all over the living room and upstairs?" Carlos's frowned. "Are you telling me you and that witch—"

"Blair. Her name is Blair, Carlos. Yes, I have knowledge of the witch. In the biblical sense, if that's what you're asking. And to answer your next question, no…I did not taste her blood."

Carlos opened his mouth then shut it again. "How? If you were intimate with her…how? It's fairly impossible, *mijo*. I should know, I tried with Trina at first, and her blood wasn't possibly lethal. Surely she had to notice your features changing."

"She did. I tried to hide my face in her hair, but Blair is too clever for that. She saw and, believe it or not, she was pretty cool about it," Eric replied.

"I know how that goes." Carlos chuckled, sipping his rum. "Been there, done that." He looked at Eric over the rim of his glass. "Did you glamour her, or, vice versa, did she spell you?"

Eric laughed out loud. "Not on your undead life. Blair is too quick on the draw for that. She's got her spells down where she can cast with one word. *Zap.* Done. *Zing,* you're flat on your back."

"Zap and zing? Those are her magical words? And I thought abracadabra was bad enough." Carlos smirked.

"Don't be daft. I was illustrating a point. Blair has proper Latin phrases—" Eric thought for a moment. "There was one that stunned and another that knocked them on their asses. *Debilito,* I think."

Carlos put his drink down and eyed Eric. "Knocked *who* on their asses, Eric?"

Eric cringed for a moment. "The youngbloods."

"So you lied to me, then."

"No. I took them out. It was me. Blair helped...restrain them." His eyes met Carlos's unconvinced stare. "We were walking together after she found me in the park. I was with Natasha—"

"The cougar?" Carlos chuckled, raising an eyebrow. "And how'd the witch handle seeing you *with* Nat, if I'm catching your meaning correctly."

"It was just blood, and, yes, it took some explaining because Blair's view of our kind is so skewed. Still, the longer we talked and walked together, the more she came around. She didn't tell me her story, but that's coming. She trusts me, or at least she's starting to."

"Good. That was the plan all along."

Eric shook his head. "No, Carlos. I know you originally said you wanted me to stalk and woo the witch, but I've gotten to know Blair since."

At Carlos's raised eyebrow and knowing grin, Eric shoved at his shoulder. "That part notwithstanding. I've gotten to know her as a person. There's way more beneath the surface. I feel it in my bones, Carlos. You have to let me get to the bottom of this. I know it goes against your oath as a member of the council, but I'm asking you as your son. Give me the time to see this through with her. She deserves it."

Carlos's eyebrow hiked even higher. "She deserves it." He nodded. "Sounds to me like you want her to be innocent for your own personal reasons."

From everyone else, Eric could poker face with the best but not with Carlos. He couldn't muffle his emotions, not when it had been a struggle to come to terms with them.

"I see." Carlos nodded. "You've fallen for the witch, and now you want her exonerated."

Eric shook his head. "Yes and no. I've fallen for the witch, but if she's guilty, then she has to pay. It'll kill my heart for the next century, but it is what it is. We don't steer our own fate when it comes to things like this, and I've weathered other heavy disappointments in both my lives."

Eric watched Carlos's face, gauging his reaction. When the elder vampire finally looked up from swirling his drink, he nodded again.

"I can see more than what you want me to see, Eric. I always have. It's why I wanted you to be with us in New York. If you think there's more to this story than a vigilante witch gone wild, then I will grant you the time to

suss out the facts. Then and only then will I approach Rémy."

"What about Julian?"

Carlos shrugged. "He's in Ireland. As far as I'm concerned, you are still investigating. He's got his own hellcat to tame."

"Funny you should use that term."

Carlos rolled his eyes. "Aren't they all, *mijo*. It's why they have our hearts and minds."

"Souls, too."

Carlos drained the rest of his rum. "That's still up for debate."

Eric lifted his own glass to shoot back the smooth whiskey. "I've got a story I've never told you that may put that argument to rest."

"Oh really."

He nodded, turning the glass upside down on the bar. "When this is over, I'll either need a drinking partner to celebrate or one to help me bury my dead heart. Either way, I'll tell you then."

Chapter Thirteen

Lizzie chuckled listening to Blair's offkey singing through the bathroom door. It was so bad, it was funny. Still, at least she was singing. The last few months she'd been so preoccupied, it was bound to take its toll. When she walked in tonight, she would have sworn her friend had hit manic bottom.

She made the daybed and folded the few clothes Blair had on top of the chair. The sketchbook sat on the desk, almost daring her to have a good look for herself without the nosy professor peering over her shoulder.

Lizzie took the book and sat on the floor, propped against the bed. Page after page, it was obvious Blair's drawings were exceptional. She captured every detail of the different supernaturals. Vampires, Weres, a few species of Faerie, and one winged being she didn't quite recognize.

"What happened? Why are you sitting on the floor?" Blair asked from the cloud of steam in the bathroom doorway.

"You just missed the hazmat team. They took samples for the CDC, but they're pretty sure you're an incubus for the plague."

Lizzie's eyes flew wide, and she flipped a few pages in the sketchbook. "Incubus!" She tapped the sketch. "I knew it. I just couldn't remember the name."

"I wish Dr. Wells hadn't gone all nosy parker on me. I was keeping those drawings private for a reason. Do me a favor and put the book in my backpack before everyone in the free world knows my business."

Lizzie nodded absently. "Sure, sure. You know Care Blair, I meant what I said. These are really, really good."

"I'm glad you like them. Now please put them away. I really didn't want anyone to see them."

Ignoring her, Lizzie flipped a couple more pages. "Why the cast of characters though? Does this have something to do with why you're here?"

"Ugh, you're doing that thing when you pretend to listen, but you don't. Is that a Southern thing, or are you still mad because I didn't tell you I was going walkabout for a few days?" Blair exhaled, toweling her hair.

"I'm not mad, and I *am* listening. It's you who's not answering. Why the supernatural lineup? You've got their details listed like some kind of criminal rap sheet."

Blair jerked her head up from towel-drying her hair. "I do not."

"Considering what your face says right now, I think I hit a nerve. Spill it, sister," Lizzie called after her as Blair went back into the bathroom.

She hung up her towel and threw on a pair of sleep shorts and a T-shirt. "I can't tell you, Lizzie," she finally replied.

"Can't or won't?"

She waited for Blair to answer, but when she didn't, Liz got up and walked to the bathroom door.

"Are you failing a class, *cher*? Is that what this is?" She gestured with the sketchbook. "Extra credit or something? It's okay if it is. Everyone struggles from time to time."

After combing her hair, Blair tied the long dark mass into a topknot and then walked into the side office.

"Lizzie, forget the sketches. I appreciate you like them, but they're not for extra credit or a research project. At least not one for school. This is personal."

"Personal. How? Are you in some kind of trouble?"

Blair walked past Lizzie in the bathroom doorway and bent for her backpack. From the top zip compartment, she took out her mother's diaries and placed them on the desk with the one she'd snatched from Lynetta. "It's personal because of these."

"And?"

Blair opened the cover to the flyleaf. "Read the inside name and date."

Liz did and then shrugged. "Again, and?"

"*Cabot*, Lizzie. Geneviève Cabot. 1942. According to the archivist at Raven House, Geneviève is my mother, and the date listed is the year she wrote that particular diary. Imagine my shock when the archivist told me she *knew* my mother. She also said she knew I was her daughter because I have this."

Blair lifted her shirt, not caring if the sight of bare breasts made Lizzie cringe. "My mother had the same exact birthmark." She traced a finger over the raised crescent-shape.

"How did the archivist at Raven House know you had a birthmark on your left breast?" Lizzie cocked her head, staring at the unusual red mark.

Blair yanked her T-shirt down. "I was wearing a camisole. How else did you think?"

"With you, I don't know anymore." Lizzie exhaled a baffled breath. "Why are you sketching supernaturals and ranking them by abilities and lifespan? What has this got to do with your mother and your shared birthmarks? Please tell me you're not thinking of adding to your nightly hit list?"

Blair picked up one of her sneakers and threw it at her friend. "I told you I went out looking for Eric that night."

She stalked past the bed to grab the sketchbook, lifting it with a frown. "And the reason I'm sketching supernaturals is because one of this immortal lot is my biological father!"

The stunned look on Lizzie's face said it all. "How can you possibly know that for certain? You don't have an actual birth certificate. An original, I mean. You said you only have the one the adoption agency issued after you were placed, and it's missing the information on your birth parents."

"That's true. I only have that document to go by, but according to Grania, my abilities aren't limited to that of the witches' sisterhood."

Lizzie stood speechless for a moment. "Who's Grania?"

"Grania is the Raven House archivist. She's the one who knew my mother." Blair lifted a hand. "Knew about my birthmark."

"So, is she saying you can shapeshift? Glamour people? Read minds? Because those are just the highlight reel from the rap sheet you've accumulated on your suspected bio-dads."

"You are so watching too much CSI."

"Blair, I'm serious. Why would you give a complete stranger so much credence?" Her eyes narrowed for a moment. "Or maybe your kissing vampire did more than just kiss you, and you're looking to see how the other half lives for real."

"Why are you suddenly being a dick? Can't you see what I'm telling you? I'm falling apart here, Lizzie, and all you care about is my artistic ability and the condition of my hair!"

"Blair—"

She shook her head. "I'm sharing the most important thing I've found out about myself since I took that goddamned DNA test and found out I'm a witch. According to Grania, I'm some sort of halfling with a very, very long life. I can't prove it yet, but why else would I scour the Raven House library and the occult section here? The only other places that could with this kind of conundrum are Hogwarts or the Talamasca, and they're both fictional!"

Blair took a calming breath. "Grania is the Raven's archivist, and she's ninety years old if she's a day. She told me my mother wrote those diaries during WWII, and that I was born during that same time frame."

Lizzie burst out laughing. "You're either insane, or this is the weirdest prank anyone's ever pulled, *cher*."

"Lizzie! Don't you think I know how nuts I sound? More so than usual and that's scaring the hell out of me, but I have to know." She sank onto the edge of the bed.

"I'm not even sure I believe it. All I have to go on are those diaries and the word of an old witchy librarian, but I gotta tell you, babe, I feel it in my gut. My dreams have always been so vivid. At first I thought Grania was feeding me her own private delusion because I had no memory of anything before my adopted family—but when I piece together remembered fragments from my dreams, it makes sense."

She whistled low. "So you're telling me you're really seventy-something years old? Wow, *cher*. Who does your facials?"

"I'm serious, and if you can't listen to me as a friend, then maybe that's all she wrote for us. I deserve the benefit of the doubt, Liz. If that's too much for you, then don't let the door hit you in the ass when you leave."

Lizzie threw a hand up. "What else am I supposed to think when you're spouting craziness? We are witches, Blair. I had a hard enough time when that truth tidbit hit me upside the head. You try finding out you're a witch in the heart of the Bible Belt."

She exhaled, crossing her arms. "It took a while, but I got used to being Sabrina the Teenage Witch. I found my way to the big bad city and claimed my place at Crow Haven House. Now you're saying we can get knocked up by immortal entities? No, ma'am. Not when two of those entities are either undead or demonic!"

Blair watched the storm of emotions on her friend's face. If the shoe was on the other foot, she would have done worse than shut Liz down with a laugh.

"I don't like the idea of this being my heritage any more than you, so I get it. It's why I need to find out the truth."

Lizzie relaxed her death grip over her chest. "I'm glad you can see how this all comes across, but you're also right. Even if I think you're batshit crazy, *cher*, I should give you the benefit of the doubt. You're my best friend."

Blair gave her a huge hug before sitting on the bed once more. "I knew you wouldn't hang me out to dry completely. Even if you are a card-carrying Southern belle busybody."

Lizzie blew a razzberry before picking up the sketchbook and nudging Blair to make room on the daybed. Flipping through the drawings one by one, she grinned. "So, who's the most likely candidate for daddy dearest so far?"

With a frayed chuckle, she took the sketchbook onto her lap. "Well, I've narrowed the field to four possibilities. One. I'm half Were. But if that was the case, other shifters

would have scented me by now. So would have Eric. But all he sensed was witch.

"Two. I'm half Sidhe or some other type of Fae. It made the most sense, but if that was the case, I would be a Raven and not a Crow. I mean, our sisterhoods are kissing cousins but still. Plus, I don't look the part. I'm curvy rather than ethereally delicate. Unless I'm not half Sidhe but some other kind of lesser Fae, like a brownie."

Blair shook her head, reading over her notes. "Nah, now that I look at the details again, a lesser Fae doesn't fit. Small, wizened, and shaggy wasn't the description Geneviève gave of the man who swept her off her feet."

Lizzie looked at her friend. "I'm going to have to read those diaries once you're done, you know."

"I know, babe. And it's fine. Just let me get through them first." She turned the page. "Candidate number three: I'm half vampire." Blair's fingers traced the sketch that just happened to look exactly like Eric.

"This possibility scared me the most, to be honest. If a vampire seduced my mother, then it makes sense I'd be crazy hot for one as well. A blood slut."

"Don't say that. Witches are very sex positive." She chuckled. "Present company excepted."

"You're fine, babe. You just need to find your inner goddess and demand to be worshiped by someone who knows what they're doing. Believe me, among the human set, they're far and few between. You'd do better with a supernatural to pop your goddess cherry." Blair frowned mid-thought. "Can you be a blood slut if you share the same blood? I mean, if I'm half vampire, then why is my blood poisonous to some vampires?"

Shaking her head again, she dismissed the possibility. More because the idea made her cringe than any other

reason. Not because Eric was undead but because of all the youngbloods who'd met her blade over the past year.

"Okay, and finally, *numero quattro*: The last and most disturbing of all the possibilities I've found so far is dark magic. A dark witch or a demon syphoning life force from other supernaturals for their own pleasure and purpose. Otherwise known as an incubus. I gotta tell you, Liz, this one left me cold."

A hollow feeling churned in Blair's gut just talking about the option. Mostly because it was the cruelest and most wicked, but it was as much a possibility as the others.

"I hate to say it, but number four runs neck and neck with the idea of a Fae or a Sidhe because Incubi and Fae are the only two true immortals. Very little can kill them, and their power to manipulate surpasses all other supernaturals."

"Jeez Louise."

Blair nodded. "You said a mouthful, babe. So, that's that. It's a tossup between one of the Fae or an incubus. I was really hoping bio-dad was a fabulous ethereal Sidhe, but after rereading this and hearing Lynetta earlier, I'm not sure anymore."

"*Cher*, it's one thing to be a halfling Fae but quite another to be demon spawn."

Blair made a face. "Ugh, Lizzie. Did you have to put it that way?"

"Demon spawn? It is what it is, right?"

"Not exactly. Technically, I would be a Cambion. A halfling demon."

Lizzie gave Blair's hand a squeeze. "Look on the bright side, *cher*. Either way, you'll be wrinkle-free and gorgeous for all eternity and outlive us all."

Blair took the playful prod, but her smile soon faded, and she inhaled another uncertain breath. "What am I going to do, Liz? I could be a half-demon Cambion with a price on my head for murdering youngblood vampires over the past year."

"Maybe your Eric can do something. I mean, the Vampire Council of New York might not want to mess with demon spawn."

"You know, I really think you enjoy saying that a little too much."

Liz laughed. "Demon spawn. Sounds like a villain from Marvel Comics." She glanced at their linked fingers and then at Blair again. "I'm sorry I was so hardheaded earlier. Chalk it up to PTSSD. Post-Traumatic-Sunday-School Disorder."

"Oh, I think the word is unhinged-bitchy."

"True but not funny."

Blair rested her head on her friend's shoulder. "It might be cool to have a demon spawn for a best friend, don'tcha think?"

Liz snorted. "One thing's for sure. Suzy will never chuck another slipper at your head."

"Now *that's* funny. Maybe I'll grow horns and really sharp teeth like one of those demons from *Charmed*."

Lizzie shivered. "Ugh. No. Not even for Suzy." She paused, thinking. "You know, if your father was an incubus, then that makes you a halfling succubus, since you're female."

"Not helping, Liz."

"No, hear me out. If you've got the whole succubus seductress thing going for you, then why not use it on Eric?"

Lizzie picked up the sketchbook one more time and flipped to the incubus page. "See, I knew I saw it earlier. Under abilities it says, enslavement kiss, a subliminal sexual manipulation and/or magnetism. You've already kissed the boy, so put a little persuasive *oomph* into it next time, and voilà!"

"Lizzie—"

With an excited grin, she tapped the book. "Why not, Blair? It makes sense. You attract men like moths to a flame, while the rest of us semi-mortals sit like wallflower lumps. Either way, if you're a halfling Fae or demon-spawn succubus, you've got the sex thing on your side. Add witch blood to the mix, and it's a trifecta of control. If your blood doesn't kill Eric, the more he takes, the more control he surrenders." Lizzie winked. "You're not the only witch who does her research."

"Listen to you, Miss Demure Witch Louisiana, talking about weaponizing sex."

"Self-defense, Blair. That changes everything. You think the Vampire Council won't be hollering for your heart in a box once they find out about your hunting expeditions? In their eyes, you're a vigilante, *cher*. They won't be forgiving. No matter how much your beau pleads."

Blair's shoulders dropped. "Maybe Eric won't tell them it's me. Maybe he'll be the reasonable, kind man he seems to be, and let the youngbloods' crimes justify the means."

"When pigs fly, *cher*."

"Eric is not like the others of his kind. I wouldn't feel this way about him if what he says isn't true."

"Of course you would. You're a witch who was traumatized by the undead in her youth, and something unfamiliar is now wreaking havoc on your sexuality."

Blair frowned. "You're saying I can't think straight because I'm a horny, hormonal beast?"

"Basically." Lizzie shrugged.

Shaking her head, Blair grinned at her friend. "I don't need an enslavement kiss or any succubi powers. I do fine on my own with Eric." She waggled her eyebrows. "We got sidetracked, so I left out a few little details."

She filled Lizzie in on Central Park, the fight, and then what happened after Grania dropped the happy birthday bomb that led her to Eric's place...and afterward.

"Holy moly, Blair! You sure he didn't nibble on you at some point, somewhere? That sounds like an awful lot of mouth-to-mouth and mouth-to-other-bits action!"

"I'm sure, but don't ask me where he and I go from here. We're supposed to get together Saturday so I can tell him about my past."

Lizzie raised an eyebrow. "You going to tell him you're possible demon spawn?"

"Cambion...and no. Not until I know for sure."

"Probably safer that way. You can't be sure he hasn't reported you to his council already. He didn't know your name at the time, but he knew you were a witch. I mean, how hard do you think it would be for them to track you if he spilled the beans? Even if he regrets it now that he's gotten to know you."

Eric's words returned in a rush. *If I wanted to find you, I could. Unlike you, all I need is your scent.* Blair looked at her friend's adamant face. "I don't know if he said anything, but I'll find out."

"How?"

Blair shrugged. "I'll ask him. He'll tell me the truth. I hope."

"Self-defense, *cher*. Remember those words, and anything goes."

Chapter Fourteen

*B*lair jerked her head off her forearms and drew a startled breath. Blinking, she unpeeled her tongue from the roof of her mouth and squinted into the dim light. Fumbling for her phone, she unlocked the screen for the time. Five p.m.

Eastern standard time had sunset in less than an hour, yet it was already gloomy out. Somehow, the afternoon had come and gone, and somewhere between Lizzie leaving and her latest sketches, she'd fallen asleep on top of her laptop. Did AppleCare cover drool damage?

Probably not.

Liz had ended up staying over. They ordered takeout and watched back-to-back movies: *Van Helsing*, and then, *The Incubus*. Very apropos or so Lizzie teased. Still, Blair hadn't had a girls' night in forever, and it was nice to cuddle under blankets and eat popcorn while watching mindless movies.

Rolling her shoulders, Blair stretched. She wasn't sore from sleeping hunched over, though she was sure she had keyboard dents in her cheek. She was edgy.

Strange dreams had plagued her mind since the bizarre shot-glass-blood-challenge nightmare the other night. Today's nap took odd to a different level. Not cruel or scary. Just peculiar.

She tried to piece the images together. A cottage along the shore. Wide green lawns set with badminton nets and croquet rings.

Men in tailored suits stood talking, as a group of women sat sipping drinks at a white wrought iron table.

They wore wide-strap summer dresses with kitten heels, stylish hats, and matching gloves. Not like a wedding party though. It was casual, as if dressing that way was expected and effortless.

Blair sighed, running a hand through her dark hair. The dream had to be a byproduct. Subliminal leftovers from everything Eric told her about his life, and what she'd recently read in her mother's diaries.

Problem was, the dream didn't feel like residual anything. The images were spotty and fragmented, like childhood memories. Only here, she was a spectator, yet the feeling of déjà vu was so strong it made her sweat.

From a distance, she watched two women and one man walk along the grassy shoreline below the summer cottage. They were together. As in *together*, together.

Intimate. A threesome.

Blair chewed her lip. Their underlying intimacy didn't bother her. To each their own. Still, there was one face that haunted. A woman's face. When she turned, it stunned so utterly it literally jerked Blair from her sleep.

It was her face. Blair watching herself in her own dream but *not as* herself.

Weird.

She shook off the creepiness, chalking it up to what she originally thought. Occam's razor. All things being equal, the simplest explanation is usually correct.

Usually.

She was either sleep-deprived, or she'd spent way too much time in the stacks. This whole *who's your baby daddy* thing was getting out of control. She wanted to know, but maybe in the long run it didn't matter. She was the captain of her own destiny. Not some random supernatural who'd

happened to donate his twenty-three chromosomes to her 23 and Me.

Getting up from the study table, she gathered her things and headed to Dr. Wells' side office for a shower and a change of clothes. It was Saturday evening, and she was due at Eric's place in an hour.

***

"I've been waiting for this all week," Eric said, slanting his lips over hers in the doorway. He breathed in Blair's heady scent, and his body reacted immediately. "Come in. We've got the house to ourselves, again."

She shrugged out of her jacket and handed it to him. "I thought you said you had a special place you wanted to go. Someplace where we could talk with no distractions." Blair raised an eyebrow and then glanced at the stairs. "Unless you had a change of plan."

"Oh boy," Eric chuckled. "I have to admit, the thought of giving my mattress another workout crossed my mind a few thousand times. I even changed the sheets and cleaned my bathroom, just in case, but I promise, no distractions." He crossed his heart and held up three fingers. "Scout's honor."

She stifled a laugh. "You cleaned the bathroom. I mean, yourself? You didn't have the housekeeper do it?"

"I know the idea of me with a scrub brush and bucket of bleachy water is hysterical, but I grew up in an orphanage, Blair. I've had to do much worse."

"I'm sorry, Eric. I forgot. Actually, that's something we have in common."

He stopped halfway from hanging up her jacket and looked at her. "Seriously?"

She nodded. "So where are we holding this pow-wow. I assume I'm not spilling my deepest darks here in the foyer."

"Of course not," he teased. "I actually have a place for us to go, but I made dinner for you. I hope you don't mind or think it presumptuous. You can eat here, or we can take it with us. It's very portable. I picked the dishes especially for that reason."

"Dishes? You make it sound so fancy. I'd be happy with soup and a sandwich."

Eric grinned, handing her back her coat. "I was hoping you'd say something like that. It's already packed and ready to go."

"*The Undead Kitchen*. Sounds like a late-night Food TV show."

Pecking her cheek, he then nodded toward the front door. "I'll grab the food and bring the car around. I'll meet you outside."

"Car?"

"It's about an hour or so ride from here."

"Eric, we're just going to talk. We can do that right here."

He shook his head. "This place is pretty special to me. It reminds me of home, and I wanted to share it with you." He brushed his knuckles over her cheek. "I promise, we will talk." Reaching for the door, he held it open. "I'll just be a moment."

The door closed behind her, and she stood in the brick entry feeling like she just got off a spinning ride. Their talk somehow morphed into a road trip with dinner thrown in just because.

Motorized gates opened at the side of the townhouse, and Blair hurried down the brick steps to the sidewalk.

Headlights glowed in the semi-dark, and a sleek black Lamborghini Sesto Elemento pulled onto the street. She stood for a moment with her mouth open before darting around to the passenger door.

"Holy Batmobile, Eric! You sure this doesn't belong to NASA or something? Jet Propulsion Labs?"

He laughed. "Shut the door. We've got a way to go yet. I hope you're up for an all-nighter."

"Why? You said it's only an hour or so from here."

He revved the engine and took off with a screech. "I lied."

Her spine hit the back of the low-slung seat, and she grinned as he peeled down the street toward 1st Avenue and the FDR Drive North entrance.

"Just for shits and giggles, where are we going?"

"Mystic Seaport."

She shifted in her seat to look at him as he shifted gears onto the highway. "As in Connecticut?"

"Yes. The fishing village reminds me so much of home. I wanted to show you my favorite spot."

"You do realize the seaport is a historic tourist attraction. It's not open this time of night."

He slid his eyes to her and shifted into high gear, opening up the engine to full speed ahead. "I know. Sometimes it's good to be a vampire."

Blair relaxed as Eric tore up the highway toward I95 north and the Connecticut shore.

"Do you like music, Blair?" he asked, activating the touchscreen on the cockpit-like dash.

"Sure, who doesn't."

"What about Claude Debussy?"

"I've never really heard much of his work other than *Clair de Lune*."

He shook his head. "Overplayed. It's part of the score for so many Hollywood movies, yet there's so much more to the man's work. Let me show you what I mean."

He hit play and then a number, and beautiful strains played from the speakers. It started soft and then grew, and it was like listening to the sunrise over the ebb and flow of water.

"This is called, *La Mer*. Debussy completed the composition in 1905. I still remember the first time I heard it played. It was transporting."

She smiled, resting her head back.

"Are you smiling because you like the piece, or because I sound like a pretentious know-it-all?"

"The title."

He looked at her for a second before shifting his eyes to the road.

She chuckled. "My first thought when the music began was it was like listening to what the sunrise over the ocean would be if put to music."

"You are something special, you know that?"

He took her hand and lifted it to his lips. Turning her palm over, he kissed the soft curve above the pulse in her wrist.

"Did you eat?" she asked as if reading his thoughts.

Eric didn't answer. "Since we're going to a place that reminds me so much of my home, I decided to make a few Nova Scotia traditions. Hodge Podge, Rappie Pie...I was going to make oysters, but they don't travel well, so I settled for cold lobster."

"Settled for lobster? Eric, are you some sort of modern-day robber baron?"

He laughed. "No, but after a century, you're bound to have put something by for a rainy day."

"Rainy day? Jeez, it must have poured the day you bought this racehorse of a car."

Le Mer ended, and *Deux Arabesques* began, and the dulcet strains of harp music lulled them both into a comfortable silence for the rest of the drive.

Eric pulled off I95 and coasted through the deserted streets leading toward the historic village.

"We're almost there. Do you want to go for a walk around the village or check into the inn first?" he asked.

"Inn? We're staying over?"

He shrugged. "I wanted to give us the option if you got too tired. I even packed toothbrushes and some toiletries, just in case."

"Is that even possible? I mean, checkout is usually around noon. You'd be taking a huge risk."

Eric glanced at her as he slowed through town. "I arranged for two nights for that very reason." He shrugged. "Comes with the territory."

"It must be hard to have to plan ahead like that."

"Traveling does require some finesse, but I get around it. At least it's not forever."

She turned at that. "What does that mean?"

"Not everything about vampire lore is recorded in those occult books your professors claim to know so well. They probably don't know that as we age, we develop a tolerance for the sun. By the time I'm an elder, I will be what's known as a daywalker."

"You're kidding, right?" she asked, stunned.

"Not at all. Carlos can tolerate early morning, until about ten a.m., and late afternoon. On overcast days, he can be out all day. At that age, though, we have to be careful we don't end up with purpura."

"That's a human condition, too, right? Bleeding beneath the skin"

Eric nodded. "Yes, but in vampires, it's much, much worse. It comes when we don't go to our rest."

"Death sleep."

He pulled into the parking lot of a large mansion. In the dark it looked ominous but beautiful. "Yes. If we end up staying, you'll know what we mean by the term. For humans or other supernaturals not familiar with my kind, it can be a little unnerving."

He cut the engine and opened the door to get out onto the gravel. His feet crunched as he made his way to open the passenger door.

Blair got out and looked up at the historical building. "I've read about this place. This is the Elias Morse Mansion."

Eric smiled, impressed, and he opened the rear passenger door and took out the overnight bag and the picnic basket he'd packed with the food. "The house is one of my favorite places to visit. It used to be the summer home of a renowned sea captain, Elias Morse, and his family. When I first came here, it was after I came to live with Carlos in New York. He brought me here hoping the sea air and the old seaport would help me regain hold of myself.

"Of course, the building didn't look this grand back then. After the good captain died, the place went to hell in a handbag. Seedy and in disrepair. It was a boarding house, a brothel, and a few other places of ill repute. Maybe it was poetic justice or simply a way to reach me, but Carlos thought since I was in hell, what better way to make me want to find my strength and crawl out on my own steam than to drop me in the mire. He stayed with

me, of course. If only to make sure I didn't murder anyone."

"Obviously, it worked."

Eric chuckled, holding his elbow out for Blair. "Indeed."

They walked up the flagstone path to the tall, narrow front doors, and Eric rang the bell.

"Mr. Fraser! I wondered when you'd arrive. Your room and your Glen Scotia are all ready and waiting for you. Francis will take your bags."

"Thank you, Sadie, but it's just the one, and I can handle it myself."

She stepped aside with a nod. "Very well. Let's get you checked in."

Blair spared a look for the woman's face and, as Eric walked past her in the door, Sadie's eyes dilated, and her lips parted. She snapped out of it relatively quickly, hurrying around to the front desk to sign them into the register.

"Wow, you've having quite an effect on our proprietress."

Eric shrugged. "Again, comes with the territory."

"I thought you were tamping down on that bit?"

"I have. I guess she remembers more than my name and my drink."

Blair snorted. "I bet. She's old enough to be your grandmother."

"She wasn't always."

Mouth open, she stared at him as he walked toward Sadie and the front desk. He glanced over his shoulder and winked.

The hound dog. He'd essentially admitted he slept with the inn manager, or whatever she was, back in the

day. Sadie had to be sixty-five if she was a day, but clearly, he knew her when.

"We're all set. We've got the top floor captain's suite complete with widow's walk so we can look out at the water and the seaport."

Blair followed him up the stairs to the third floor. "You know, traditionally, the third floor was for servants. During the summer, they were the hottest rooms in the house, and they froze in winter."

"I know. My orphanage was like that. Luckily for us, Sadie installed central heating and cooling."

"I bet that's not all she installed," Blair mumbled, but Eric turned around on the stair ahead of her with a smirk.

"You're jealous of an old lady."

Blair sniffed. "She wasn't always," she repeated, mimicking him.

He laughed out loud and scooped her up and over his shoulder, sprinting to the top floor.

"Eric! Put me down! Eric, *jeez.*"

With a chuckle, he let her slide to the floor, making sure every one of her soft curves met its match against his hard body.

"You are going to make this talk very hard to get through, aren't you?" She took a step from him as he unlocked their room.

"It's not my intention, but hey. It's a beautiful, starry night. The air is full and crisp with a kiss of the sea. Anything's possible with you."

He swept his arm around her waist and pulled her in close. His lips slanted over hers, soft yet demanding. She opened for him, their breath mingling as her tongue met his for a quick swipe.

Blair broke their kiss and stepped back, her stomach rumbling.

"Wow, that was loud," he said with a laugh.

"I know. I didn't want it to gurgle when I was kissing you. I think I better try some of your hodgepodge." She took his hand and tugged him into the room. "Think you can ask your girlfriend if she got a good bottle of Shiraz?"

"I've gone one better." He pulled a bottle of Vampire Wine from the side of the picnic basket.

He nudged his head toward the inside door that led up to the widow's walk, and they climbed the narrow circular staircase to the top door.

"Damn, I'd hate to do those steps drunk," she said, closing the door.

Eric opened the basket and put out the food on the café table set for two. He uncorked the wine and poured two glasses before walking to where Blair stood looking out at the view.

"You were right. This place is beautiful. History has always been my forte. I love it. From the ancient world, straight up to the twentieth century. I picture myself in whatever time has captured my imagination at the moment. Right now, I'm post-Civil War, standing on the dock, waiting for my lover to return home from his latest whaling adventure."

He handed her one of the wineglasses. "Fast-forward fifty years from then, and you could've been waiting for me." He paused. "If things had gone differently."

She sipped her wine, keeping her eyes on the lights gleaming on the dark water and the shadows of historic buildings dotting the seaport.

"I'm an orphan, too," she began without preamble. "My biological mother died giving birth to me, and I never

knew my bio-dad. I was adopted right away, so I was lucky. For a little while, at least. That is until I ended up back in the orphanage."

Eric was genuinely shocked. "I'm so sorry, Blair. That's unconscionable."

"I was too young to remember, and to this day I don't know what happened. Maybe my first family couldn't afford to keep me, or maybe they got divorced." She shrugged. "Fate was on my side, though, so I can't complain. After that, I was placed relatively quickly with the family who raised me. I was a little over three years old."

"Wow. Talk about jumping in with both feet."

"Well, you shared yours, so fair is fair. Plus, it's getting late."

"Is Cabot your adopted family's name?" he asked.

Blair shook her head. Almost all of my biological information was left off the birth certificate the agency issued to my adoptive family. The only thing that was included was the name Cabot. I was lucky in that my mother and father opted to let me keep my birth name as a middle name. My full name is Blair Cabot Moore, but I legally changed it to Blair Cabot after my family died."

He didn't comment. It wasn't his place at this point. Offering condolences now was a moot point, so he let her continue.

"I've been having such weird dreams lately. Especially since I met you," she said, shifting gears.

Eric nodded. "That's funny because I have as well. Memories I haven't thought about in decades are suddenly haunting my brain."

Blair slanted her head to look at him. "Yeah, but my dreams have to do with you on one hand, and my past on the other."

"Maybe it's because of our unusual connection and the obstacles we face. Perhaps it's the threat of your blood and how it connects to your past and what you've felt compelled to do."

"Compelled. That's the perfect word. It didn't start that way, but more and more if feels as though I was driven to my hunting sprees."

She told Eric everything about her past. About her parents and her brother. About the camping trip and how the vampires attacked. How they saved her for last and how she watched them burn after they drank her blood.

"I was the only one to survive that awful night. After that, every time I left my grandmother's house, I felt as though the entire town looked at me like I was a freak. Either that, or I didn't deserve to survive. Of course, I know those were my own feelings bubbling up to torment me."

"How old were you?"

She took a big gulp of her wine. "Whew, I didn't think saying that out loud would bother me as much as it did."

"It's okay if you want to stop. You haven't eaten."

She shook her head. *"Well begun is half done.* It's better to plod through the facts and then let you ask your questions."

"Did you just quote *Mary Poppins*?"

Grinning, she held out her glass for a top up. "I did. I guess thinking about my mother reminded me she used to quote that movie a lot."

Eric filled her glass again and then dragged over two Adirondack chairs. He grabbed a blanket from the basket and wrapped it around Blair's shoulders when she sat.

"To answer your question, I was seventeen when the vampires killed my family. I had just graduated high school and was glad to be going to college early. After that, I rarely went home. A year or so later, my grandmother died as well, so there really wasn't any reason left after that."

"I don't blame you. Did you hunt then?"

She shook her head. "I didn't even know I was a witch at that point. After my family died in the woods, I knew for sure there were supernatural entities living among us, but I never thought about hunting them. Not until last year. I was busy with school. I was a history major and earned my Bachelor of Arts from NYU. I don't know why, but eventually I was invited to join the master's program in occult studies. Dr. Lynetta Wells is the head of mythological studies. She offered me a spot in the program even though it wasn't my major course of study. I really enjoy it, so I'm not complaining."

"When did you find out you were a witch? You were well past puberty, so it couldn't have been the onset of your powers."

Blair chuckled at that. "Like I said. I took an ancestry DNA test. Dr. Wells knew some of my story, and she suggested the test to see if I could locate my biological parents. I didn't locate my parents, but I did find out I was a Crow. The Supreme of our coven set up some kind of alert when certain markers are met. She contacted me, and the rest is history."

Eric froze with his glass halfway to his lips. "Did you say you are a Crow? As in Crow Haven House?"

Blair nodded. "Yeah, why?"

"It's nothing, I suppose. It's just I knew someone from your coven house many, many years ago."

"Well, Crow Haven and Raven House, our coven cousin, go back a long time. In fact, I've been researching my history at Raven House with their archivist, a crazy old witch named Grania. Believe it or not, she was able to pinpoint my bio-mom's name. It was Geneviève." Blair smiled a quiet, absentee smile. "Pretty name, really. I'm just finding out about her, so I don't want to get into it, but there it is. My story to date."

Eric stared at Blair like it was the first time. "Genny," he murmured. "I should have known."

"Eric, are you all right?"

"Blair, the Crow I told you about. The one I knew so long ago. Her name was Geneviève. I called her Genny."

Blair's wineglass slipped from her hand, but Eric caught it before it smashed to the ground. Not caring, she stared at him openmouthed.

"Eric, for God's sake. Please tell me you are *not* my father."

He shook his head. "No, Blair. I am not your father."

She exhaled the breath she'd been holding. "Thank God for that. I was looking at a millennium of therapy otherwise."

"Genny was a kind soul, happy. She was one of the only people outside Carlos and my family to show me kindness. She wasn't afraid of me." He smiled at the memory. "Probably because she knew her blood kept her safe from my otherwise untamed thirst. As time went on, she seemed to grow distant. Melancholy. Even sad. When I realized what was happening, it was too late. She had been seduced by an incubus. His name was Tolan. He

drained every ounce of soul energy from her over three years. I tried to intervene, but Genny refused to listen. He owned her. Body, mind, and soul.

"I kept my distance until I found out she was pregnant. What you were told was the truth. She died giving birth to you. Personally, I think she sacrificed her own life and her own spirit to give you the strength you needed to survive.

"You were such a tiny thing, but feisty and fierce. Tolan showed up with his sister, Xylana, to claim you. He said you were his spawn. His to do with as he wanted. I wouldn't let him touch you. We fought, and I killed him. Simple as that."

She blinked, hanging on every word. "Incubi and Succubi are immortal, Eric. How can they be killed?"

"Vampires are immortal as well, but you know plenty of ways to kill us. It's a matter of angles. How you look at the problem. Incubi and Succubi are demons. Demons are technically entities from a dark realm. Not Hell. Not the underworld. Just a dark realm. The opposite of light. They have no link to humanity like most supernaturals. So if they come from the dark, the way to kill them is with light. I was prepared when Tolan and his bitch sister came for you.

"I'd had months to consult tomes and speak with our elders. Dominic De'Lessep has been a vampire for a millennium. He's the one I spoke about who helped teach Carlos how to hold onto his humanity. He also collects artifacts and has done so since he was turned. If anyone would have a weapon to use against an incubus, it would be Dominic.

"Obviously he gave you something to use or I wouldn't be sitting here. What kind of weapon could a vampire have that would kill a demon?"

"He gave me a blade forged from light."

"How can you forge a blade from something intangible? Light is made of waves. Photon devoid of elements. It's non-substantive."

He shrugged. "It's like I said. It's a matter of how you look at things. Everything you said is true, but let me ask you a question. In our world, for supernaturals...what light source can be both life giving and bring death?"

Blair's eyes widened. "The sun."

"Yes, and what is the sun, but a very large star. Dominic gave me a blade forged from a fallen star. It is the only thing that can kill an incubus, or his even more lethal counterpart, a succubus. It's what I used to kill Tolan."

"What happened afterward?"

Eric exhaled, handing Blair her wine. "Xylana vowed revenge, of course, but then ran away like a little bitch. I haven't seen or heard from her since. I wrapped you up in a blanket and took you to the only other person I knew who could help."

"Let me guess. Grania."

He nodded. "You were and still are a Cambion. The reason you don't have any of their abilities other than extreme longevity is because Grania bound your demon side, not your witch side. She wanted to keep you with her, but it was prohibited. Things then were not like they are now. The lines between supernaturals were very strong and just as impenetrable. The fact Genny and I were friends, and that Grania helped me with you, was a miracle. Anyway, she bound your dark side and then we took you to the orphanage together. I worked my glamour on social services though. I wanted to make sure you were placed in a good home.

"Now that you told me your first adopted family sent you back, it makes me wonder if Xylana came looking for you and got to them through their dreams. It's how that bitch works."

The blanket had fallen from Blair's shoulders, and she shivered but not from the cold. "Eric, do you think it's possible the strange dreams we've been having lately might be her?"

"Maybe. But I doubt it."

She didn't need a veritas spell to know everything he said was truth. The revelation should have made her head spin, but instead she was very calm. The pieces of her puzzle were finally fitting together.

It was all she could do not to jump into his arms and squeal. All that time in the library, cooped up like some manic hermit, when the answers were right here waiting on Eric's tongue.

His very talented tongue.

Ooh, baby.

Don't go there.

Why not. You hinted at it before we left the city.

"Grania did a great job binding your Cambion side. After all, I couldn't tell you, and I've been up close and personal in your milk and cookies."

Yeah, you have!

Okay already. Just shut it.

She chewed on her lip. "Speaking of which, I think I'd like to try letting you snack on me a little more than what we've done so far."

"Now that I know you're only half witch, I might stand even more of a chance, but let's wait until others of my kind are close by, just in case."

She glanced at the harbor and the dark shadows across the water. "Then how about plain old milk and cookies?"

He grinned. "Al fresco?"

"I've got a spell that can warm us up if you want."

Eric pulled her to her feet, letting the blanket drop to the chair. "Let's see if we can't heat things up the old-fashioned way, my pretty witch."

Chapter Fifteen

Blair sank into one of the widow's walk's Adirondack chairs, while Eric went to top off their wine. "Here's to our brand of magic." He handed her a glass and then touched his to hers with a soft clink.

She drained the entire glass and then licked her lips.

Wow, you've got it bad, demon spawn.

Shut up.

Who's complaining?

Shush, I can't think.

It's about doing, babe. Not thinking.

Eric's mouth was mesmerizing as he spoke. Not that she heard a word he said. There were too many revelations for one night, and her subconscious was right. No more thinking.

The moon was high above the water, casting the balustraded widow's walk in silver light. Eric stood in front of her, every inch a supernatural god. Even with so many revelations, there wasn't enough wine in the world to keep her thoughts away from him and what she wanted. She watched him polish off his wine, his tongue darting to catch a single drop on his lip. That innocent, yet utterly sexy swipe, sent the butterflies winging in her stomach into a kamikaze dive straight for her nether regions.

The anticipation was almost illicit, though it shouldn't have been. After all, this wasn't their sexual maiden voyage and not because of the threat of a little fang in the mix. This, their unnerving attraction, felt right. As though, it, too, was part of the bigger puzzle fitting together. All

this time she was critical of his kind, when her own kind…her real kind…was even worse. She should've been racked with guilt, but she wasn't.

Not because she was callous, but because the reality of who she was and what she was, finally gave her a reason *why* that fit. It wasn't an all-consuming hate. Something she had to justify to herself over and over again. She wasn't a borderline sociopath, and that meant everything. She was born demon spawn, but she was still very much a witch as well. Now that she had answers, she could control her nature instead of letting it control her.

Her fingers closed over the crystal stem, nearly snapping the pretty glass. When she got in the car with Eric tonight, she expected a frank discussion, a little wine, and maybe sex. Not a night of epiphanies. Certainly not one regarding her feelings for Eric. She could have gone home, or back to the library when he said the words road trip, but she wanted to be here with him. The reality was intoxicating, even without the wine.

She sighed. Truth was, Eric was all she thought of—well, that and whether or not she was demon spawn, and that was no longer a question. So that left Eric. All she wanted from this was—Blair cut the thought short.

All she wanted.

Period.

There wasn't more to the notion. Eric was all she wanted. The clarity of it floored her, even as he took the glass from her hand and set it on the small, round table next to the Adirondack chair.

"Is there room for me, or are your moods too big to share?" he asked with a soft grin.

She smiled up at him. "There's plenty of room.

"You sure? You look like you're chasing thoughts."

Eric's sexy voice sent shivers from the base of her spine to her private parts even when he was being polite. The way he looked at her incinerated any last vestiges of doubt, and her heart squeezed. "I'd rather chase you around that big bed downstairs. Much more satisfying than my jumbled mind."

"I know you initially made the invitation, but—" Without another word, he scooped her up and carried her down the spiral stairs to their suite and the king-sized bed waiting for them. He placed her on the edge of the mattress and then stepped back.

"Strip for me, Blair. No clothes, no barriers between us tonight."

His eyes darkened with desire as she got to her feet and walked him backward to the couch across from the bed. She turned with an inner wince. Was she really going to strip tease for her vampire lover?

Yup.

And she was going to enjoy every raunchy second. A low chuckle bubbled. Maybe there was an upside to being demon spawn because right now she felt oh so bad, yet oh so good.

She wasn't dressed for a striptease but to hell with convention. Just a button-down top, black leggings, and ankle boots. At least the boots had a heel. Turning to face him, she met Eric's hazel eyes. They were rimmed with dark red and watching her like she was something to eat.

Now, that's funny.

Funny is not what we're going for here.

I'll shut up.

Thank you.

She curled a corner of her lip at the errant inner dialogue, and the effect must have been unconsciously

sexy because Eric's hand went to the bulge at the front of his pants.

Encouraged, she slipped out of her boots, barefoot.

Wow, no white gym socks?

What happened to shutting up?

One by one, she unbuttoned her shirt, keeping a few intact for a tease as the soft cotton fell over one shoulder. She was braless. Not that she had too much to worry about in that department. Turning her back to him again, she slipped her hands under her legging waistband and wiggled the wide band over her hips in a figure eight. She twisted the snug Lycra to her knees, but that was all she wrote.

With a snap, she lost her balance.

Ugh, and we were doing so well.

Shut the fuck up already!

She was going down, hard. And not in a good way. Eric was off the couch in a blur. He caught her just in time, and the two tumbled backward onto the bed in a tangle of arms and bound knees.

"Those pants should come with a warning label, though I love the way they showcase every one of your luscious curves." He chuckled, brushing her hair from her face.

Blair blew the last few strands from her forehead. "They're built for comfort not speed. Definitely not striptease material. Sort of like me."

"Sort of like you." He shook his head. His eyes were still dark with unspoken want, even with the comedy of errors playing instead of a seduction scene. "There is no sort of, Blair. I most certainly like you. Demon spawn striptease notwithstanding.

"Ha, ha." Her lips pushed to one side in a teasing smirk.

The humor stayed in his eyes, but his grin softened, and he lifted his fingers to her cheek. "Actually, since we're baring scars and souls tonight, the truth is I more than like you, sweetheart. I've fallen in love. Something I never thought would happen in any lifetime, let alone an undead one."

Before she could answer, his lips claimed her mouth. Deep but not insistent. Not yet. He broke their kiss, letting his tongue trace her lower lip. "I'll never get enough of the way you taste." He untangled himself from their jumble and stood, his eyes scanning her naked waist and what teased below.

"You're completely commando under those skimpy pants?" He raised an eyebrow.

She slipped the Lycra the rest of the way from her legs. "I didn't want panty lines. I've been holed up in the library for the past couple of days. I had to do something to be sort of sexy with my limited wardrobe." She wiggled pretty pink toes. "I glommed my professor's nail polish from her drawer. Considering I usually wear ugly white gym socks under my boots, I should get partial credit for trying."

"Gym socks? No problem. As long as you're not wearing anything else." He laughed out loud. "No panties under those torturous hose?" He reached for her shirt and finished unbuttoning the rest until the soft cotton fell to either side of her waist.

"No lacy bits, either. You mean to tell me we drove all this way, and you were naked as a jaybird under your skimpy clothes? The whole time in the car? Woman, if I'd

known that, we'd never have made it out of the driveway."

"Well, now you know. So shut up about it and kiss me."

Eric slid his arm around her waist and pulled her against his hard length. Blair's pulse raced in her chest when a deep-throated chuckle fanned against her lips.

He nuzzled the tender flesh. "No lacy undergarment to help with friction this time around. I'll have to think of something else."

He nipped her lip.

"You're playing with fire, vampire. You forget I'm a half-demon witch." She bit him as well, and he growled.

"Blair Cabot, you are a wanton tease."

"I try."

A low rumble formed in his throat, rough and full of desire. "Come play in the dark with me, my little demon. You have possessed me, utterly. I want your heart as much as I want your body and your blood. Say you're mine, no matter what the consequence."

His mouth took hers again before she could argue, his tongue delving deep into her moist cavern, this time demanding and hungry. She met his urgency and matched it as his hand found the nape of her neck, urging their kiss even deeper.

"Eric, please—" She pulled back with a gasp.

He caressed the nape of her neck. "It's okay, Blair. Tonight has been full of surprises and disclosures. Maybe mine was too much, too soon."

The hard bar of his member pressed against her softness. She shook her head and snaked her arm around his neck, urging his mouth closer. Disclosures and truths.

Taking her lead, he slid his free hand over her hip, his fingertips brushing her soft fluff between her legs. "After all this, if all you want is a little release, I'm sure I can accommodate."

"Of course I want *that*, but it's not all I want, Eric. I want you, too. Not just your body, and not because you make mine quiver."

His eyes held her gaze with such intensity it nearly broke her heart. She realized then he was waiting for the *but* in her statement.

"Eric, stop looking at me like I'm about to deliver a sentence of hard labor. I'm trying to tell you, you're not the only one who's fallen hard—and I'm not talking about tripping over my striptease."

He studied her face, his nostrils flaring slightly, and she smacked his shoulder. "Oh my God! I'm trying to tell you I've fallen in love with you, and you're busy scenting the air to see if I'm lying? Dude!"

"Well, you polished off that bottle of wine pretty quickly, not that I was counting."

She had to laugh. Talk about sticking to their comedy of errors.

"You do realize with one word I could compel you to spill your deepest darks, right? I may be demon spawn, but I'm still a witch, so don't make me get out my flying monkeys."

He kissed the tip of her nose. "Wouldn't do any good. I already spilled plenty, free of charge, my twitchy witch."

"What am I going to do with you, vampire? You occupy my thoughts to the point I can't concentrate. It's clear to me the fates have been toying with us since the day I was born."

"And you have crept into my everyday world, holding me utterly captive. The fates have a way of bringing things full circle. But with this, I can't fathom why," he replied softly.

"What do they want?"

"They will reveal their master plan in time, Blair." He brushed his lips to hers, whispering into his kiss, "As for me, the only thing I want right now is you."

His hand slipped between her legs, to her slick seam. Separating her folds, he stroked the tender flesh, gently teasing her nub.

His lips hovered close to her mouth. Their breath mingled. "What do you want, Blair?" He slipped two fingers into her slippery cleft. "I said no barriers tonight. Physical or emotional. Forget the outside world for now. It's just you and me. The consequences be damned."

Blair's breath hitched in her throat. She clung to his wide shoulders as he pressed small kisses to her mouth, working her inner spot as his thumb circled her hard nub.

"Let go, Blair. I want to feel your walls to squeeze my hand as you come. I want to lick your slick juice from my fingers again. To tease you until you beg for my cock. I want to taste you for real this time. No holding back."

Eric lifted his head enough for their eyes to meet.

"No holding back," she repeated his words. "You mean—"

He nodded. "Blood and sex, Blair. I know I said I wanted to wait, but now I need to know. I want you with every fiber of my being. I want you to know me. The truth of me. Not just the humanity you see and love but the darkness, too. You need to see the whole of me. The good, the bad, and the ugly."

A smirk tweaked the corner of her mouth, and she squelched it but not before he saw it.

"You really are a little demon bitch." He bit her lip.

She whistled the iconic theme to the Clint Eastwood classic, and he rolled his eyes.

"Sorry, babe. I couldn't help it. You walked right into that."

"So this is what life is going to be like. I bare my soul, and you laugh."

"I thought you said vampire souls were up for debate."

He kissed her again, rolling with her on the wide bed until he pinned her beneath him, her legs open and his cock pressed to her slick entrance.

"That" — he pressed another short kiss to her mouth — "is a conversation for another time."

"How about no more conversation for a bit, eh?" She teased, mimicking his Canadian accent.

"Definitely a demon bitch."

With a single thrust, he drove his cock through her folds and deep into her sex but then pulled out just as fast. His swollen head hovered at her entrance as he kissed her mouth, his tongue teasing and tasting every bit of her sweetness.

His fangs descended, not fully but enough for him to graze her lower lip, drawing blood. Eric pulled back as Blair froze. Tiny red droplets formed and pooled into a single trickle.

"Eric, no. My blood could kill you."

"Witch blood is a crapshoot for any vampire, Blair. I'm not waiting any longer."

"Please, wait. I don't want to risk it. I love you."

Without hesitation, Eric dipped the tip of his tongue to the tiny crimson rivulet. He closed his eyes and lapped the

tangy copper. The moment her blood hit his tongue, colors exploded behind his lids. Every nerve ending quivered, sparking with life and unbelievable desire. His cock thickened to near bursting, and he moaned.

"Eric?" Blair shook him. "Eric!"

A small smile tugged at the corner of his mouth and he opened his eyes. Smacking his lips, he bent to lick the residual, sealing the small abrasion. "You taste even better than I hoped."

She headbutted him.

"Ow!" His hand went to his forehead. "What was that for?"

"For making me worry. For not giving me a vote in your little death wish experiment. I tell you I love you, and you go ahead and pull something that could kill you? How would I explain the pile of ash on the sheets to Mrs. Whatshername downstairs? Besides that, what the hell would I do without you?"

Rant over, Blair was panting by the time she finished, but Eric's stupid grin only made her angry all over again. "Stop looking at me like that!"

"I'm sorry, love, but you're not one to talk about having a death wish."

She smacked his arm. "Yeah, but I didn't love you then."

Gathering her in his arms, he kissed her soft and deep. "Don't you realize this means I'm immune to your blood? It means we can have it all."

She sniffed. "You mean you can have it all. I get to be a walking-talking Red Cross bloodmobile."

"With all the cookies and orange juice you want." He traced the seam of her closed lips with the tip of his tongue. "Plus, you get all of me."

He thrust his full thickness between her folds again, taking her mouth as he teased her with inches, slow and torturous. He pulled back from her sex again, letting his lips trace from her mouth to her chin and the tender underside beside her swift pulse.

Working his way past her collarbone to her breasts, he slid his hand from her neck to cup one breast. He kneaded her stiff, bare nipple, pinching the hard peak while teasing the other pink bud with his tongue and teeth. He drew a little more blood, sucking and licking until Blair gasped, her head falling between her shoulder blades.

"Your scent tells me everything, love. Exactly what you want and where." He trailed his mouth over her belly to the soft fluff of her sex.

Sliding her knees wide, she reached for the top of his head. Digging her fingers into his hair, she groaned as he blew on the dark curls between her legs, his warm breath teasing her higher.

"Eric!" she ground out.

"What, Blair?" His tongue darted to her sensitive nub. "Is this what you want?"

She moaned as he dipped his head to her sex and teased her folds, his tongue pushing them apart with soft rasps. He licked her straight up, drawing his tongue across the tender flesh to her tight bud.

Grazing his teeth across her sensitive flesh, he was careful not to draw blood. Her need dripped slick and wet, but his breath caught when Blair pushed her legs wider and urged his head from her sex to her inner thigh and the pulsing artery glistening below her smooth, sex-sheened skin.

He groaned, lifting his face to look at her. Eyes dark and lips wet, she nodded. "Do it, Eric. Now."

He drove three fingers deep into her wet cleft. Heat skittered across her skin as he curled them farther inside, working her hard and deep. She cried out as she crested, her climax flushing her blood to the surface, thick with adrenaline and release.

There was no turning back. The scent of her climax forced his fangs to descend fully, and their sharp tips penetrated her thick artery. A rush of copper hit his tongue, and he groaned as the sweet crimson filled his mouth.

Blair cried out as she came again as he took deep pulls from her artery. In that moment, she choked out two words. *Vim vitae.* Their auras shimmered, tangible, together yet apart.

The shock of the spell pulled his fangs from her vein, and he blinked at the living orbs. He sealed her wound, and then pulled his hand from her sex before gathering her in his arms.

"You, hard and deep! Please!"

Eric drove his full length deep into her soaked sex.

She cried out as he plunged full inches, his member swelling and stretching her to boneless pleasure. She met him thrust for thrust, her body grinding for more.

Eric bit the inside of his cheek and then took her mouth, his blood coating her lips and tongue. Not much but enough.

Colors exploded behind her eyes as she went weightless, her body on fire at the alien sensations rocking and ripping through her body as she came yet again.

Panting, she managed one more spell. *Immesceo.*

The shimmering spheres vibrated and rippled, merging into one pulsing union, encircling them both. Eric's body suffused with light and warmth. The feel of his

body joined with Blair's, and their auras as one had him crying out.

He floated in bliss, the feel of sunshine on his skin and life coursing through his body. True life. Not the stolen semblance a vampire gleans from living blood. Every sense animated with the particles of life. Every whisper of breath and hope, seen, heard, felt.

Wrapping his arms around Blair, he lifted her to him. He wanted her as close as their joined bodies would allow.

He pressed his forehead to hers and let his mind merge with hers, and she gasped at the feel of him. Hope and love feathered through their linked auras and into her mind, and her body quivered at the immensity of the feeling.

They moved together, tension building both rigid and fluid at once. Their combined auras tingled and vibrated, their warmth turning to heat. It enveloped them in a swirl as Eric rolled with Blair on the bed once more, until she was beneath him in a frenzy of thrusts and sweat.

He took her lips, kissing her hard and deep until he ripped his mouth from hers with a ragged breath. Blair's head dropped between her shoulders, and delicious pain sluiced through her flesh as his fangs bit deep into her throat.

Their auras swirled gold and red as their essences merged. Their coupled minds spun with colors and images. A fragile mesh connecting them to one another. Each slender thread attached to their very core. He was hers, and she was his. In body. In soul. And in blood.

He drove his full length, pumping harder, faster until he could no longer hold on. He pulled his fangs from her throat. Red rivulets dripped from the wound as he threw his head back. With a shuddering gasp, hot jets burst from his swollen head as he emptied himself deep inside.

Blair's body quaked, her legs shaking as she crested, her body tensed as waves radiated from her sex up her belly and spine.

Eric held tight, his body riding out every last aftershock until his shoulders slumped. He opened his eyes and rushed to seal the wounds at Blair's throat, licking the drips clean.

The shimmering air around them faded as their auras withdrew, separate but forever connected. His member slipped from her body, but he shifted around to gather her onto his lap.

"That was the single most incredible experience of my life, human or undead."

She chuckled, nuzzling his throat. "I should get you a T-shirt that reads, *I survived the demon-witch*...or what about *demon-witch blood slave*."

"Don't joke about that. Witch blood isn't just poisonous to some vampires. It also makes the undead very, very biddable."

Nipping his neck, she traced the spot where his pulse should be but wasn't. "Biddable, huh? Is it like go fetch? Or more like, peel me a grape?"

He growled, flipping her onto her back again. "More, as in—" His still-hard cock slipped between her tender folds again. "More."

She inhaled, fisting the rumpled bedspread as he filled her again. Eric rolled again, this time with Blair landing in a straddle over his hips.

"I feel the thrum of your pulse even without touching you, Blair." He thrust up, and she rolled her hips, grinding her spot on his thick length. "I sense your every emotion. Your adrenaline, your exhaustion, and everything in between."

She gasped and rolled her hips faster.

"Like, I know you're about to come again…right now…"

Her hands gripped his chest as she milked his member, rolling her hips as her body spasmed into another climax before crashing to utter spent exhaustion.

Slumping to his chest, she inhaled their mingled scent, resting her chin between his pecs. "So it wasn't just me who felt a real connection. I don't mean we had a meeting of the minds, or you're my new BFF. I mean a real, honest-to-God connection. Like linked."

"No, there was a definite connection, or how else would I be so attuned to you. This strange enmeshment tells me you're mine, Blair. Now and always. My lover, my everything. Flesh. Blood. Soul. All shared."

"You're saying we're soul mates, then? Is that what the fates are playing at with us?"

He pulled her up his chest to kiss her nose and then her mouth. "Exactly. And it's up to us to see it through. Blood hurtle, down. Now it's just a matter of what to do about the Vampire Council."

She chewed on her lip. "Maybe I should have Grania unbind my demon side. That might discourage them from messing with a spawn." She chuckled. "At least that's what my friend Lizzie says."

"Oh, so you've been telling people about this…about me?" He grinned, shoving his hand behind his head on one of the pillows.

"Yes and no. She knows about you." Blair grinned. "She calls you the kissing vampire."

He laughed out loud. "Why ever?"

"Because I told her about our first kiss that night in the alley."

His grin sobered for a moment. "So she knows about your vigilantism?"

"I suppose," Blair hedged.

Eric sat up. "This is important, Blair. You've got to tell me the truth. If others know about what you've done, it will not go over well with the council. They will feel compelled to make an example of you just to show solidarity and force to the other supernaturals."

"You mean save face." She frowned, sitting up as well.

"Couch it whichever way you want, it doesn't change it." He slipped two fingers under her chin. "Does your friend Lizzie know the whole truth?"

Blair nodded. "She knows what happened to my adoptive family, she knows what Grania told me, and she knows I've been doing research to find out about my parentage. She knows I've been hunting, but she also knows I've stopped since meeting you. She calls you the kissing vampire because you kissed me back to my senses."

He spared her a small close-lipped smile. "Well, that's something, then."

"Lizzie is my best friend in the world. Besides, I know you told Carlos. Would he tell the council even though he knew it would crush your heart?"

Eric shook his head. "In fact, he was the one who told me to pursue you."

"See? People who love us understand. Like Carlos would never betray you to the council, Lizzie would never betray me. In fact, she's the one who told me to use my demon abilities on you. Something called an enslavement kiss. I told her I didn't need it, that you were already as enslaved to me as I was to you." She giggled. "Lizzie loved it. She's a hopeless romantic, even if she is still a virgin."

Eric raised an eyebrow. "A witch who's a virgin? I thought sex was part of your earth rituals and sabbats?"

"It is, but Lizzie hasn't come full circle yet. It was hard enough on her finding out she was a witch. Did you know she thought it meant she had to worship the devil?"

"Really."

Blair nodded. "And to quote my favorite witchy move, there is no devil in the craft."

"*Practical Magic*, right?"

A grin split Blair's face from ear to ear. "Eric Fraser, I think I just fell in love with you all over again."

She cuddled up, tucking herself under his arm as he pulled the bedspread over their naked bodies. Linking her hand with his, she bounced his fingers up and down.

"Tell me, Blair. I can sense your uncertainty."

"I'm just wondering what's next, I mean besides the council."

He kissed the top of her head. "One sunset at a time, one dawn at a time." He closed his eyes. "Starting with this one. One thing a vampire can always sense is daybreak. Dawn isn't too far off, love. You ask what's next? Death sleep…at least for me. You should get some shut-eye, too. I've already put the Do Not Disturb sign on the door, but tomorrow when you rise, don't open the curtains. Unless you prefer your lovers charbroiled."

She snickered. "Hot, yes. But that might be taking it too far." Throwing the covers off, she slipped out of bed.

"Where are you going?"

"To check the curtains and shut the door to the widow's walk. I'm not taking any chances." She paused at the base of the circular stairs. "Tomorrow night, do you think you could come with me to the library? I want to

pack up my things and take them back to Crow House, but there's something I'd like to show you."

Eyes closed again, he nodded. "Of course, but in the meantime, you'd better give me a kiss good night. I feel myself fading."

Blair rushed to the bed and smoothed Eric's hair from his face, brushing his lips with hers, but they were already cold.

"Death sleep." She shook her head. "Damn. He wasn't kidding."

Tomorrow they'd come up with a plan of attack. She frowned. Bad choice of words. A strategy. She nodded to herself. And she'd get to show Eric the drawing she did of him, too. One way or the other, she had to clear out of Dr. Wells' side office. Fall break was over, and classes began first thing Monday morning.

She glanced at Eric again. He was so still, it was unnerving. Would it be weird sharing a bed with him when he was tantamount to dead?

One sunset at a time.

One dawn at a time.

She shivered. At least it was a king-sized bed.

Chapter Sixteen

"Are you going to tell me what it is you want to show me?" Eric asked, following Blair off the elevator.

"Nope. You'll just have to wait. It's in Dr. Wells' side office where I've been holed up."

He followed her through the stacks toward the wide, floor-to-ceiling windows overlooking the street and Washington Square Park.

"Wow, if you had to play at being a hermit, at least you had a terrific view."

"I guess, except for the never-ending construction." Blair pointed toward the last row of stacks. "The office is just around this bend."

Leading the way, she gestured toward the large corner office at the end of the section. "Dr. Wells prefers small, intimate classes. She holds a lot of them here, hence the large office. It's unusual, but then again, Dr. Wells isn't usual."

"How so?"

Blair shrugged. "I'm not sure how to explain it. She's just unusual. Most of her students are male. Obviously present company excepted in that assessment. She seemed to pop up unexpectedly, too, whenever you happen to think of her. Like she's been lurking or something, when you know she's not. I gotta tell you, it's unnerving."

"As unnerving as waking up before I rose this evening?" he asked, pulling her to a stop right before the end of the row of shelves. "I've always wondered about students who have sex in the stacks. Like the Mile High Club. It's a pretty exclusive group, eh?"

Blair rolled her eyes as he pressed her against the shelves, and the hard bar in his pants against her. "Not as exclusive as you'd think, Eric. All it takes is one adventure junkie idiot or an exhibitionist looking for a public thrill and you have liftoff. Most times, it's morons too stoned to realize they're in a public place. You gotta laugh because they're usually too high to seal the deal." She held a pencil straight out by its eraser and then let it droop to her palm. "If you get my drift."

"Now that's a visual," he said, stepping back.

Taking him by the hand, she towed him toward the office door as she dug in her purse for the keys. "I hope I remembered to lock the door. I shot out of here so fast last night, I don't remember."

She put the key in the lock, and it snicked open. "Guess I'm not as flighty as I thought."

Opening, the door, she walked with him through Dr. Wells' main space and through to the side office.

The room was relatively neat, and Blair was suddenly grateful Lizzie had a cleaning OCD thing, or she would have been very embarrassed.

"Pretty sweet, huh?" She put her keys and purse on the desk and then went to grab her overnight bag. "I'll just be a sec."

Blair went into the bathroom for her toiletries, and when she walked out, Eric was sitting on the daybed with one of her mother's diaries in hand.

"I was surprised she didn't mention you, considering you were such good friends," she said, putting her toiletries in the overnight bag.

"She mentions me a lot, but you wouldn't have known that." He pointed to an excerpt.

"Rikky asked me to go to the pictures with him tonight, but I said no. I feel bad for him. He's always alone. I don't know why though. He's such a kind man...well, for a vampire. He's been through so much, I'm just happy he has a family he can depend on. Vampires having families. It's an odd concept, but then, no odder than a witch befriending the lonely hearts club undead. Maybe he'll go to the pictures with Julian or one of the others. He needs to get out more, or he'll never master his thirst completely.

I need to stay put in case you-know-who drops by. He's so dreamy. I can barely sit still just thinking about him. Why he wants me, I'll never understand. You'd think being a witch would automatically make a person brave, exotic, and interesting, but I'm just an ordinary girl. Rik says I'm just shy. We make a great team, Rik and me. A mousy witch who can barely squeak in public, and a vampire who might slaughter an entire theater if someone looks at him the wrong way. I often wonder what happened to Rikky before he was turned and then afterward to give him such a hair trigger. He's always peaceful when he's with me. Funny, even. Like the big brother I never had.

Sigh. I wish I could tell Rik about you-know-who. I don't even dare write his name for fear of upsetting him. I don't know why he wants me to keep him a secret, but I keep hoping he'll come around. Rikky knows I'm seeing someone. He's asked me to introduce him a hundred times. Probably so he could use his vampy powers like that military truth serum I saw in the movies. I keep avoiding the conversation, so much so, Rik jokes my suitor is either fictional or married. Funny really, considering my best friends are a witch and a vampire. I haven't even told Grania about you-know-who. She'd definitely scry for him and then show up unannounced. When Rik teased you-know-who was

214

probably married, I teased maybe I didn't want to risk introducing my red-blooded boyfriend to a vampire...

"You're Rikky?"

Eric nodded. "Didn't the fact she was talking about a vampire give it away?"

"No, not really. You said the two of you were friends, so I chalked it up to something usual, at least for Geneviève."

"Genny was one of the sweetest people I ever met. I'm sorry you never got to know your mother."

"I don't even know what she looked like. Grania says I look just like her, but then again, if that was the case, wouldn't she have recognized me before she saw my birthmark?"

Eric lifted a hand to his pec in the same place Blair had her mark. "I knew your mother had a mark, but to be honest, I forgot all about it until you told me just now."

He cocked his head, studying Blair.

"The last time you looked at me that way was in the alley. What is it?"

"You resemble you mother but not exactly. Her face was a little more heart shaped than yours, and her hair a little lighter. Yours is a richer chestnut. More reddish highlights. But your eyes are hers. Same cat's-eye shape. Same brightness. Same gorgeous amber."

Blair picked up her sketchbook from the desk and flipped to the page with Eric's portrait. "This is what I wanted to show you. I drew it from memory. If I had a picture of my mother, I could draw one of her, too."

Eric took the book from Blair's hand and turned it around. Lips parted, he stared at the detailed sketch.

"Blair, I don't know what to say. This is incredible." He flipped through the other drawings. "You did all of these this week?"

She nodded. "I was trying to put together a catalog of possible bio-dads."

"So you added me to the list of choices?" He shook his head. "That's going to haunt me in my nightmares."

She went to snatch the book from him, but he pulled it out of reach. "C'mon, I didn't add you as a possible bio-dad. It was just the category. Undead. And since you're the only vampire I know, my head and my hand sort of went there…on their own."

He had to laugh, but they both turned when the main office door opened and closed.

"It's only me, Blair."

They listened to the sound of keys, and a desk drawer opening and closing. Eric shut Blair's sketchbook and then handed it to her before getting up from the daybed.

"It's okay, it's only Dr. Wells. Relax." Blair winked. "I told you, she just pops up, like Where's Waldo."

"Just checking to make sure you were packing up because tomorrow I have student meetings in here." Lynetta stopped in the doorway to the side office. "Oh, I didn't realize you had—"

Eric pushed Blair behind him. "Xylana." His voice was low and lethal. "I shouldn't be surprised, but from the look on your face, you're just as stunned. I not surprised you hold private tête-à-têtes here. Makes for easy feeding, eh? Makes sense a predator like you would install yourself in a place with an ever-replenishing stream of young innocents."

Eric?" Blair tried to move to past him. "What's going on? How do you know—"

Lynetta's face changed. It grew sharper, longer, and her teeth very sharp. Her skin was still smooth, but in the sheen from the overhead lights, it almost looked as though it had a roughness to it, like shark skin.

Blair blinked. "I'd ask who you are, but I think I'd rather know what you are?"

"Stay behind me, Blair. Your Doctor Wells is a succubus. If my guess is correct, she's been feeding off her students. Didn't you say it was unusual for a professor of Mythological Studies to have so many male students?"

"They're not all male," Xylana replied. "Ms. Cabot is a student of mine and a very deliciously souled student at that."

"Really. And I thought even demons drew the line at feeding off family."

Xylana blinked, confused for a moment, and Blair cringed at the weird double-lidded, almost reptilian blink.

The succubus stared at Blair, taking a step closer. She leaned in and sniffed. "You lie, vampire. I would smell Tolan on her if she were his spawn."

"The word is Cambion, and if Tolan the incubus was your brother, then I am your niece. Wow, my own auntie feeding off my soul. Huh. I wonder what the rest of *your* kind will think of that because, as far as I'm concerned, I am all witch. One hundred percent Geneviève's daughter. Your brother was nothing but a sperm donor."

Lynetta's face changed completely. Her clothes shredded, and black wings unfurled with snake-like skin that spread across her body.

"You were always a fashion-forward kind of gal, Lynetta, but even you have to admit the Jimmy Choos are a bit out of place with naked snakeskin and demon wings." Blair snorted crossing her arms.

"What would you know of our kind," she ground out. "You're no Cambion. I doubt you could find the soul in a virgin, let alone the creature standing beside you."

Blair finally slipped around Eric's side but stayed close. "Well, who would know more about vampire souls than you, Auntie X. Seems you let the cat out of the bag about that demon secret. You're two-for-two strikes. Feeding off family and spilling demon deepest darks."

"You were useful when you were my puppet, Blair Cabot, but I'll see you dead before you can draw attention to me."

Xylana's wings spread, sending papers flying around the room. She opened her mouth, showing rows and rows of jagged teeth.

"Cover your ears, Blair! Now!" Eric stepped in front of Blair just as the succubus let out an earsplitting screech. The office windows facing the street shattered outward, and she launched herself from the ledge, wings flapping.

Blair jerked from Eric's grip and rushed to the window, but Xylana was gone. She whirled on her heel.

"We have to go after her, Eric! You heard her. I was her puppet. She's my mitigating circumstance! What if she compelled me into killing those youngbloods? It'll prove I'm not some heartless vigilante. We need to find her."

He nodded. "Yes, we need to find her but not to question her. We need to find her and kill her, Blair, or she will come to you every time you close your eyes and torture you, just enough so you don't die, but enough to drive you insane for the rest of your life. She needs to die, or neither of us is safe, nor are the people we love."

"Everything makes sense now. I never thought to hunt until I joined Dr. Wells' department a year ago. After that, it was as though I was obsessed."

"More like possessed."

Blair sat on the edge of the daybed. "I guess my mother and I aren't that different after all."

"Demon attacks are not uncommon, love. Most humans don't even believe they exist, let alone that they can prey on humanity through their dreams. They attribute their exhaustion and malaise to poor diet and stress. Once night terrors start, it's too late. The succubus or incubus have you good and tight."

"I never felt that malaise. Just exhaustion and overwhelming anger and resentment. Did she feed that, too?" Blair raked a hand through her hair. "We'd better get out of here. With shattered glass all over the sidewalk, it's only a matter of time before the police show up."

Eric pulled her to her feet and wrapped his arms around her shoulders. "You pack up. Let me worry about the police. If you're not up to casting a ward, I can always toss a little glamour around to throw them off the scent. Figuratively, of course. I only know of one detective who's a half-Were, but he moved to California."

"Where do we go? The last thing I want is to bring trouble to Crow Haven House—" She looked up, panic rising. "Oh my God. Lizzie."

She whirled from his arms. "Lynetta...Xylana...or whatever the fuck her name, she met Lizzie. In fact, she teased her about being so innocent." Blair looked at him, and her throat tightened. "She's my friend, Eric. The virgin witch, remember? We have to find her and take her someplace safe."

"You can both come to my place. We'll figure this out, together."

"What about Carlos? What's he going to say about having a vigilante witch and her BFF under his roof?"

"It's my roof, too…and you are not a vigilante witch. You're my lover, and my life. He won't bat an eye."

***

"*Mijo*, are you sure this is the same succubus you knew from when you were friends with Geneviève?"

Eric kept Blair's hand in his for her sake as much as his own. "Without a doubt. It was Xylana."

He pursed his lips, looking at Blair before shifting his eyes to Liz. "Well, if my son says you are in danger from this demon, then you are welcome to stay here until we figure out what to do."

"We need to lure her out, Carlos. Xylana swore revenge when I took Tolan's life. I would bet my fangs youngblood deaths over the years have been her doing, and that Blair is just the latest victim of her machinations and manipulation. She couldn't find me to exact her revenge directly, so she took it out on any vampire she could find but in a cunning and very demonesque manner."

Lizzie's knuckles were white in her lap. "She got someone else to do her dirty work."

"Exactly, Liz. Me. She used me." Blair looked at her friend's anxious face. "You need to relax, babe. No one is going to hurt you here. You're safe as kittens. I warded the townhouse myself before you got here."

"Blair's right. No one is getting in or out who doesn't belong to this household," Eric reassured. "The human staff Xylana could manipulate have been given temporary paid leave, so they're no problem. They just hit the vacation lottery. Time off with pay they didn't have to ask for."

Liz looked from Blair to the vampires and back again. "What I don't understand is how she got to you in the first place, *cher*. Are you sure she didn't know you were her brother's spawn?"

"*Jesus*." Blair got up, pulling her hand from Eric's a little too roughly. "Can we all agree to stop calling me *that*? Please. If you have to refer to my paternal lineage at all, use the right terminology. Cambion. At least it sounds less...less...I don't know... Demonic."

Liz bristled. "You call yourself spawn. We joked about it."

"I know." Blair exhaled, giving her friend what she hoped was an apologetic look. "But now, not so much. The paternal side of my family is threatening the people I love. It's enough to make me want to crawl out my skin."

Carlos got up and poured two Jameson's double shots from Eric's stash. He handed one to her and one to Liz. "Drink this in one go, ladies. You both need to calm down."

Blair shot the whiskey back, draining the tumbler, but Liz nursed hers, obviously thinking.

"Dr. Wells must have read your thoughts to be able to play on your emotions so well." Liz nodded almost to herself. "It's like she pinpointed the exact nerve to tweak."

Eric shook his head. "Not Blair's thoughts. Sleep Demons, as Succubi and Incubi are sometimes called, are not mind readers. They have preternatural strength and speed, they can dream walk, and they have one skill they only share with the Fae—rippling."

"Rippling. Does it have to do with water? Like spirit entities supposedly can't cross a body of water?" Liz asked.

Carlos answered. "No, rippling is the ability to imagine a place and then be there. The Fae have a similar, but much more powerful ability, called *sieving*. They can imagine not only place, but time, and move backward and forward at whim."

Liz took a swig of her whiskey, wincing. "Smooth." She coughed, before using the edge of her glass to point at Blair. "You could still be a halfling Fae, right? Maybe we've got this succubi/incubi thing wrong, *cher*. You could do the sieve-thing and go back in time and save your mother."

"That's a nice thought, Liz, but I'm a Cambion. Too much evidence points to it being the only truth." Blair sat again, sliding an arm around her friend.

"We have to keep in mind that demons, like succubi and incubi are not attached to the human realm in any material way. Unlike vampires, they were never human. They are immortal beings with no prior humanity, and they can heal from almost any injury." Carlos shrugged. "In that, they are very much like the Fae. Same tree, just an evil branch. Even the Unseelie have no truck with demons. Not unless there's an advantage and the Dark Sidhe can keep the upper hand."

Liz finished her drink, putting the empty tumbler on the coffee table. "So if this succubus didn't read Blair's thoughts, then how did she know how to manipulate her so seamlessly?"

"My dreams. Or more likely, my nightmares. Suzy didn't chuck her slippers at me for nothing. My dreams are horror blockbusters up there with *Nightmare on Elm Street*."

"If that's the case," Carlos replied, "then she used your trauma to feed your underlying hate for the undead. I'm

sorry, *mija*, but those emotions would have had to exist in order for Xylana to twist them and flame them. She can't plant nightmares, not ones like that. She can become a nightmare herself. Allow her victims to watch as she ravages their bodies, draining their life force and soul energy, but she cannot concoct a nightmare such as yours.

"If a Sleep Demon is very adept, victims watch themselves age decades as their life force is stripped, until there's nothing left but a lifeless corpse. They steal soul energy and life force to prolong their own existence. They are immortal, but they still need to feed to maintain themselves."

Blair chewed on her lip. "Xylana was stunned to see Eric, and even more stunned when he told her about me. She didn't believe him at first because she couldn't sense my Cambion side."

"Grania did a bang-up job. I remember watching her in action. Of course, she was much younger then, but she was a powerful practitioner."

"She still is," Blair replied.

Carlos left the room for a moment, and, when he returned, he had a small platter with slices of cake and a few cookies.

"You're chewing on your lip like a little mouse, so I thought you might be hungry." He placed the plate on the coffee table. "You'll have to forgive us. We don't partake, so we sometimes forget our manners. It's not much, but you are welcome to it."

Blair and Liz both helped themselves.

"Thank you, Carlos. Sweets are comfort food when I'm stressed," Liz replied, taking a slice of banana bread.

Munching on a slice of butter pound cake, Blair pointed to Eric. "Grania's an elder now. She might be able to help us."

Carlos shook his head. "Leave the elder witch out of this, for now. Her skills may come in handy later."

Eric and Carlos shared a look, and the veiled gist wasn't lost on Blair. "Eric...I saw that look. If there's something I should know, you have to tell me."

"It's nothing of importance, *mija*. Not yet," Carlos replied. "Trust we will tell you if it becomes necessary. The less people who know about this, the better."

Blair had no choice but to accept the elder vampire's word. She trusted Eric, and he trusted Carlos like no other.

"Okay, then. What do we do?" she asked. "We've more or less figured out Xylana's tactic for taking backhanded revenge on Eric, which inadvertently led her to me. The fates are rolling the dice with us, and I would like to change the odds. What now?"

"I told you the only way to kill a succubus or an incubus is with pure light. Luckily, I still have the Star Sword Dominic gave me all those years ago."

Lizzie scrolled through her phone and then looked up at the group. "Look at what it says here." She read the passage. "Even though succubi are extremely powerful demons, they prefer not to engage in battle. They would rather hide in their human form and only fight in extreme cases."

Blair snorted. "Makes sense and fits Xylana to a tee. She posed as Dr. Lynetta Wells for years, feasting on the life force and souls of God knows how many students. Still, when Eric confronted her, she dropped her human guise but didn't attack. She flew the coop, literally."

"What else does the article say," Eric prompted.

Liz enlarged the screen for the rest. "Once threatened, a succubus will go underground. They are stealth beings and will wait out their quarry for centuries if necessary, lulling them into a state of forgetfulness. The only way to lure a succubus is with a pure soul. Untouched. It is the one thing they cannot resist. To do so, an object of value treasured by the demon must be used in a summoning."

Blair made a face again. "Anything else?" She leaned over to peer across Liz's shoulder.

"A succubus's heart is their most vulnerable organ. If pierced through, a succubus can falter, but the injury is only fatal if they are impaled with a sword of light. Ancient texts mention the weapon, but one has yet to be located. If a succubus is struck with a fatal blow, a bitten victim becomes a potential vessel for her spirit, provided she can get to them before she expires."

Blair took Lizzie's phone and scrolled through the rest of the article, reading where it spoke about incubi. "It took you all of five minutes to find this site, yet I sat in a dusty library in the lair of a Sleep Demon and came up empty until Eric made his connections." She handed the phone to her with a huff.

"Beginner's luck, I guess." Liz chuckled.

"The Internet isn't very reliable anyway." Blair waved one hand. "Anyone could have written that article."

Liz looked at her phone again and then at Blair.

"Ugh, don't tell me." Blair covered Liz's hand as she held up her phone for the accreditation. Blair closed her eyes, with a hard exhale.

"Dr. Lynetta Wells?" Eric asked.

Lizzie nodded.

Carlos sat in his chair. "Whatever the article says, Xylana has gone underground. I think we have no choice

but to wait her out. She knows Eric will defend Blair with his life, and she knows he has access to a fatal weapon."

"Not necessarily," Lizzie began, locking her cell phone screen and stuffing it in her purse. "She says an innocent. Pure and untouched."

Blair shook her head, her eyes tracking Lizzie's resolute expression. "If you're saying what I think you're saying, then no, Liz. Not on your life."

Carlos watched the interaction. "I'm not following. If Liz has an idea, we should hear it."

Lizzie eyeballed her friend. "Please don't make me embarrass myself, Care Blair."

Eric coughed, spewing his drink.

"One word, vamp boy, and you sleep on the couch." Blair addressed Eric's snicker but kept her eyes on Lizzie. "No, Liz. I won't let you do this."

"What won't you allow, *mija*?" Carlos asked.

"Liz wants to use herself as bait. She is…untouched," Blair replied, delicately.

The meaning dawned on the elder vampire, and he nodded. "That's very brave of you, *mija*. But no. It's too dangerous."

Eric agreed, mopping the front of his shirt and the coffee table. "Blair can forgive me teasing her about a nickname, but she could never forgive *herself* if something happened to you."

"What could happen with you three there to have my back," Liz asked, looking to each.

Blair was incredulous. "You just read off a laundry list of what that succubus bitch could do. What if Xylana bites you and then takes over your body? Or, more likely, she drains your life force, leaving you a dried husk?" She

shook her head. "I agree with Carlos and Eric. It's too dangerous."

"I appreciate their chivalry and your loyalty, *cher*, but this is my decision. If Xylana can't resist a pure soul, then I'm about as pure as you're going to get in New York. You and I will go to the demon's office and swipe something of hers. There has to be something she treasures in those offices. Like you said, it was her lair."

Blair didn't have a choice. If she didn't say yes, Liz would just go it alone. "Okay, but you and I go to her office by ourselves. I don't want any of Dr. Lynetta Wells' minions to get suspicious."

Chapter Seventeen

"Maintenance is going to shit twice once I lift the wards and they see what happened. Lynetta blew the windows out, for fuck's sake. I'd like to see her try and explain that without glamour." Blair fumbled with her keys, thankful the staff knew she was a Wells' favorite and didn't raise an eyebrow.

She and Lizzie walked through the door, making sure to close it against prying eyes. Leading the way, Blair stopped short with a jump.

"Eric! What the hell?"

"Fancy meeting you here." Eric chuckled. "We took the vampire way up instead of the elevator." He pointed to the still-shattered window.

Carlos sat on the daybed, thumbing through a magazine. "This succubus is well published. I'm impressed. They aren't usually productive entities." He closed the glossy book, tossing it to the side.

"What are you two doing here? I thought we said Lizzie and I would handle the treasure hunt."

"That's my fault," Liz said sheepishly. "You're always talking about stacking the odds in our favor, *cher*." She shrugged. "So I did."

"What I want to know is why the window is still in a shattered state? Doesn't the school have a maintenance crew?" Carlos asked, brushing shards of glass from his pants, his tiny sliver wounds healing immediately.

"That one's on me. I warded the office so people would think everything was in order." Blair gave Eric a guilty grin. "I should have told you."

"You think? Why would you ward the office, knowing it might tip off the succubus?"

"I didn't think of that. I only wanted to keep her minions from snooping around. If she manipulated me into killing youngblood vampires, God knows what she could compel one of them to do."

Carlos nodded. "Smart." He stood and looked around at the art and the books in the cases. "This succubus left us much to choose from." He pointed to the ancient fertility sculptures and the ancient Viking rings and belt embellishments.

"What about these?" Liz pointed to Shakespeare folios in the locked bookcase.

Blair shook her head. "All good ideas, but I know this bitch better than anyone. There's only one thing in this lair she treasures more than anything. I didn't understand its significance until I learned about my biological father."

She went to the locked bookcase and pressed her thumb to the ID keypad. The electronic lock snicked, and she slid open the glass. Reaching inside, she took the most nondescript item in the case. A silver tie pin with a blood-red carnelian at the top, making it look like a miniature wand or mystical walking stick.

"I admired this once, and Dr. Wells actually got a little misty as she told me about her brother, and how he was viciously murdered trying to save his only child from abduction." Blair snorted. "Talk about delusional." Closing the case, she stuck the tie pin in her purse.

"Well, that went a hex of a lot faster than I expected." Lizzie grinned.

Blair chuckled. "I told you we didn't need team testosterone."

"Yeah, standing right here, ladies." Eric cleared his throat. "So, what should we do now?"

Blair took Liz by the hand and gave it a squeeze. "We help my amazing best friend summon a demon."

***

Blair and Liz set the circle, lighting sage candles at the five points of the salt pentacle. Along the inner cross sections, Blair put obelisks of labradorite and obsidian for protection and diversion.

"Those are lovely, *mija*. I understand the salt and the star, but I've never seen such small, beautiful towers. What are they for?"

"The vibrant colored obelisk is made from labradorite. It is a mystical stone that can illuminate the darkness and remove the evil eye. It diverts harmful energies and acts as a shield to keep the circle protected."

"And the black one? It's obsidian, yes?"

She nodded, flashing Carlos an appreciative smile. "Yes. Obsidian is a powerful stone used to absorb negativity. We place it at the points on the pentale that channel ley line energy. The crystals will form a protective shield, kind of like a bubble. It will trap Xylana when she answers the summons, but it will also protect our auras from attack. Other stones can do the same job, but I chose obsidian because it has one specific property we need."

"What's that?"

She inhaled, straightening her shoulders. "It will stop Xylana from influencing or manipulating me. She's done so in the past, so I need to make sure she doesn't use me to harm any of you."

Carlos touched Blair's cheek. "Eric is lucky to have found such a clever mate."

Heat tickled her cheeks, and, as if taking her cue, Carlos dropped his hand to his side.

"I want to thank you for letting us do this in your courtyard. I didn't want to use your house, but I think we'll be okay outside. You have lots of raw soil surrounding the patio to redirect energy if necessary, plus it's always a good ground for witches to keep close to Mother Earth."

Lizzie brought the last of the crystals and placed them beside the sage candles. Amethyst for clarity and focus.

"Blair, I really wish we had one more woman with us. Two is just not enough feminine energy. Especially not when we're fighting a female. You should have let me call Tara."

She shook her head. "No. Like I said the first five times we discussed this, Carlos said the fewer people who know, the better it will be all around—"

"Blair," Eric interrupted. "I couldn't help but overhear your argument earlier. So I took it upon myself to find someone to help."

Natasha stepped out of the sliding glass doors from the townhouse and onto the moonlit patio.

"Remember me?" she asked.

Blair nodded. "Of course, I remember. How did Eric find you? Are you sure you want to help us with this? You know we're trying to kill a demon, right?"

Natasha laughed. "Slow down. One question at a time, please."

"Of course. I'm sorry." Blair turned, calling Lizzie over. "Liz, this is Natasha. She's a Were Cougar, and one of Eric's…" she paused.

"Friends." Nat finished the sentence. "To answer your questions. One, Eric can find me anytime he wants. Once you share blood with a vampire, you wear their mark, sort of like GPS. You have one on your throat as well. I can see it, though it's very faint. Two, of course I want to help. I've even memorized your summons...and three, demons need to have their butts kicked from time to time, if only to remind them that our realm is not their playground nor their toilet."

Liz laughed. "Oh, *cher*. I like you. A whole lot."

"Okay then, let's get started. I think it best if we do this sky clad," Blair nodded. "What do you think?"

Natasha shrugged. "I'm a Were. The cold doesn't bother me, and I love being naked. Makes for a much easier shift."

"Do we have to?" Lizzie asked. "I'm not used to your northern cold yet. Hex, I wear socks to bed in summer."

Blair eyeballed her, and she exhaled. "Fine, but one of you had better get me a double shot of whatever whiskey Carlos gave me last night."

"I anticipated as much," Eric said carrying a tray with three large tumblers filled with his Glen Scotia.

The three took their glasses, each touching the other with a soft clink. "To feminine energy."

Blair downed hers in one shot, going up on tiptoe to peck Eric's lips. "You have our secret weapon?"

He patted the inside pocket of his jacket. "Carlos and I will be outside your circle waiting for your signal, if you need us. You have to do this, Blair. I could, but this is your bloodline, so it will be final if you strike the blow."

She nodded. "I understand."

Eric handed her the Star Sword, and she placed it on the outer rim of the pentagram, well within the circle and still within her reach.

The three women stood naked on the inside ring. At the center, Blair placed Tolan's tie pin. With a nod, they held their hands out, palms up, and began the summons.

Demon of sleep and dreams beyond,
Flesh of your flesh a child spawned.
Your darkness chained; your appetite bound,
We summon you here this circle round.

The air swirled, bitter cold. It whipped at the candles, trying to douse their flames. Lizzie smirked. "She can bluster and blow all she wants, but candle magic is my thing."

"You go, girl," Natasha chuckled. "I wish I could do this. All I get to do is shift to my cat and hope I don't end up with fleas."

"I think you get to do a lot more than that, but I don't think Eric will be making trips to the park anytime soon. Not unless he's with me."

"*Ah ha.* I told you!" Nat grinned. "I guess if he doesn't need me anymore, then he must have passed the blood test."

"With flying colors."

The ground shook, rattling the flagstones, but they held the circle tight. Blair winked at Liz. "Now, that one is me. I figured she'd try to suck us into her hidey-hole, so I warded the property and everywhere in between."

"Heads up, ladies." Lizzie swore as the inner circle swirled with a black mist. It curled like fingers searching for something to latch onto, but it found nothing and evaporated with a wrenching groan.

"Which one of you was that?" Nat asked.

"Both," Liz replied. She looked at Blair. "Part two?"

She nodded, and they began the second chant.

Come with haste, no time to waste,

Your demon ass into this place.

Your mouth will water, some juicy bits,

The innocence here, you can't resist.

A token waits, a treasure stolen,

If you want it back, get a rollin'.

Blair had to bite the inside of her cheek. The second half of the summons wasn't exactly orthodox, but it gave them a chuckle writing it. And why not? The task ahead was dangerous and heavy enough.

The center circle blackened as though scorched from the inside out, and Blair darted forward, snatching the tie pin before it melted.

The charred slate reeked of paraffin and burnt wood, but the odor faded when a puddle formed in the smaller circle. It filled the space, spreading until it hit the salt and sage. With a hiss, it receded, swirling and eddying in a mini whirlpool until a figure rose from the black pool.

Xylana stood, levitating over the tainted liquid. "How dare you summon me, spawn!"

"Nice to see you, too, Auntie X." Blair tossed the tie pin in her hand. "I decided to take the tie pin from your office. It's only fair, right? Technically, Tolan was my father, so the family heirloom should go to me."

Xylana shrieked, banshee-like as she did when she'd shattered the office window, but now there was no sound. Her hand shot to her throat, and red eyes narrowed at Blair.

"Yup. All me. I bound your powers while you're in our circle, and since we've got you in an obsidian bubble,

layered with wards and other witchy goodies, you aren't going anywhere."

The succubus gnashed her sharp teeth, her lips peeling over black gums.

"God, you're ugly. How long did it take for you to do up your glamour every day for school? Must have been so uncomfortable. Like wearing double Spanx all day. Betcha couldn't wait to rip that human condom from your body, huh?"

"Let me go, spawn. You're my flesh. My blood. I could teach you so much." Xylana's tongue darted snakelike, testing the air. She reached a hand toward Blair, her finger twirling as if trying to reel in a thread she'd planted.

Blair shook her head. "It's gone, Xylana. It severed the moment I learned the truth about myself, you, and your shit-heel brother."

The succubus swiped at Blair with razor claws, her eyes frantic at being held captive. She whirled but then stopped, her eyes shifting from red to black and then to a human brown. She straightened, and, with a whoosh, transformed to her human form.

"Lizzie, so nice to see you again." Her eyes glinted as she tried to keep her snakelike tongue from hissing, but it wouldn't cooperate.

The woman's eyes dilated. "So fresh. I do believe you are the only virgin over the age of twenty-one in the entire metropolitan area."

She laughed, and the sound was tinny and harsh. "Once in a while, I get lucky, and find a delicious freshman, still young and untouched. I usually have to get to them before the school year gets into full swing, or it's too late. But, you. A virgin witch!" Her eyes glittered to red and black, and her snake's tongue darted again. "You

will be worth every one of my brother's spawn's degradations."

She turned to Blair. "She's your offering, no? Wasn't that part of your summons?"

"So? You're powerless to do anything about it."

Xylana nodded. "True. Now. But the moment you release me, your virgin friend is mine. When you tempt a demon to a summons, what you use as a lure belongs to that demon once released."

Lizzie's face fell, and she glanced toward Eric and Carlos.

"Don't worry, Lizzie. She lies. Can't you tell?" Blair nodded. "Do you remember the spell I told you earlier? The one I used on Eric to see his true colors."

Liz licked her lips and repeated the words.

Magic forces here and now
Lend your sight, the truth allow
Show this witch her evil heart
Her motives show, so there's no doubt.

Xylana's human guise dissolved instantly, and her normally reddish skin was mottled black. Her swirling aura showed murky, with streaks of a sickly yellow.

Like vomit.

"See?" Blair said, lifting a hand to the deceit. "She holds no claim on you or anyone else."

Xylana opened her mouth for a banshee-like screech again, only this time the wards cracked. Not enough to set her free but enough to embolden the demon.

With a snarl, she spread her wings, and the great scaled span flapped, sending leaves and lawn furniture flying, but the candles stayed lit and glowing. She flew at Blair with clawed fingers and a scream on her lips.

"Eric!" Blair yelled.

He dove for the knife at the outer circle, tossing it to Blair. She issued a silent prayer she didn't drop the damn thing or, worse, let Xylana catch it.

Blair leaped, snatching it from the air just as Xylana broke through the wards. Seeing the blade, the demon pivoted last minute and aimed for the skies.

"Blair! Stop her! She's getting away!" Lizzie yelled.

The witch's voice caught the demon's attention, and she changed direction again, making straight for the Cajun witch.

Her clawed feet sank deep into Lizzie's shoulder and she rotated in a whirl, yanking her from the circle.

Liz screamed, and Blair hurled spell after spell, trying not to hit her friend. White energy scorched Xylana's wings so she couldn't fly, but the demon held tight, aiming for the black pool portal.

Blair chased her, throwing out her hand.

"Obliviscatur!"

She yelled the last spell, closing the portal, but Natasha got there first, shifting to animal form on the fly.

With a piercing cat's shriek, the sleek animal launched from powerful hind legs. She leapt, sinking lethal canines into the demon's leg, dragging her down to the circle again. The succubus hit the ground, clawed fingers slashing at the magnificent cat, scoring her gut.

The cougar dropped to the ground, blood pooling with the salt in the pentagram. Blood spilled on spelled earth was never a good thing. The ground beneath the circle steamed and cracked.

Blair fisted the Star Sword. She had to strike before a magical recoil sent them all hurtling. She lunged for Xylana's heart, but she was too late.

Lizzie's throat was ripped wide, and the demon laughed at her with her friend's blood staining her razor teeth.

"No!" Rage, white hot and scorching, bubbled in Blair's chest. Her skin rippled and prickled in the heat, and when she looked, she saw the outline of scales across her flesh.

Grania's bonds were unraveling. Maybe this was the magical backlash. Either way, she had to act fast. Xylana was high on Lizzie's soul energy. If there was a chance at all to save her friend, it was now.

Blair bolted, using the demon speed unfettered in her blood to plunge the blade straight through Xylana's heart. The demon screamed, and the sound was jarring. Her red scaled body undulated, her muscles twisting unnaturally. With a final jagged screech, the succubus slumped to the ground.

Blair twisted the blade in her chest to make sure the bitch was dead. Pulling it loose, she frowned at the black sludge coating the blade. It hissed, steam rising until it burst into flame.

The ground where Xylana fell was coated with the same fluid, and, in seconds, the demon's body melted into the same dark muck.

Eric and Carlos rushed into the circle—Eric taking Lizzie, and Carlos taking Natasha.

"Hurry, *mijo*. We have no time!"

Biting his wrist, Eric held the welling blood over Liz's mouth. He squeezed his fist, forcing it to come faster.

It ran into her mouth and over her chin, but, finally, she coughed, taking hold of his arm for more.

"You're going to be okay now, Liz," he said with a chuckle. "Any more and you might end up a member of the undead."

Carlos motioned for Eric to help him. Natasha's wounds were much more severe. It took both of them to heal her enough to move her inside.

Eric stayed behind with Blair, helping her burn what was left of the succubus and her blood and restore the earth to its pristine state.

"It's over, love," he said, opening his arms to her.

She tucked herself against his chest and drew in a ragged breath. "No, it's not. My demon side broke through tonight. Something's happening, and I don't know what it is. Maybe it's a repercussion for turning on my own blood."

"Blair—" He slipped his fingers under her chin, forcing her to look at him. "Your blood is fine. In fact, it's delicious. What happened holds no magical corollary. It was fury and fear, and every emotion in-between tearing at you in the moment. The last time you faced that you were too young to understand what was happening to you or why you survived. This time, you controlled the situation and saved both Lizzie and Natasha."

"Maybe, but Natasha's injuries are going to involve the Alpha of the Brethren. There's no keeping what happened or what I've done from the Vampire Council now. I'm sure Carlos would agree."

"I do, *mija*," Carlos replied from the sliding doors leading inside. "I said it before, and I meant it. Eric is lucky to have such a clever mate, but you need to let us handle the council and the Alpha of the Brethren. You show up when called and let us take care of the rest. *Comprendes*?"

She nodded. "I understand."

Eric exchanged another look with Carlos, and this time all she could do was bite her tongue and hope they had things under control.

Chapter Eighteen

*R*émy sat in one of the three council chairs in *Le Sanctuaire*, the vampire heart of the Red Veil and the seat of the Vampire Council of New York. Carlos sat beside him, along with Dominic De'Lessep, who'd made the trip especially.

Blair stood in front of the three with Tara and Caitlan. Lizzie stayed in the background. Neither Supreme looked happy, but their presence was required as heads of both coven houses, Crow and Raven.

Rémy looked imposing in the center chair. It signified him as Master Vampire and Adjudicator General. He sat cross-legged with the ruined side of his face turned toward the stone hearth. The fireplace blazed, accenting the ornate room in a warm glow. The soft glimmer cast the vampires in a forgiving light, but their faces said otherwise. This meeting was no trifling matter, and Blair's sweaty palms and the damp trickle between her breasts proved that.

"Blair Cabot, do you understand the charges leveled against you?" The question was basically rhetorical, but nonetheless, it required asking for protocol's sake.

"Yes." Her answer was direct. No ands or buts or rambling explanations. Again, protocol. All evidence had been presented beforehand, but judgement had been withheld awaiting Dominic's arrival.

"Is there anyone who wishes to speak on the Cambion's behalf?" Rémy scanned the small group.

Blair cringed at the word, but as it was the truth of her parentage, there was no arguing with the reality.

Sean Leighton stood at the back with Natasha. As Alpha of the Brethren, he wanted to be present whenever a Were was called before any council, especially the vampires. Nat wasn't under indictment, but she was called nonetheless.

Eric stepped forward. "I would speak on Blair's behalf."

"As would I," Natasha replied stepping to Eric's side.

Rémy spared a look for Sean who inclined his head, before addressing the cougar. "You have given your statement, and it is appreciated. You may stay, if you wish, but we ask no interference. Lives have been lost, and reparations need to be paid."

"Reparations." Natasha lifted her chin. "That's a little one-sided, don't you think? Do humans or Weres have the right to reparations for the lives taken by the few undead scumbags the witch took out?"

"Natasha—"

Sean eyed the shifter, but she lifted a hand to signal she would behave.

"Go on," Carlos prompted.

Nat spared a look for Sean and then looked at Carlos directly. "I run the Rambles often, not just to chase the full moon. I myself have been surrounded by two, three rogue vampires all looking for more than a nip from my neck. No pretext of friendship or communion, just a wham, bam, thank you ma'am. I've left claw marks across more than one pale, translucent face.

"I've seen youngbloods terrorize the homeless in the park and have had to come to their rescue along with a few others of my kind. We can't race the moon under any phase with peace. Once Blair began hunting, the park calmed, and its residents relaxed. I didn't know it was her

doing when I met her, but I thank her for doing what you three should have been doing from the beginning."

Three sets of undead eyes watched her, unblinking. Sean stepped forward and gently took Natasha by the arm, making her step back.

Settling her, the Alpha met Rémy's eyes and nodded. "Weres have been reporting these facts to me for months now. It's why I insisted on coming tonight. Not just to be here for Natasha but to reiterate her claims. The HepZ virus cast our world into a panicked frenzy for survival, but the fallout hasn't been just infected donors and rabid Weres. Inattention has been a consequence."

"Inattention," Carlos reiterated. "Are you saying the council and elders have neglected our youth?"

Sean shrugged. "You called this tribunal and even flew in an ancient elder to sit in judgement over someone you deemed a vigilante. Might I remind you, my mate was also deemed such yet was never called before you in this manner. Was that because her blood held the cure for HepZ, or because mitigating circumstances called for leniency and understanding?

"As I don't know the particulars of this case, I can only assume you are here to determine if there are also mitigating circumstances that apply here. I can't speak for Blair Cabot or the reasons for her actions, but I can speak to secondary circumstances that gave rise to another so-called vigilante, and that is the inattention of the vampire elder population. Beginning with Sebastién, you were all concerned with saving your own hides and providing for your own sustenance when the donor wells ran dry. My Weres and hunters were called in, and rightly so, to help find and eradicate infection. One of mine was responsible

for the virus, so we gladly offered that help. But that's beside the point.

"Elders, and even older youngbloods, did nothing to stem the wanton creation of new fledglings, and even less to teach them respect for other supernaturals or even respect for your own laws and territories. It only follows, this new generation of undead were bound to run wild, wreaking havoc. When taboos were lifted, I took responsibility for all species of Weres and made sure my kind understood the limitations and risks inherent with mixing with the undead. Blair Cabot may be guilty, I don't know, but you share accountability in events as they unfolded, from your inaction regarding your own."

Dominic raised an eyebrow, a tiny curl at the corner of his full lips. "I can see why you are the Alpha of the Brethren of all Weres. Very astute, and, of course, very correct. We have been remiss, but—" He turned his eyes to Blair. "Our neglect does not absolve your actions, young woman. Does anyone else have anything to add?"

The elder eyed Eric, and the young vampire nodded. "As I said earlier, I do."

"Eric, you asked the council to wait for your oral testimony, but now I ask for it for the benefit of our guest adjudicator." Rémy gestured to Dominic. "Please go ahead."

"Thank you, Rémy. I bear witness to the fact Blair Cabot acted not of her own will but under a compulsion placed on her by a succubus. A demoness she unwittingly encountered and befriended, by the name of Xylana." He met each set of eyes directly. "I know this to be true because I also encountered her. Twice. Once at the NYU library where she worked under the guise of a professor

by the name of Dr. Lynetta Wells and once in 1944 when she targeted me as prey."

Carlos's brows pulled together. "Prey. That makes no sense, *mijo*. In 1944 you were already undead for decades. You have no soul, so you would be of no interest to a succubus other than for sexual gratification."

"Carlos, you and I have been arguing for nearly seventy-five years about whether or not vampires have souls. I'm here to tell you we do. I know because Xylana tried to seduce me for mine. She entered my dreams to try and feed from my soul energy, much in the same way she would a human or a witch.

"Fortunately for me, she didn't count on undead thirst or on this particular vampire's survival reflexes. Demon blood is foul, but it won't kill. Or so I found out the hard way. It was then Xylana let me in on a guarded secret. That a vampire's soul is no longer in a protected state of grace. It exists in limbo. Not damned but in a perpetual state of waiting. Because of that, if a succubus or an incubus is so inclined, they feed off that soul at whim."

The buzz in the room was audible, and Rémy had to bang his fist on his chair to silence the undead gallery.

"How does this relate to the Cambion's actions?" Dominic asked.

"In 1944, I learned the reason for Xylana's attentions. She wanted to keep me from Geneviève Cabot, Blair Cabot's biological mother. Genny, as I called her, was a friend. She was also a witch. A member of Crow Haven House coven. Xylana's brother, an incubus named Tolan, had seduced my friend body and soul, stealing her life force and her will over the course of three years. When I found out, I tried to put a stop to it. It ended badly."

Eric told the council the entire story, including how Dominic had given him the Star Sword. How he returned to save Genny, but it was too late. She had died giving birth to Blair.

"I killed Tolan when he tried to claim the baby. Xylana vowed revenge, but I had gone underground by then. As Carlos will attest, I had a hard time processing loss and rage then."

Carlos gave Eric a soft smile. "Even now, *mijo*. Under extreme circumstances."

Rémy looked from one to the other and then shared a look with Dominic. "Rosa. Of course," he added. "But those were extenuating circumstances."

"And so are these, Rémy," Eric countered. "Xylana found Blair by sheer chance. In her own lair, at the NYU Mythological Studies department. Plenty of fresh young men and women with beautiful souls to reap. She targeted Blair as prey, only to discover her true Cambion nature. From there, it wasn't a far reach for the succubus to put the puzzle pieces together once she realized Blair was also a witch.

"She used her, manipulating emotions linked to tragic events from her pasts into revenge. Blair Cabot was compelled to action. Xylana couldn't get to me directly, so she avenged herself on the next best thing. Youngbloods."

Rémy considered Eric's words but held himself in reserve. "Is there any way to prove this?"

Natasha moved to speak again, and Rémy was about to stop her, but Carlos intervened. "You have something else to add, Natasha?"

"Yes. I witnessed this demon firsthand and carry her scars across my flank. I would be dead if it wasn't for Eric and Carlos. They witnessed the succubus as well, heard

what she said to Blair, her manipulations even until the end. She's dead by Blair Cabot's hand, but I still stand with what I said before. I'm glad Blair inadvertently enforced your laws while you were preoccupied elsewhere.

"Your new youngbloods are cruel and out of control. They kill and torture for sport. No elegance in their feeding or thought for anything but their own desires. If you don't act to check them, you three will be responsible for setting vampire kind back hundreds of years."

Sean tugged her arm this time with a look that said, "enough." With a nod to the three adjudicators, he left the council room with Natasha in tow.

Dominic stood. "I, too, can offer proof. I gave Eric the Star Sword, as he said, but I can also scan his mind to see if the record needs further irrefutable proof."

"Adjudicators, I ask for what's just, not what some might demand to save vampiric face." Eric turned to stare at those grumbling from the gallery. "Blair Cabot doesn't deserve to die for her actions. If consequences are to be levied, they should come from her Supremes, not us."

Rémy eyed Eric, and he shut up. "You make an impassioned speech, but this is a verdict the adjudicators will decide. Not you, and not the witches."

Dominic held his hand out, and Eric stepped forward. "Give me something of yours. Something attached to the events would be best."

Eric reached into his pocket and pulled out a photo of him and Genny. He'd planned to give it to Blair once this was over.

Dominic looked at the old black-and-white snapshot. With a soft smile, he nodded. "This will do perfectly."

The elder closed his eyes, and Eric held his breath. Seconds ticked by, and finally Dominic lifted his lids. He returned the photo to Eric and then stood.

"Eric Fraser speaks the truth. I saw everything just as he said. Minute by minute, day by day, year by year. The succubus he saw at the NYU library was the same one who tried to drain his soul. I watched him kill her sibling, the incubus Tolan, and then watched as the succubus rail in her need for revenge. I also witnessed what he saw in the demon's face when she recognized him. The evil in her eyes and how she tried to compel Blair to take silver to him. Blair Cabot is guilty of one thing, and that is being too susceptible to her Cambion side. It must be stripped from her, or she runs the risk of falling prey again, or, worse, coming into her own as spawn." He looked to Rémy and Carlos. "What say you?"

They both nodded. "Agreed."

Blair kept her face impassive. She had to trust Eric and Carlos, yet Caitlan slipped her arm through her elbow as if to say, no way.

The Supreme lifted her chin. "You make it sound as though powers and abilities can be cherry-picked, like a mix-and-match menu. Stripping Blair's inherent nature, albeit bound, is likely to be very painful, Dominic. It might even kill her. Or at the very least, leave her completely powerless. She would no longer be a witch."

Dominic lifted a conciliatory hand to the Supreme as he took his seat once more. "I am aware of the possible consequences for your young witch, and I am sorry for her, but, compelled or not, she willfully killed at least a dozen youngbloods over the past year, if not more.

"I, and the other elders, will own our culpability with our fledgling undead, and will rectify that. You and Tara,

as Supremes, must own yours and rectify your end as well. That means stripping your witch. The end result will be as fate decrees, but our verdict has been decided. You can either abide by our ruling, or we will exact justice *our* way."

Caitlan and Tara each linked their arms around Blair as she faced the three vampire elders.

"Blair Cabot, what say you?"

She met the adjudicators' eyes. "I understand your verdict, and I accept the consequences of my actions. I know I am not in a position to ask for anything, but I will anyway."

The room buzzed again, but one look from Dominic quieted them in seconds.

"Go on," he said, inclining his head.

She untangled herself from Caitlan and Tara and then moved to stand beside Eric. She didn't reach for his hand or link her arm with his because she knew it would be viewed as unseemly. Just standing beside him made her point.

"If the fates bless me, and I survive my ordeal, whether as a witch or as a powerless human, I ask that you give Eric and I leave to explore what destiny holds for us. Without bile or fear of reprisal. It seems I began life with Eric as my safe haven. I'd like to see if that holds for my future as well."

Carlos didn't wait for his brother adjudicators. "Granted."

The set to Eric's mouth softened a fraction, but his lips stayed a thin line. Even if he could change things, Blair had accepted the consequence. His hands were tied.

It was déjà vu from when he faced his own judge all those years ago. Like him, Blair had one choice. To take the odds and roll the dice for life.

Epilogue

*B*lair stood in the Raven motherhouse library with Grania, her mother's diaries safely stowed in the old Raven's warded bookshelf.

"Are you ready, sweetheart?" the old woman asked.

Blair lifted one shoulder. "As ready as I'll ever be." She paused, helping Grania from her seat. "Will it hurt much? The stripping, I mean."

"Who told you it would hurt?" Grania asked, reaching for her cane.

Blair's brows pulled together. "Caitlan. She told Dominic it was very painful, and it might even kill me."

"Tosh. Stripping a witch's power is light-years easier than binding them. I could do a stripping in my sleep."

Eric met them in the doorway. "I told Blair you were a force to be reckoned with." He pecked the old witch's cheek. "I'm glad you're doing this for Blair. I wouldn't trust anyone else with her well-being."

"Still a charmer, I see." She patted his cheek. "Is everything ready? Exactly as I requested?"

"Yes, ma'am."

She nodded. "Good. Then let's not waste another minute. If I see one more scale pop up on that beautiful child's skin, I swear I'm going to lose my shit!"

Blair nearly choked on her tongue. "Grania. Language!"

"Now you sound like your mother. I loved her like a sister, but she was definitely Miss Prissy Pants. Just like your friend Liz, God help her. It's unnatural for a witch to be a virgin."

Blair helped the old woman into the narrow elevator and then shut the old-fashioned gate. "Geneviève had an illicit affair with a demon and gave birth to his illegitimate spawn. That doesn't sound like someone very prissy. And as for Liz, she'll be fine. She'll meet the right one, and nature will take it from there."

Shutting the gate, Blair pushed the button for the top floor. She had opted for the roof to have the ritual done. If she wasn't meant to stay a witch, then the last thing she wanted to see before her powers faded was the full moon and its silver light.

The elevator bumped to a stop, and she pulled the gate open, getting out first so she could help Grania. The old witch squinted into the dark as they moved at a snail's pace up the short flight of steps to the rooftop.

"You know, Eric could have flown you up here, or jumped or something. I can't keep his abilities straight. It seems the older vampires get, the more talents they acquire, including daywalking, as in walk in the sun again."

Grania chuckled. "I know, dear. Who do you think helped Carlos with him back in the day?"

Blair's mouth dropped, and Grania pursed her lips. "Close your mouth, Blair. We are not a cod fish."

The young witch smiled wide. "You sound like my mom...well, my adopted mom."

"I know. I chose her for you, too." She patted Blair's hand. "I told you a little fib when I gave you your mother's diaries. I always knew who you were. I've been keeping a gentle eye on you all these years. I haven't gone to my rest because I couldn't. My job wasn't done. You see, I promised your mother I would keep you safe. Despite

Of Blood and Magic

Xylana and all her machinations, I managed to do just that, for decades.

"I knew Tolan's blood would give you extreme longevity. Not quite immortal but close. Even longer than a Were. I had to live so you would be safe. The vampires have helped me over the years. Their blood sustaining me so I could keep my promise to Genny."

Blair's mouth dropped again. "So it was Xylana who got to my first set of adopted parents."

"Unfortunately, yes. I had to do some quick thinking on that one. I not only bound your Cambion side, I augmented your witchy side to camouflage you even more. Eric had glamoured the orphanage and the adoption agency personnel, so when you showed up on their books again, they scrambled to find you another home.

"I paid the Moore family a visit after you were placed with them. I don't remember under what pretext, but they let me see you. You were only about three or four years old at the time…or at least that's how old you appeared. I had to do some fancy magical footwork to get you to age normally after your placement with them. I didn't need them hauling you from doctor to doctor, trying to figure out why you weren't aging.

"Now, if the stripping is a success, I can reverse that spell, and you will return to aging slowly." She winked. "Give you all the time you want with your vampire, without having to face growing old while he still looks so yummy."

"Grania, you dirty girl."

"I may not have any money in my pocket, but I can still window-shop, little girl."

They got to the top level, finally, and Blair waited while the old witch caught her breath.

"Grania, if you're successful, and you strip my demon side, won't I start aging immediately? You know, have it all catch up, or if not that, won't I age like a regular human?"

She shook her head. "No. Your blood is your blood. A Cambion's longevity isn't linked to their demon abilities, it's part of your DNA. Stop worrying. You and Eric will be together a very, very long time, and you will never have to make the choice to become undead in order to be with him."

They stepped out onto the roof, and there in the center of the circle of salt were Caitlan, Tara, and Lizzie. Standing at each point were Eric, Carlos, Rémy, Dominic, and another vampire she didn't recognize.

She raised an eyebrow as Eric came to help her with Grania. "Who's the sandy-haired vamp?"

Grania answered first. "That's Julian. Eric's brother. He's here because you finally gave Eric a reason to stop scowling."

The tiny smirk on Julian's lips told Blair his vampire ears heard everything, so she whispered, "It's nice to meet you, too, and you're welcome!"

His grin widened, and he inclined his head.

"Stop talking about me," Eric teased, pressing a kiss to her temple. "I'm right here."

"So am I, and according to Grania, I will be for a very, very long time." Blair motioned toward old Raven. "Provided the stripping works."

With a wink, Grania left them on their own to go and greet Tara and the other Crows.

"It will work, love," Eric said, pressing another kiss to her hair. "And after it's all over, I want you to do something for me."

"What? Something kinky?"

He shook his head. "A handfast."

"A handfast." Blair blinked. "Eric Fraser, are you asking me to marry you?"

He nodded, pulling her into his arms. "Yes. To all of the above. I'm asking you to marry me, and if you want do something kinky, I'm all in."

"Let's get my demon side exorcised first. If Lizzie calls me demon spawn one more time, I'm going to give the girl a tail."

He slipped his arms around her waist, locking her in tight. "Nope. Not until I get an answer. Blair Cabot, will you marry me and be my own personal demon?"

"Yes, but without the scaly skin." Laughing, she nodded but then lifted her chin to search his eyes. "I'll be okay, right?"

"Grania's got this covered, love. Carlos and I already knew what the verdict would be. Would I have agreed if I didn't know you'd be safe as kittens?" He shook his head. "I would have secreted you away, and we'd have lived happily ever after as two hermits."

"After you killed Xylana, Carlos and I consulted with Rémy and Dominic. Everyone agreed this was the safest way for all involved. The mob-mentality vampires would have their symbolic pound of flesh, but you would still be exonerated. Most importantly, we could live our happily ever after without the hermit bit."

She chuckled. "Hey, don't knock the solitude. As long as there's take-out Chinese, I'm good."

Kissing her mouth, he whispered, "You're more than good, Blair. You're mesmerizing."

"And we'll be okay, right?"

He nodded, brushing her lips once more. "With you, there's nothing a little blood and magic can't handle."

Acknowledgements

When an author publishes a book, whether it's their first or their five hundredth, it's nothing less than a defining moment in their life. Since I began this writer's journey, I've run the gamut in terms of emotion…from *no excuses, do the work…* to *what was I thinking? To be careful what you ask for because you just might get it!*

This is my eighth book in the Cursed by Blood saga, and I still have to pinch myself. So many people have helped and encouraged me, even when the writing dragon had me spewing fire and belching smoke at every turn.

My unbelievably patient husband, Bill, for putting up with the insanity and verbal barrages that accompany being glued to my laptop for hours. Our three kids for knowing enough to leave Mom alone when she's writing, despite laundry piling up and pasta for dinner, yet again.

My amazing alpha readers: Kathryn Parson, Patricia Statham, Lisa Errion, Bonnie Jean Aurigemma, Rene Hurt, and Sherily Toledo. Without you guys I would be lost.

My editor, Kate Richards and her staff at Wizards in Publishing, including line editor/proofreader, Nanette Sipe. Whether it's a full content edit, line edit, a proofread, or content brainstorming, you guys rock!

And last but certainly not least, I want to thank God for all his blessings. The longer I live, the more I learn to appreciate what could very easily be taken for granted. God bless. I hope you enjoy the book.

Like FREEBIES and SWAG and info on contests and new releases? SIGN UP FOR MY MONTHLY NEWSLETTER! http://www.mariannemorea.com/contact-me.html

If you enjoyed the story, please feel free to email me. Reviews are always welcome, especially on Amazon, iBooks and Goodreads!

About the Author

 Marianne Morea was born and raised in New York. Inspired by the dichotomies that define the "city that never sleeps," she began her career after college as a budding journalist. Later, earning a MFA, from The School of Visual Arts in Manhattan, she moved on to the graphic arts. But it was her lifelong love affair with words, and the fantasies and "what ifs'" they stir, that finally brought her back to writing.

More by Marianne Morea

THE RED VEIL DIARIES

(Reading Order)

Choose Me

Tempt Me

Tease Me

Taste Me

Bewitch Me

THE CURSED BY BLOOD SAGA

Hunter's Blood (Shifter Romantic Suspense!)

Fever Play (Short, fast, and HOT!)

Twice Cursed (Vamp/Were…Book hangover possible!)

Blood Legacy (Icy hot vamp romance)

Lion's Den (Will make you cry happy tears!)

Power Play (Hot and Suspenseful!)

Collateral Blood (Vampire Suspense!)

Condemned (Vampire Suspense!)

Of Blood and Magic (Vampire/Witch Suspense!)

THE LEGEND SERIES

Hollow's End (Witch Suspense)

Time Turner (Time Travel Suspense)

Spook Rock (Ghost Suspense)

THE BLESSED

My Soul to Keep (Angels and Demons)

MT PRESS BOOKS

Sass Master
(Sassy Ever After-The Catamount Shifters)

Lucky Sass
(Sassy Ever After-The Catamount Shifters)

Sass in the City
(Sassy Ever After-The Catamount Shifters)

HOWLS ROMANCE

Her Fairytale Wolf
(Modern twist on Cinderella)

The Wolf's Dream Mate
(Modern twist on Sleeping Beauty)

Her Winter Wolves
(Modern twist on Snow White)

The Alpha's Chase
(Marriage of Convenience)

Made in the USA
Middletown, DE
06 October 2023

40111703R00149